Timothy Hillmer

TIMOTHY HILLMER
RAVENHILL

12/25/07

For Brad —

I hope you enjoy the novel, and best of luck with your new work endeavors.

Tim & Nancy

University of New Mexico Press
ALBUQUERQUE

YEAR						PRINTING					
12	11	10	09	08	07	1	2	3	4	5	6

Library of Congress Cataloging-in-Publication Data

Hillmer, Timothy, 1958–
  Ravenhill / Timothy Hillmer.
    p. cm.
  ISBN-13: 978-0-8263-3985-0 (pbk. : alk. paper)
  1. High school students—Fiction. 2. Teenagers—Conduct of
life—Fiction. I. Title.
  PS3558.I4532R38 2007
  813'.54—dc22
                                        2006033643

■ ■ ■

Book design and composition by Damien Shay
Body type is Trump Mediaeval 10/15
Display is Frutiger

■ ■ ■

For
NANCY
and
RACHEL
and
CARLY

■ ■ ■

ACKNOWLEDGMENTS

MANY thanks to the teachers and students who have shared the classroom with me; to my parents, Vernon and Catherine Hillmer, for providing a legacy of hard work and of love; to Tom Jones and Robert McBrearty for their friendship; to my colleagues at the Colorado Writing Project, especially Karen Hartman; to Glenda & Mark Allinson and Margaret Brewster & Chris Matthews for their long distance support from New Zealand; to Paul & Brenda Lilly, Andy Aiken, and Alan Olds for generously offering quiet places to write at critical times; and to Luther Wilson at the University of New Mexico Press for having faith in my work.

This novel could never have been completed without the help and support of Karen Palmer, Darrin Pratt, Cheryl Dorsey, Michael Hillmer, Don Williams, Charlotte & Marshall Arlin, Jaye & John Zola, Jane Patton, Lisa Cech, and especially Lloyd Kropp and Father Robert Meyer, the finest men I've ever known.

Finally, a special thanks to my wife, Nancy, and to my daughters, Rachel and Carly, for their patience and love over the years.

■ ■ ■

Did heaven look on and
would not take their part?
— *Macbeth*

■ ■ ■

...and behold,
a great wind came
from across the wilderness
and struck the four corners
of the house and it fell
on the young people
and they died;
and I alone
have escaped
to tell you.
— *The Book of Job*

*R*AVENHILL *High School was originally constructed after World War II in 1950. It was a source of pride for the community, which back then was made up mostly of farmers and miners and shop owners. To many of them it represented a fresh start after the war years, a clean slate, and the first step in becoming a place admired by all who passed through. A few of the realtors pitched in to help with fund-raising for some of the special features the school board couldn't afford, like a larger library and a full gymnasium. "After all," they told the newspaper, "a quality institution is an investment for all of us."*

The school was built over a two year period by Driscoll and Sons, a local construction outfit that cut no corners. "Only the best for our kids," they told the school board. The best included mahogany seats in the auditorium, tiled floors in all the restrooms and locker rooms, a wooden basketball court in the gym made with Maine timber, a carpeted library to keep things quiet for studying, and five hundred combination lockers. On opening day, the newspapers touted it as the finest school in the county. Hundreds lined the sidewalk and parking lot to watch State Senator Edwards cut the ribbon. Afterward, refreshments were served in the cafeteria and the senator gave a speech. Then the hallways and classrooms were opened up for parents and students so they could admire the clean, white lavatories, the shiny red lockers, the stacks of new textbooks that filled the shelves. It was a beautiful school and the parents were proud that their sons and daughters would have this opportunity. They had a chance to shake hands with Senator Edwards and Mayor Fontaine and say things to the local reporters like, "For once the taxpayers got their money's worth."

Five years after the school opened, a miracle occurred. A group of local boys, mostly the sons of miners, went undefeated as a football team and won the state championship by beating one of the big city high schools. There were pictures from the game on the sports pages of every paper in the state and the team became known as "The Miracle Miners." The town welcomed them home with a parade down Main Street and the boys rode on the fire engine with police cars leading the way. They canceled classes in order to hold a huge celebration on the athletic field behind the school and practically everyone in town showed up. All the players were introduced to the crowd, and Coach Fitz held the championship trophy aloft and shouted, "We won this for the town, for each and every one of you!" They displayed the trophy in a new oak showcase in the main lobby and eventually a sign was posted in the front of the school that said, "1955 State Football Champions—Home of The Miracle Miners."

In the years that followed, the school was the gathering place for all the annual parades before they headed downtown on Main Street. Whether on the Fourth of July or Veterans Day or Halloween, the parking lot was always filled with floats and costumed marchers and the municipal brass band. The city held political fund-raisers for local candidates in the auditorium during elections. The school was used as a county voting station, and for nearly thirty years people cast their ballots in the lobby next to the trophy case. The town booked the gymnasium each month for dances, while community organizations and clubs like Home Extension and the Farm Bureau held their classes and meetings during the evening in the same rooms where their members' children studied during the day. On many Sundays the loud, exultant voices of preachers and choirs could be heard up and down the block as the auditorium was transformed by a local church into a place of worship. In 1965, when the five seniors were killed drag racing out on Ravenhill Road, they held the funeral in the gym because it was the only place big enough to hold all the mourners. The school was like the hub of a great wheel, always spinning and gathering momentum for the next event, whatever that might be.

■ ■ ■

FRIDAY, DECEMBER 19, 1997
4:00 P.M.

Officer Bradford

AFTER the County Shoot Team arrived at the high school and secured the area, Chief Gibson pulled officers Leary and Jamison aside and asked them to take Bradford back to the station. They were standing in the hallway of the karate studio across the street from Ravenhill. The police had taken over the building and set up debrief and triage in the workout rooms. They'd already shut down Main Street and through the glass front door, Leary could see the lineup of fire trucks, police cars, ambulances, and EMT vans, all parked directly in front of the school. The bomb squad had arrived with their dogs and were headed into the building. Gibson had a walkie-talkie in his right hand that sputtered with static and voices, and for a moment he glared out at the action in the street and shook his head in disbelief. Then he turned back to the officers. "Get Bradford out of here before the place turns into a circus," he said gruffly. "Where are you parked?"

"In the alley," Jamison answered.

"Good," the chief said. "Take him out the back through the locker room. Make sure he doesn't talk to anyone. Call the

Association and get a lawyer over to the station ASAP." He paused and ran a hand through his silver hair, then lowered his voice. "No mistakes on this one, gentlemen," he said. "We do it by the book. We want Bradford with us for a long time. It's good for our image." *Good for your image*, thought Leary, knowing full well that Gibson was worried about the town's "white flight" reputation and loved having a black cop on the street.

The chief stepped away and joined a group of Shoot Team detectives. Leary and Jamison moved closer to the large glass doors at the entrance. They could see the huge crowds already forming outside the border of yellow tape and knew the media would be arriving soon with their cameras and reporters and satellite dish vans and lengths of cable that spread across the ground like black pythons.

"The last thing Bradford needs," Leary said, "is to have a bunch of TV vultures gawking at him."

"Absolutely," Jamison answered, nodding in agreement. He and Leary knew what needed to be done to shield the officer, at least until they could get him back to the station. "It's tough enough to be the shooter," Jamison continued. "You don't need to get home and see your face on the tube on top of everything else."

They left the hallway and entered the studio, its walls encased in floor to ceiling mirrors. It was bustling with police, EMTs, firemen in their burly uniforms, and plainclothesmen with gleaming silver badges affixed to their coats. Soon a small cluster of detectives moved away and they saw Bradford seated in one corner in a plastic chair, his elbows on his knees as he leaned forward, staring down at the floor. Leary checked and saw that the Shoot Team had already relieved him of his 9 mm handgun. They went over and squatted down next to him so they were at eye level. Bradford was a big man with wide shoulders, probably a linebacker in high school, and he dwarfed the chair he sat in. He lifted his head up for a moment and saw Leary and

Jamison. His eyes were red and tired-looking and his dark hands shook with small tremors as he ran them back and forth across the black pants.

"How are you holding up?" Leary asked.

Bradford looked at him for a moment, then said, "Been better."

Leary nodded, dipped his head down for a moment. "The chief asked us to take you down to the station. It's going to get crazy around here with the press and all."

Bradford glanced over at Jamison, then back to Leary. He didn't say anything, just gave a quick nod, then rose from the chair.

"We're taking him," Leary said to one of the detectives, a heavyset fellow with a bushy mustache that looked like steel wool.

"Okay," the man said. "Set him up in one of the back rooms, and tell the tech guy that we'll need the video camera ready when we get there."

Leary stepped away from Bradford and moved closer to the detective. "How soon before you question him?" he asked softly.

The big detective motioned toward the entrance with his arm. "It'll be a few hours. This is a messy one. We got the kids who witnessed it in the small studio. A lot of loose ends to tie up before we can send them home. Guess it's like that any time kids are involved. It's tough to get a straight answer out of some of them. They're pretty shook-up."

Leary nodded, then turned back to Bradford and Jamison and the three of them walked to the rear of the large room. Leary went first, going ahead of Bradford, while Jamison stayed right behind. They turned in through a door labeled "Men" and entered a narrow hallway lined with metal lockers. Their footsteps echoed in the stillness as they moved across the concrete floor.

Suddenly Bradford stopped walking. He stood there quietly, his hands at his sides, and stared at the far end of the locker room where there was an Exit sign above the door.

"I had to fire," Bradford said, shaking his head. "No doubt about it."

Leary stepped back and put a hand on the officer's shoulder. "Better keep it to yourself," he said. "At least until we can get to the station and set you up with someone from the Association."

"I fired one shot," Bradford said. "No choice. I had a clear line of fire but could hear kids screaming all over the damn place. I had to shoot."

"Save it for the Shoot Team," Jamison said. "Trust me. It's for the best."

Bradford stared at each of them for a moment, his jaw clenched tight. Then he slowly nodded and continued walking to the metal door at the far end. When they got to it, Leary paused, his hand on the steel push-bar. "Once we're outside, we're going straight to the squad car," he told Bradford. "Jamison will follow in his own vehicle. There might be some media waiting to ambush us, maybe even a few cameras. Don't say anything. Just keep your head down and get to the front of the cruiser."

Bradford took a step back, any defiance now replaced by fear. "They're going to know it's me," he said. "What if my family sees it on the news?"

"We're five minutes from the station," Jamison said. "Once we're inside, we'll get you a phone so you can make some calls."

"Thanks," Bradford said.

Leary paused momentarily and gazed at the two officers in silence. Then he said, "Let's go," and snapped the door open.

He mumbled a low curse under his breath when he saw the reporters as they walked out. There were more than he'd expected, maybe twenty or thirty. They must have checked the alley and knew they'd bring him through the back. A camera-man was sitting on a curb smoking and when they burst from the door, he flung the cigarette away and scrambled for his gear.

The officers were too quick for him, however, and rushed past before he could hoist the camera to his shoulder. Jamison was on one side of Bradford, Leary on the other.

"Is this the officer involved?" someone shouted. "Is he the shooter?" They could hear the camera motor drives clicking as the photographers pushed forward to try and get a decent head shot for the front page.

"No comment!" Leary shouted as they moved to his squad car. He flung the door open and Bradford ducked inside. Within seconds they were speeding away on a side street and heading toward the station. Leary looked across the seat and saw Bradford in the place usually reserved for his partner. He was crouched low, his head in his hands as if hiding from someone. Leary didn't like seeing an officer behaving like a scared drunk or a cheap felon. It didn't seem right. Then again, a shooting at a high school didn't seem right either.

When they reached the station, Leary parked in the covered lot and brought Bradford in through the squad door. Jamison was waiting and took them to a windowless room that had been set up for questioning where they had Bradford take a seat. It was all pretty textbook. On the center table was a cassette recorder with blank tapes, a microphone, and some legal pads and pens. A video camera was mounted on a tripod at the far end with the lens aimed directly at the table where they had Bradford sit down.

"How about some coffee?" Jamison asked.

"Sure," Bradford said.

"And I'll get a phone from the front desk. You'll want to call the Association first and request a lawyer, then contact your family."

Bradford didn't respond, instead putting his hands on the table and staring at the camera.

Leary stayed with him while Jamison went for the coffee and the phone. The room was hot and stuffy so he cracked a door to let in some air. "The Shoot Team will be here later for the questioning," Leary said. "Just remember that everyone's on your side. Even the detectives. They want to help you out, so tell them everything you remember down to the smallest detail." Leary motioned at the pens and paper on the table. "You may want to start jotting down a few details while you wait. It could be a while before they arrive."

"I'll do that," Bradford said, taking a pen and legal pad. His hand was shaking as he tried to write, and he couldn't hold the pen steady.

"It's okay," Leary said. "Shooter shakes. It'll pass."

"How many dead?" Bradford suddenly asked, setting the pen down.

"It's unofficial," Leary said.

"How many?"

"Five."

"And wounded?"

"I heard at least three on the police radio. There could be more. They took everyone to County. I can call over there later and check with a friend in the ER."

"Thanks," Bradford said. "I'd appreciate it." He raised the pen again and held it over the paper, staring down at the blank sheet. "Never thought it would be like this," he said, looking up at Leary. "Not in some damn school."

"It doesn't make sense," Leary said.

Again Bradford tried to write. His hand was still trembling, but a little less so, and he seemed to be pulling it together. Leary had seen good police officers break down and cry in this room after an incident.

He got up from his chair and sat down next to Bradford, then reached over and picked up another pen. "I'll help you out. I'll do the writing until you settle down. Just tell me what happened and I'll put it on paper."

"I've never been much of a writer," Bradford said.

"It's okay," Leary said. "Just tell me what you remember."

"There's too much. Besides, it's all jumbled up in my head."

Leary leaned forward. "So think of it as a story. Go back to the beginning."

"When I arrived at the school?"

"That's a good place to start."

"But I don't remember the exact time I got there."

"Don't sweat it. Tell me why you went."

Bradford hesitated and ran a hand through his short hair. "I got a call from the assistant principal, Kathie Romero. It was the last day before the holiday break and I guess the students were pretty cranked up."

"And you went there without your partner?"

"I didn't think I'd be there long. Maybe fifteen or twenty minutes. I told Crawford just to drop me off. He had to go back to the station to pick up some paperwork."

"What did the assistant principal want?"

"She asked me to come by for a few minutes because she was concerned about a student and his connection to some vandalism on school grounds."

"And what was the student's name?"

Bradford paused and stared intently at the far wall. His brow furrowed as he concentrated. For a moment Leary thought he might not be able to remember the name. Sometimes it happened like that after a shooting. The details just don't click and the officer involved draws a blank when it comes to names, dates, times, even where he was standing when he fired his weapon.

"Leonard Lamb," Bradford finally said. "She called about Leonard Lamb. A ninth grader."

"That's good," Leary said, writing it down. "Let's start with Leonard Lamb and work from there. Tell me about him."

So he did. It went on like that, Bradford talking and Leary writing, until Jamison brought the coffee and the phone so the officer could make his calls. And when the Shoot Team arrived later, Bradford's hand was no longer shaking and he was ready to face them with the facts of what happened in Room 222 at Ravenhill High School at or around 2:30 P.M. on Friday, December 19, 1997.

■ ■ ■

FRIDAY, DECEMBER 19, 1997
5:00 A.M.

Paul

HE was awakened by the sounds from upstairs. He lived in a
small apartment in the basement of the Catholic church's
rectory and each morning heard his old friend, Father Lou, shuffling across the hardwood floor in his soft slippers. This was followed by the clicking of sharp toenails that belonged to Lou's
companion, Judas, an ancient basset hound whose enormous
belly dragged the ground as he walked. He knew they were
preparing for their morning march, as Lou liked to say, and it
was as much a part of their daily ritual as the 7:00 A.M. Mass
Father Lou celebrated most days of the year. Paul lay in bed for
a few minutes, listening to them moving above and found comfort in the reassurance that he was not alone.

When he finally rose and stood at the high window near his
bed, he could see that a light snow had fallen during the night
and covered the yard with a fine white down. It was a cold morning in December, a few days before Christmas. He stared at the
ice on the window and thought of Robert Frost and his poem,
"Stopping by Woods on a Snowy Evening," with its final lines:
"But I have promises to keep, and miles to go before I sleep, and

miles to go before I sleep." Paul had a job to do that day, and he, too, had promises to keep.

He had once been a priest but was now a custodian at the local high school. He was also an alcoholic, which was one of the reasons he'd left the priesthood. Paul had been sober for three years, the same amount of time he'd been employed as a janitor, and his weekly AA meetings were held at the school in one of the classrooms, which was convenient since he didn't own a car. Father Lou had helped him get the job by making a few phone calls on his behalf after he'd gotten out of rehab. "It's a start," Lou had told him. "It'll keep you busy." Paul had thanked him and moved his things into the basement apartment the following day.

He was forty-two-years-old and celibate and had spent most of his adult life in the seminary or priesthood where maids and parish women had cleaned and cooked for him. As a result, he'd learned to enjoy the everyday tasks of his new life. In the morning he always prayed, then showered and dressed for work. The basement was often cold and damp in the winter, but he had an electric heater to offset the chill. On most days, after fixing a lunch, Paul walked to the school and usually worked until three in the afternoon. Then he returned to his apartment and spent a few hours with his woodcarving. The shop teacher at school kept him supplied with leftovers of pine and spruce and the occasional scrap of maple. He had a special carving knife and loved the feel of the blade as it peeled away the wood shards as easily as the skin of an apple.

He made small things that could fit into the palm of his hand. At Christmas he liked to carve ornaments and painted them to give away as gifts: tiny sleds pulled by reindeer; a pot-bellied Santa Claus; a Christmas tree with a gold star at the top; a snowy dove. Last night Paul had stayed up late to wrap the ornaments in white tissue paper and attach name tags so that later in the day he could give them away as presents to certain teachers and students that he'd befriended.

Paul left the apartment at 5:30 A.M., carrying the gifts in a brown grocery bag. It was still dark and the warm light from a few select kitchens illuminated the block like yellow beacons at sea. His breath was ghostly with cold, and the steam swirled upward. He had dressed warmly for the day ahead: thermal boots and wool socks; thick corduroy pants; a long-sleeved shirt and heavy sweater; a down parka. When he reached the football field behind the high school, he paused before crossing. It stretched out like a frozen sheet cake encased in a layer of white frosting. He could see the back of Ravenhill, with its brick exterior looming behind the grandstands, then noticed that his hands were trembling. It was not the cold, nor did he suffer from physical tremors. It was simple nerves, the shakes. He could almost taste the bourbon on his tongue, the sweet burning in the back of his throat. It's what he craved now. When he was a priest and still drinking, there were mornings when he shunned the liquor and attempted to offer the Mass sober. He'd last until Communion and then the shaking would set in as he tried to place the Body of Christ on the tongues of his parishioners. And so he would pray. *Forsake me not, O Lord; my God, be not far from me. Make haste to help me, O Lord my salvation.* He repeated it now over and over, a simple chant whispered to the demons as he crossed the white field.

When Paul reached the building, he did not enter it. Instead, out of habit, he walked around the structure in a slow, studious loop in order to inspect the grounds and do a facilities check. Right away he noticed that a few of the windows near the gym were cracked. Perhaps some local boys had raced by on their bikes and hurled pop cans filled with stones overhead like hand grenades at the glass. He turned the corner and saw the gray portable trailers on the north lot that were used as classrooms to ease the crowding in the main building.

For the last three years the hallways had overflowed with students during passing period, all due to the area's tremendous growth as businesses and homes moved west toward the interstate and away from the old part of the city. Many shops in Old Town had closed because they couldn't compete with the big superstores. Then a referendum passed over a year ago and construction began on a state-of-the-art high school out near the new subdivisions. A rumor circulated among the teachers that the Ravenhill building would be closed for good and torn down and that all students would be required to attend the new site with its spacious classrooms and the latest computer technology. "Why not make a fresh start?" Paul had overheard a few of the parents say at the beginning of the year. "Our kids' futures are at stake here. Let's bury the old and get on with the new."

He reached the front of the school but then suddenly stopped and glanced to his right. Something had been written on the brick exterior next to the main entrance. Paul moved closer and in the faint light saw the words scrawled with spray paint in huge letters on the outside wall: **I RAPED LARA**. As dark and red as blood. He looked toward the street and knew the message would be easily visible to drivers making their way downtown. And right away he had a hunch who'd done it. Leonard Lamb.

Paul did his best to get along with the students. Most were good kids, especially when they came from homes where the parents gave a damn. But Leonard Lamb had always been different. He transferred to Ravenhill last year from another school and right away Paul could tell that the other kids were scared of him. He was bigger than most of them and used his size to intimidate and frighten the students. Because he'd failed most of his classes, he was repeating ninth grade this year. With the girls, he was always making comments about the way they dressed or walked. When a cute one went by his locker, he liked to grab his crotch and howl like a wolf. From the first day of school, teachers had been after him for pinching bottoms and snapping bras.

Once Paul saw Leonard and Kathie Romero, the assistant principal, go nose to nose over something he'd said to Mr. Hardin, the English teacher. Mrs. Romero wanted Leonard in her office, and he wouldn't budge from his locker. When Leonard turned away and shouted, "Back off bitch!" Mrs. Romero pulled the cell phone off her hip, dialed a number, then handed it to him. Calmly she said, "Please talk with Officer Bradford about the conversation we were just having." Leonard clutched the phone in his big hand for a moment, hesitant about what to do next. Then he slowly passed it back to Mrs. Romero and shuffled away to her office.

Paul had confronted Leonard a number of times and certainly had his share of run-ins with him. Once Leonard brought a length of steel chain to school and Paul caught him going up and down the halls before classes, swinging the chain over his head and forcing other kids to duck as he ran by. He got suspended for three days after that one. The most recent incident was last Monday during passing period when the halls were jammed with students trying to squeeze by to get to class. A pretty girl with a red scarf tied around her neck walked past Leonard. He said something to her and she ignored him, so he reached out and grabbed the scarf and jerked her back to his locker. Paul had been doing some work in one of the restrooms and was standing in the doorway. He saw the girl slap at Leonard as he twisted the scarf even tighter. "You gonna miss my kiss?" he yelled at her. Paul rushed through the crowd and told him to let her go. Leonard released the girl, cackled with laughter, and said, "Mr. Janitor's cracking down." Then he quickly grabbed his books, slammed his locker shut, and swaggered off to class. The next day Paul found his custodian's closet broken into and noticed that some cans of red spray paint were missing. It was classic Leonard. Hit and run and hide.

As he stood next to the school, Paul knew that a crazy day awaited him. The last day before the Christmas holidays was always like this. The students were wired because of the impending break, and the teachers were wiped out from trying to keep a little order in their classrooms. He also knew that some hard work lay ahead as well. The hallways would be a wet, muddy mess from the snow and would need mopping throughout the day. The red graffiti on the wall was an entirely different story. If he had the right cleaner and the graffiti paint was still fresh, then he might be able to scrub it off the brick with a wire brush. He hesitated, thinking of the students and teachers as they awakened this morning. Especially Leonard.

As a priest, Paul always knew his role when trouble or even tragedy loomed. The specifics didn't really matter; it was usually about pain or loss or sudden, irretrievable regret. Whether it was the midnight heart attack or the long siege with cancer or the freak accident or the suicide, he knew what to bring when the phone call arrived. The black leather pouch was the size of a toiletry bag and he carried it snugly in his hand the way he'd once carried a baseball glove as a boy. Inside was the prayer book with the frayed green cover, the tiny glass bottle filled with holy water, the small tarnished canister containing the fragrant, scented oil. No matter what the circumstances, one thing was clear to him: during a shocking, unexpected crisis, he was the voice of compassion and sanity. It was what he did best.

So he placed his hand on the cold wall and prayed for Leonard, for all the students and teachers at the school. The morning was hushed and still. No cars passed in the street. No wind. The brick was icy to the touch. His prayer was simple and lasted only a few seconds. And when he was done, Paul unlocked the front door and entered the school. He went straight to the central electrical box near the office and used a small key to open the metal panel. Even in the pitch black, his finger found the main circuit and he paused, thinking momentarily of his prayer and all that awaited him today. Then he flipped the switch and watched with satisfaction as the darkened hallways came alive with light.

■ ■ ■

FRIDAY, DECEMBER 19, 1997
6:00 A.M.

Hardin

IN Kent Hardin's dream, memory flashed before him in a ghostly train of images, a subway of regret speeding by like a stream of boxcars, the siding of each illuminated with moments from his life as if he were staring at the screen of a drive-in movie: his mother's crooked tooth, visible only when she smiled; his father's hammer, the handle worn and burnished like bronze; his friend's three-legged dog, Apollo, and how it valiantly hopped down the block; his daughter's skin, as white and soft as an orchid.

Then the alarm sounded and he bolted upright, gasping. He stared down at the pulsing green numbers on the clock at his bedside: 6:00 A.M. His eyes throbbed under the canopy of each eyelid. He felt wiped out. *Whacked to the gnarl*, as one of his students might say. Except for the nuclear glow of the clock face, it was pitch black in the trailer, and he could feel the damp cold seeping in the top of the sleeping bag as it chilled his throat and shoulders.

He'd been using the sleeping bag most of the winter, and it had been a warm friend to him ever since he moved into the mobile home. It was a four-season, Snow Lion mummy bag that he bought years ago when he went into the Peace Corps. Initially, he imagined using it in some godforsaken, frozen wasteland like Siberia. Instead, he ended up being assigned to the Pacific island of Motu as a teacher, and the last thing he needed was a goose down cocoon in the tropics.

He stirred and felt the gun under his pillow. It was an old target pistol that he always kept loaded in case there was trouble. It gave him a little extra comfort at night so he could sleep. Some punks had broken into his trailer last month and ransacked the place. He'd walked in and found drawers pulled out and furniture overturned and shelves busted down. They hadn't taken much. Then again, there wasn't much to take. After that he started keeping the gun close by at night. Nothing wrong with being prepared. That's what he was always telling his students. "You never know," he was fond of saying as they rolled their eyes, "there could be a test or quiz waiting for you just around the corner. Expect the unexpected."

On mornings like this, when the cold was too unbearable to face right away, he liked to stay tucked in the sleeping bag, eyes closed, and remember Motu with its intense sun and white beaches. During the past year, not a day went by when he didn't think of the place at least once. He'd been fresh out of college, without even a year of teaching experience under his belt, when he joined the Peace Corps. And what he discovered was unlike anything he'd ever seen or imagined before. The sweet taste of ripe fruit each morning. The silhouette of tattered palm fronds against the turquoise blue of the ocean. The salt smell of the water and the sting between his toes when he went for long walks on the beach. The crunch of shells underfoot as seabirds wheeled across the sky in great, winged arcs.

More than anything, he could still hear the voices of the students when they came to say good-bye on that last day. They lined the path from the school to the boat dock where he was to be picked up, forming a gauntlet of smiles and waving arms. *"Hai konea ra, kaiwhakaako,"* he heard, over and over, as the students reached out to shake his hand and touch his shoulder. *Farewell to you, teacher.* They handed him gifts as he passed. A fragrant bundle of flowers. A necklace made of ocean shells. A carving of a dolphin whittled from a rare jungle wood. A scrapbook filled with their finest writing and drawings. And finally, when he reached the dock, the principal was waiting with a handmade quilt consisting of seventy-five squares of colored fabric, each piece decorated by a student with his or her name sewed into the cloth.

Nothing's perfect, Hardin thought, nestling deeper into the sleeping bag. *Not my life. Not even memories.* Motu wasn't a complete paradise. When he first arrived, he saw a flat, one story building patched together with wood, stone, shingles, tin siding, and whatever else the builders could get their hands on. Teaching resources were almost nonexistent. No TVs or VCRs or cassette decks. No copying or mimeograph machines. No overhead projectors. No textbooks. Instead there was a small, ragged set of encyclopedias and a few shards of chalk for the single blackboard in his room. His only real supplies had been the boxes he'd shipped from the States, all crammed with paper and pens and crayons, as well as his own personal library of favorite books.

After a few days at the school, he quickly discovered that the other teachers, all native to the island, kept control of the children through sheer force by lashing out at them for even the slightest hint of disrespect. They used thin, wooden rods that stung like a wasp and left purple welts on the students' dark skin. If a child received a particularly harsh whipping, the parents might show up the next day to berate the teacher and chaos would ensue as the adults screamed at each other. Once Kent witnessed an irate father who grabbed the rod and started flogging an instructor right in the classroom. Suddenly the principal, an enormous ex-rugby player named Mr. Jonah, appeared in the doorway. He stepped in, snatched the rod away from the angry parent, then grabbed the father by the seat of his trousers and hustled him out of the school.

In the beginning Kent was treated suspiciously by the other teachers. He was, after all, an American who wore fancy clothes, never screamed at his students, and refused to use the rod to discipline them.

"Kindness will make them lazy and you crazy," one veteran teacher told him after that first week. "They need to see the rod, not your happy smile."

Kent would simply nod in appreciation for the advice, then close his classroom door and go about the business of teaching. When he stood in front of the students, he didn't see a group of primitive, uneducated islanders living in poverty. They seemed proud to have "The Yankee" as their teacher and asked a hundred questions about his country and the world he came from. *Do you carry a gun? Don't all Americans carry guns? What kind of sports car do you drive? Which Hollywood stars do you know?*

"We need to make a deal," he told them during that first week. They stared back at him with puzzled expressions. "A trade," he explained. "I'll teach you what I know as long as you teach me about your home." At first his class couldn't possibly understand. After all, wasn't he from America, land of the free, home of the brave? Didn't he travel thousands of miles to teach *them?* "America is just one small part of the planet," he said, holding up a dented, plastic globe. "I want to learn about your world too."

So, once a month, he organized a field trip to the beach or the jungle or the high country, where volcanic rock formations loomed like black towers. On these excursions, he became the student in their classroom and asked them to name the speckled bugs he found clinging to his shirt sleeves, the shrieking, crimson birds that soared through the jungle, the quick, lime-green lizards that darted between his feet when hiking, and the leopard-spotted ferns that flourished along the stream and made his skin burn when he brushed against them. He asked the students to teach him their songs and stories and they told him about the beginning of time when there was Te Kore, the Nothingness, and Te Po, the Night.

"*Te Po nui,*" they sang. "*Te Po roa, Tep Po uriuri, Te Po kerekere, Te Po tiwha, Te Po tangotango, Te Po te kitea...*"

They told him of Rangi nui, the Sky, and Papa tu a nuku, the Earth, and how they were joined and created offspring such as Tane mahuta, the god of forests, Tawhiri matea, the god of winds and storms, and Tangaroa, the god of all things that live in the sea. In return, he taught them English and how to read some other great storytellers. They memorized poems like "The Highwayman" and "The Midnight Ride of Paul Revere" and recited them aloud in a thunderous chorus of voices until the other teachers complained of the noise pouring through the flimsy walls. They acted out scenes from *Macbeth* and *Romeo and Juliet* and performed them in special evening shows for the parents. Most importantly, he showed them how to write stories, speeches, poetry, then hung the best papers on the classroom walls and ceiling and windows and doors until the small room was overflowing with their words and pictures.

More than anything, Kent adored the students. Even though his room was small, the principal still crammed at least seventy-five kids into the space, ranging in age from ten to eighteen. The school had a population of close to three hundred, with at least another two hundred children on a waiting list to get in. His room was always packed with students sitting on the floor, on the windowsill, sometimes on each other's shoulders. Yet he seldom had discipline problems. Education was a precious gift to them, possibly a way off Motu, and they knew that to misbehave could mean being easily replaced by someone on the waiting list. And Kent had never seen students so hungry to learn. All he had to do was ask a simple question and he was greeted with a swarm of arms thrust upward. It seemed as if all that he shared with them, whether it was the opening chapter of *The Last of the Mohicans* or a photograph of his parents on their family farm, was met with an excitement unlike anything he'd ever witnessed before.

It had been twenty years since leaving Motu, and Kent had never gone back. He tried to return a number of times, but something always came up and he was never able to pull it off. Complications. Commitments. A lack of savings for the expensive round trip ticket. In the months that followed his return to the States, he wrote letters to the students and tried to keep in touch as best he could. Then he met Claire, a colleague at a nearby school, and got his first teaching job. They were married within the year and put a down payment on a house. For their honeymoon, he wanted to take her to Motu, but Claire was a reasonable woman and convinced him that New Mexico was more in tune with their budget so they settled on a weekend in Santa Fe. Once he started writing a novel about his experiences in the Peace Corps but never finished it due to the extra night classes and summer school courses he taught to make ends meet.

He never forgot Motu, however, and even created small, daily rituals that helped him to remember the place. He kept the farewell quilt in mint condition and displayed it on the wall in every classroom he ever taught in. He stored the necklace and wooden dolphin and scrapbook in the middle drawer of his desk. On certain late afternoons, when the students were gone and he was nearly finished with his grading, he took them out and held them in his hands as if each item was a magic talisman that had the power to bring him good fortune. He closed his eyes and tried to remember the students and their voices, the electric hum and chatter of their questions and conversations as they worked, the steady beat of the winter rain on the tin roof of the classroom like a thousand tiny drummers pounding away overhead, and the scent of the ocean breeze blowing into his classroom through the windows. "Sail wind," they'd often sing. "Storm wind. Stay-close-to-home wind."

Hardin unzipped the sleeping bag and slid out so his legs hung over the side of the mattress. He was forty-eight years old and his right knee cracked every time he got up, the result of an old injury from a school rugby match he agreed to play in while living on Motu. He rose three times a night to piss and there were moments when his abdomen felt like a heavy, burning stone. He hadn't had a physical in ten years and was damn sure that no preppie doctor, fresh out of medical school, was going to stick a hand up Hardin's ass and announce to the world that he had an enlarged prostate. The hell with it all. Humiliation was something he got plenty of each and every day at Ravenhill. He didn't need to pay somebody to give him a little more.

He took the pistol out from under his pillow and set it on the nightstand, then turned on the lamp. The first thing he saw were the papers stacked on his wooden desk in the middle of the room. *Damn.* Thirty-five essays on *A Christmas Carol* from his eighth period class. Thirty-five *ungraded* essays. For two weeks he'd promised his students that he would get all the essays scored and returned before the holiday break. One more day of school remained and only eighth hour was still unfinished.

Then he saw the overturned wine bottle and glass and remembered last night when he'd settled down to try and finish the papers. He'd pulled all-nighters before and thought he could do it again. As he drove home after school, he stopped at the Liquor Barn, thinking that a 1996 Chardonnay from New Zealand might ease the pressure. During the past year, he found that a few glasses of wine in the evening helped soften the monotony of correcting the endless parade of incomplete sentences, fragments, run-ons, misspellings, and punctuation mistakes. The wine made bearable the weekly barrage of worksheets and comprehension quizzes and vocabulary tests that seemed to flood the correction basket until it was stuffed with paper, an endless wave of paper that had to be checked, evaluated, commented upon, marked, and recorded in his red grading log that he protected like a secret code book that could never fall into the hands of the enemy.

Now Hardin noticed that a small pool of wine had seeped across the desk, then dripped down to form a stain on the carpet below. He got up from the bed in his long underwear and saw that the eighth hour papers, neatly bundled together with a rubber band, were soaked with alcohol. Thirty-five wine-drenched essays. He slipped on a flannel shirt to offset the cold, then picked up one of the papers, which was damp and smeared, the ink running down the page in tiny black rivulets. Last night he must have accidentally bumped the table on his way to the toilet. No other explanation. He grabbed a bath towel and tried to wipe up the remaining wine in an attempt to salvage some of the papers, but it was no use.

After a while he stopped and sat down and stared at the pile in front of him. What would he say? How would he explain what had happened to thirty-five essays that represented one hundred points and might be the difference in a full letter grade on their semester evaluations? How would he explain it to the parents who often left messages in his mailbox in the faculty lounge, each yellow reminder slip labeled URGENT!? How would he explain it to the students, especially those under academic contracts, whose grades were on the border between a C and a D, who had ski trips and entertainment centers riding on whether they made the grade, whether they survived the cut, whether they had *what it takes* as their parents liked to say.

A sudden, cool draft in the trailer made him shiver. It had been a frigid night and ice had formed on the inside of the mobile home's windows. He grabbed his red wool robe and pulled it on. *My own damn fault.* He'd made the mistake of turning on the TV after dinner. *Just a few minutes*, he told himself. *I've earned a little down time. It's a Wonderful Life* was on, and Hardin vowed to only watch a few scenes before tackling the grading. But he didn't turn it off and had a few more sips of wine, all the while knowing that the papers were waiting for him.

After the movie, he poured himself another glass and sat down to grade. He was going to take a shortcut and just skim each one, then look in the grade book at the student's previous mark and give them a score that was a few points higher than the last. *If you're not sure, then grade high and keep them happy.* He'd burn the midnight oil and crank out the grades. He'd done it before and could do it again. After all, there was only one more day of school before the holidays. He'd be a good soldier and march through the night and have these papers graded and recorded by morning, then slog through the day. Only there had been a slight problem. At some point he must have gone to bed for a quick nap and had fallen into a deep sleep from which he never awakened.

This morning Kent knew he needed to think fast or his classes were going to eat him alive. He tried some oatmeal for breakfast, but it tasted like paste and he couldn't stomach it. The back of his neck was already tightening up, throbbing, and he felt a migraine coming on, so he went into the bathroom and popped three Advil. His head spun with possibilities for what to say about the ruined papers: *they were stolen from my car; the janitor accidentally threw them out; my trailer was vandalized and thieves took them.* But it all sounded like bullshit, the kind that high school kids would detect in a heartbeat. More than anything, he wanted to get on the phone and call in sick and just avoid the whole mess. But he knew the chances were poor of getting a substitute on such short notice on the last day before winter break, and if he didn't show, the students would suspect that he didn't get the papers done and was merely avoiding their wrath. *Old Hard On's going soft,* they'd say.

An unopened bottle of wine rested on the kitchen counter next to the microwave. Maybe a quick one would settle him down, take off the proverbial edge. But he dismissed the idea, still feeling the effects of last night on his head and stomach. What he needed was a fresh start, a new attitude about the day. Perhaps a surprise was in order. Throw the students a little curve ball. Start with his appearance. He'd put on a jacket and tie, his best slacks, even the new black shoes he'd recently bought. It's important to project an image of confidence. The students and staff would see him coming down the hall and know something was different, that he was there to tackle the day head on with authority and expertise. Set a visual tone and grab the bull by the balls.

He went to his closet and switched on the light then began to rummage through the clothes that hung from a metal pipe. His foot bumped against something and he bent down to slide it out of the way. It was a cardboard liquor box filled with odds and ends. Dusty mugs. Glass Christmas ornaments. A plaque with his name written in gold above a bold heading: *WORLD'S GREATEST TEACHER.* Some of the gifts were rustic and hand-made. A crude clay bowl. A small cedar box with his name woodburned onto the surface. A cracked ornamental plate.

At his previous schools, Kent had always looked forward to the final day before winter break when students brought pres-ents for him and left them on his desk. Red plastic trays with fudge and cookies or jars of homemade salsa and jam. Sometimes even a gift certificate to a local restaurant or book-store. He would always try to thank the students individually yet was wise enough not to make a big deal out of it. He knew that many of the gifts were bought by caring parents who felt it was an obligation to show their support in some way.

But today he was sure that nothing would be left on his desk. Not for Mr. Hard On. Despite the lack of appreciation, Kent still needed to maintain a consistent atmosphere of disci-pline and responsibility, no matter what the personal cost. He needed to put the lost papers behind him and start the day strong. So he picked up the box of old gifts, then went to the lone door of the trailer, where he flung it open and stepped outside into the biting cold.

When Kent hit the first metal step, his right foot slipped on the caked ice and he went down hard on his tailbone. The fall knocked the wind out of him and he gasped for air as he lay sprawled in the snow. The box he was carrying had been thrown to his right, its contents strewn across the white ground in a trail of brightly colored relics. After a few seconds of panic, he finally caught his breath and started to move, slowly probing his back for any sign of injury. Nothing seemed to be broken. At the most, a bruised hip. For a moment, Kent actually felt a slight letdown. He'd secretly hoped for a fractured pelvis, even a ruptured disc. Something serious that might put him in a warm hospital bed for a while. Maybe he'd have a pretty nurse who would drop by and deliver his pain meds, adjust his pillow. He could sleep in every day, watch some TV, or even catch up on his reading. More importantly, there would be no lessons to plan or papers to grade, no students to deal with. A paid vacation, courtesy of the school district's insurance plan. A part of him longed to call 911 and whisper into the phone, *I've fallen and I can't get up* . . .

Then he saw the faces of his students. Not the ones at Ravenhill, but those from previous schools he'd taught at. Each day they would stare at him, study his every move, analyze him in order to test his patience, his resilience, his character. *Mr. H*, they called him with affection. Or even, *Mr. Hard-ass*, on those days when he pushed them to write with more conviction and passion. What might they write *now* if they saw him collapsed on the icy ground and daydreaming about vacation plans at Holy Family Hospital? What strong adjectives might they use to describe his sorry state of existence: *woeful—pathetic—wretched*?

Kent used the metal railing next to the steps to finally pull himself up from the ground. After gathering together the old gifts and placing them back into the box, he set out once again. More snow had fallen during the night and his slippers made fresh prints as he trudged across the yard. In the distance he could see the farm of his nearest neighbor, Mr. Boaz, which was over a quarter mile away. He'd be up, as always, to take care of his cows. The early morning was still shadowy and a full moon lingered low in the sky. *Full moon madness*. He shrugged, thinking of werewolves, of his high school students who were always cranked up and nearly impossible to teach when the moon was full. *When the crazies come out*.

Across the gravel driveway was a squat farmhouse that had been his parents' home. It had been three years since his mother's death, and nearly eight since his father's. Icicles hung from the frost-covered gutters like glass bayonets. The windows were dark and covered with plastic. When he bought the trailer and parked it here, he'd hoped to renovate the place and make it his own. But that was before the divorce, before things turned bad for him in the school district and he was asked to transfer. Before he came to Ravenhill.

Daylight was beginning to seep across the landscape and he knew he had to hurry. He walked to the wooden fence at the back of the yard. It was a strong one that he and his father put in years ago by using a posthole digger to burrow down through the hard, clay-riddled soil. He set the box down and began to remove the contents, taking each object out one by one and balancing them carefully on the top rail of the fence. When he was nearly finished, he saw one item left, a tiny, ragged doll that he recognized as one of his daughter's toys. The doll was faceless with a mop of purple hair and a frayed, orange jacket that was tattered around the edges. He didn't touch it and couldn't remember the last time he'd seen this doll or how it had gotten here with these other things. He left it in the box, then stepped back about ten feet and turned toward the fence to admire the display. He liked the even spacing between the objects, the way dappled sunlight played across the colored surfaces. *A good morning gallery,* he thought.

Kent removed the target pistol from his coat pocket, then assumed a classic shooter pose, his left arm supporting the right elbow, and took careful aim. He was a good shot and worked in a mechanized fashion. It didn't take long to finish. With each jerk of the pistol, each pop of the bullet finding its mark, he felt somehow lighter, more in control, more steady. For a while he'd been coming out in the early morning with soup cans and wine bottles. It felt good to fire again. A clean start to the day. Almost holy. In control. A steady hand. A pure aim. Breathe in; squeeze the trigger; breathe out.

When he was finished, he walked along the fence and picked up the enamel shards, the strips of wood, the pieces of broken glass. He cleaned up the mess and put the remains back in the box. Before he dropped it in the trash, he took out the purple doll and slipped it into the pocket of his robe. Then he returned to the trailer in order to finish preparing for the long day ahead.

■ ■ ■

FRIDAY, DECEMBER 19, 1997
6:45 A.M.

Lara

IN the Technicolor dream of Lara Wright—age fifteen—she *was* the *Titanic* queen, strutting on Leonardo DiCaprio's arm across the stage of the great ship in her spangled evening gown as that towering dagger of ice loomed in the background. Only her voice sounded like Celine Dion and as the ship tilted, she hit that high note in the song, the one that made everyone on deck stop and check her out and even the boat paused in appreciation before taking its big plunge into the frigid waters.

Now she was half awake and thinking about the dream while sitting on the east side steps of Ravenhill High. She'd seen the movie *Titanic* twelve times and was wondering if Leonardo actually did the drawings of Kate Winslet in the nude, or whether the director hired some Hollywood artist to do them and DiCaprio just faked it. *Shannon will know*, thought Lara. Shannon had seen *Titanic* twenty-one times and had an enormous collage on the wall in her room that contained hundreds of scenes from the film and its stars. She'd read every book available on the subject and had even ordered a $19.95 imitation of the "Heart of the Ocean" necklace that Kate wore in the movie because "it draws unforgettable attention to anyone seen wearing it."

Lara was waiting for Kelly and Shannon, her "weird sisters." She was in drama class with them in the fall and they chose the witches scene from *Macbeth* for a group project. They got an A and the teacher, Mr. Sweeney, said it was brilliant, and the trio had been inseparable ever since. Two days ago they decided not to cut school on Friday, but instead to dress up like the twisted, Goth witches once again and add a little dark Christmas cheer to the Ravenhill climate. Shannon loaned Lara a few things to take home. Black platforms and hose. Black leather jacket. Black miniskirt and black silk top with the flared sleeves. They planned to finish up this morning in the bathroom at school with the makeup mistress, Kelly, who was bringing her complete vamp collection to give each of them a unique look.

Lara left the house early before Teresa returned from the morning paper route because she didn't want her mom to see the outfit she had on. Lara was usually up by 4:00 A.M. to help her mom deliver 250 newspapers. Teresa always drove the old station wagon while Lara threw from the side window as they raced through the dark streets. But last night Teresa had told her to sleep in. "You look exhausted, honey," she'd said. "Get some rest. I'll do the papers by myself." There'd been problems in September with Social Services when Lara had been falling asleep in class, and she knew Teresa didn't want them calling at the house again.

After her mom left on the route, Lara spent an hour getting dressed, then slipped out. She couldn't handle seeing her mother at the kitchen table all pissed off, her face and neck streaked with red, shouting, "If I'm paying for the roof over your head, then I can say whether or not you can march off to school looking like some hooker witch."

Once outside, Lara almost fell on her ass on the icy sidewalk because of the platform shoes. Every few minutes she looked over her shoulder at the street behind, hoping she wouldn't see Leonard Lamb. He didn't live far from their home and about two months ago he'd started following her. It was usually after school, but there had been a few times in the morning when she caught him stalking her as she walked to Ravenhill. He would hang back a block and act like he wasn't watching her, but she knew he was. Once she got up the nerve to whirl and scream, "Leonard, keep it up and Gary'll kick your ass!" Gary was her big brother, a former boxer, who had just gotten out of rehab for a drinking problem and was living back home for a while.

But when Lara had turned around, Leonard was gone. No sign of him anywhere on the street. *Creepy bastard*, she'd thought, then hustled to school to make the bell.

Lara had seen clips on *Jerry Springer* about stalkers and how they chased old girlfriends and ex-wives, sometimes murdering them in their sleep. She wanted to tell someone about Leonard, maybe Gary or the police, but she waited and hoped he'd just go away. Then the weekend phone calls began. At first Leonard was calling her and asking to go to the movies or to hang out at the mall. She made up excuses; she was already doing something with her friends, or she had to go somewhere with her family. After a while though, the calls got weird. She'd pick up the phone and there would be a shrill scream that sounded more like a woman than a man. Then slurred words like "bitch" or "slut" or "whore." One syllable crap that he'd say before she could hang up. She knew it was him even though he never identified himself. Leonard the Lurker. No doubt about it.

Last week, Lara got another prank call and decided to tell Gary. After dinner, she went to the basement where he was working out. Her big brother, almost thirty, exercised each day by punching the heavy bag. He'd boxed Golden Gloves until an eye injury had forced him to quit and start working construction. His arms were like hammers when they drilled the canvas and made it pop, his feet shuffling and dancing around the red cylinder that swung from the steel ceiling beam. He always wore a camouflage tank top and shorts when he boxed, and Lara knew that training had been his salvation since he'd quit drinking six months ago.

Gary stopped punching when he saw her come down the steps, his chest heaving from the exertion and the muscles in his biceps seemingly ready to burst from the strain. He sat with her on some folding chairs and held her hand and listened as she told him everything about Leonard. "I don't know what else to do," she finally said in a tearful voice. "I just want him to leave me alone."

"I'm proud of you for telling me," he said. "You did the right thing. Now let your big brother help you out." She wasn't sure what he meant by that but figured Gary would know how to handle a situation like this. She also trusted him to keep it a secret. Before she went back upstairs, he gave her a strong hug that lifted her off the ground and she felt safe in his powerful arms.

"Thanks," she whispered to him.

"I'll always be there for you," he said. "You can count on it."

Later that weekend, Gary invited her back down to the basement. "It's time you learned to defend yourself," he said. "Guys like Leonard will always be around, and you need to know how to handle them." He showed her how to punch and kick, using the heavy bag as a target. "When you kick, aim for the crotch," he told her. "Hit him in the nuts and he'll go down." She started training with Gary at night and would do back-to-back reps of twenty-five until her arms and legs throbbed and she had to rest. "Be strong," he would say, coaching her on technique and positioning, "and never let your guard down." She liked working out with her big brother and felt powerful each time she smacked the heavy bag and thought of Leonard's face recoiling from one of her punches.

One night after training, Gary went over to a metal footlocker in the corner of the basement. He removed a small object wrapped in cloth and came back to where Lara was standing. "This is serious stuff," he said solemnly, "but I think you're ready."

Then he uncovered it and Lara saw the gun in its leather holster. Gary placed it in her hand so she could feel the black casing, surprisingly cold to the touch, and the dark, pebbled handle. "It's a nine millimeter I bought when I used to live in a rough neighborhood. "He showed her how to hold it, arms outstretched like a steel rod as she supported the weapon with both hands, then how to load the bullets and flip the safety off and on. "I always keep it loaded," he said. "Just in case."

For the next few evenings, he drove her to an isolated field outside of town and had her practice shooting. She liked the heft of the pistol in her hand, how powerful she felt aiming down the barrel and squeezing the trigger. "It's a bad ass world out there," Gary said. "A woman's got to be able to take care of herself." They practiced close range stuff, firing at pop cans and beer bottles that were ten or fifteen feet away, and Lara loved the rush of seeing the glass explode as she hit her mark dead-on. Afterward, when they drove home at dusk in Gary's Camaro, they listened to Los Lobos on the stereo and Lara tried to remember the last time she'd felt this safe and warm and strong. Sometimes Gary turned the music up even louder and howled like a wolf and she laughed at her crazy brother, at his wild ways, and knew that he loved her and would always be there for her no matter what the cost.

Lara was shivering on the cold steps of the school as she waited for Kelly and Shannon so she jammed her icy fingers deep into the coat pockets. She watched a few cars roll into the school parking lot as the rich kids from Snob Hill started to arrive. Their vehicles had sleek, curved exteriors and tinted windows and rode low to the ground. As they eased past where she was sitting, their stereos throbbing with bass, Lara wondered if sports car side panels were bulletproof and whether they could withstand a full round from a 9 mm at close range. She'd seen this old movie on TV called *Bonnie and Clyde* about some out-laws in the Depression. At the end, Bonnie, who was pregnant with Clyde's baby, got all shot up while she was sitting in her car, and Lara thought about how her body danced like some dying puppet as the bullets pierced her skin over and over. Lara closed her eyes and tried to imagine what the bullets could do to one of the Snob Hill guys while he sat in the plush, leather-seated comfort of his new Mustang.

Last night on the phone Shannon had said, "You got a death wish, girl," after Lara had told her about the lump on her breast. She'd found it earlier that morning in the shower and was sure it was cancer, the same disease that had killed her grandma and forced Teresa to have her left breast sliced off the way a butcher lops a ham in half with his meat cleaver. "Nothing but a zit on your tit," Shannon said, giggling. "I wish I had two big lumps on my chest like yours." Even though Lara laughed with her, she still spent most of the night probing her breast again for the lump she was certain was there. This time she found nothing and tried to put the possibility of cancer out of her mind. But it kept creeping back in. So she got up and wrote in her diary:

> death is in the air
> poison on my tongue
> welcome to my lair
> where death is everywhere

It sounded like a song and she decided to call it "Black Widow" and work on it later. The spider could be a symbol for cancer and the song could be about how it traps everyone in its net. She put the diary in her backpack next to the bed so she could show it to Kelly at school. Kelly was always looking for catchy song lyrics. Lara wanted to start an all-girl band called Vampire Planet and was trying to talk Kelly and Shannon into taking gui-tar lessons with her at the music shop in Old Town. Lara was going to ask her mom about it as a possible Christmas gift even though she knew money was tight at home. Along with the morning paper route, Teresa worked as a stylist at Hairem in Old Town. Business had dropped off since they put in the new Klip'N'Curl chain stores and she was afraid the shop was going to fold.

Lara's legs were going numb from sitting on the frozen steps and she stood up to move around. *Where the hell are they?* she wondered, glancing toward the front of the school for any sign of Kelly or Shannon. She thought about asking her dad, Ernie, for the guitar lesson money this weekend, but then decided against it. Ernie worked long hours in Denver and ran heavy equipment for Cruz Construction. He often left early for work and didn't get home until late at night after Lara had gone to sleep. Even if she did ask him for the money, she was pretty sure she knew what the answer would be. The same answer he'd given her for weeks now. His excuses had become all too familiar.

"I don't have that kind of cash, baby, I swear," he'd tell her. "I haven't seen a paycheck for over three months. Business is hurting 'cause all the damn West coast outfits are moving in and stealing the contracts. Ask me again next month and I'll see what I can do. That's a promise." Then he'd wink at her and smile and flip on the TV.

Lara slung the backpack over her shoulder and started walking toward the main entrance. She'd gone about thirty feet when she glanced over and saw the red graffiti sprayed on the brick next to the door: **I RAPED LARA**, it said. For a moment she couldn't catch her breath. She looked away at the parking lot, then back again. The letters were still there and seemed bigger than before, like a banner written in blood that carried her name. *A deed without a name*, she thought with a shudder. There was already a small crowd and kids were pointing and laughing at the message. She wanted to run home and hide in her room, under the bed, where it was dark and quiet and warm. But she saw the words and looked at herself and the way she was dressed and knew she couldn't go home while Teresa was still there. She moved quickly back to the entrance next to the auditorium and slipped inside.

The nearest girls' bathroom was on the second floor so she hurried up the stairs, careful not to trip. Once inside, she went to the farthest stall and bolted the door, then sat on the toilet seat and began to cry. The tears were hot and her eyes suddenly felt exhausted. She slammed a hand against the metal divider and felt the sting on her palm. She'd told Kelly and Shannon about Leonard and the phone calls. She'd wanted to tell someone at the school before now and had even thought about going to Mrs. Romero, the assistant principal. But she'd hoped it wouldn't get to that point, that Leonard would just go away and find someone else to bother. Besides, if she did tell Mrs. Romero, she didn't want Leonard coming after her if he found out. There was talk around school that he'd almost gone to juvie because he tried to rape someone. And Lara didn't dare tell her mom. Teresa had already made it clear that she didn't like Lara's new friends or the way she'd been dressing. She threatened to send her to St. Cecelia's, an all-girl Catholic school, if her grades and attitude didn't improve.

She heard someone come into the bathroom and she froze, trying to stay as quiet as possible. Then there was a knock on the stall door.

"Lara?" Kelly whispered. "Are you in there?"

Lara didn't say a word, just sat on the toilet with her head down and stared at the cracked floor. All she wanted was to slip into some other clothes and head out. She could hang at the mall for the rest of the day, then take some back streets home after three o'clock.

Suddenly she saw Kelly's face slide under the stall door, an outlandish clown of a face that was half-white, half black, with a red crescent moon around one eye and a purple diamond around the other. Lara smiled at the black lipstick and the tiny gold skulls that dangled from Kelly's ears.

"Where hast thou been sister?" Kelly said, sliding the rest of the way into the stall. She was impossibly skinny, a dancer and actress who rebelled against the daily grind of lessons and auditions and told her parents to shove it so she could do her own thing. They'd become friends after meeting in one of the ballet classes run by Madame Fifi, the local dance matron, who all the parents adored and all the kids hated. Kelly had been kicked out of the studio when, after being yelled at for her wild, jazzy moves, she'd yanked off Madame Fifi's peroxide blond wig in a fit of anger and hurled it into the trash.

Kelly pulled herself off the floor, grinned, and said, "Sister, where art thou?"

Lara tried to smile, then said, "Let's cut? We could go to the mall."

Kelly frowned. "And miss another day at Raving Hell?" she replied. She gave Lara a stern look. "Miss Wright, as your legal counsel regarding the slander splattered across the front of the school, I'd strongly advise you to find one Leonard, a bastard of the first order, ask him if he understands the consequences for attempted rape and harassment, then sue his ass."

Lara didn't smile. "I can't go in the halls," she said. "They're all laughing. And he's out there laughing with them."

"So screw 'em," Kelly said. She reached over and squeezed Lara's arm. "Truth?" Lara looked at her and nodded. "Leonard's a psycho whose day is coming. You can't bail and show him you're scared. If you do, he wins." Kelly reached out and traced something invisible on the metal panel with her finger. "Easy for me to say. My name's not out there on the wall." She looked at Lara with her aqua blue eyes. "But I wish it was my name and not yours so you didn't have to put up with this shit. I mean that."

"I know you do," Lara said.

"We can't kick his ass like he deserves, but we can outthink him. The problem is that he's no dummy. We got to set him up. Make him feel some pain in return. Payback."

"I don't know," said Lara. "I'd just as soon let Mrs. Romero deal with it. She's been after him all year."

"And how's she gonna deal with *it*? What evidence does she have that Leonard wrote it? Any witnesses? No. And when she asks Leonard if he was involved, all he'll say is 'Hell no, I was at home watching *da tube*.' End of the interrogation. Romero strikes out."

Lara was quiet. She looked around at the stall. She felt as if she were trapped in a steel box with all exits blocked. She just wanted to get through the day and then have the next two weeks to lay low and hope people would forget about the graffiti.

"Leonard needs to learn a lesson. He needs some instruction," said Kelly.

"Like what?" asked Lara.

"Eighth period with Hard On. It's perfect. He and Leonard have been at each other for the last two months. We're gonna set him up so Hard On does the work for us. All we do is sit back and watch."

Hard On was Mr. Hardin, their English teacher. A real head case. He'd been at Ravenhill for half a year after transferring from some school in Eagle Ridge. Rumor was that he'd hit a student and the district was trying to avoid a lawsuit. Hardin spent the first day of classes telling stories about when he worked in the Peace Corps on some tropical island in the Pacific. He talked about how respectful all the native kids were and how much they appreciated their education until Lara thought she was gonna barf. Then he said, "If there's one thing I love, it's teaching the English language. I hope by the end of the year we'll be in agreement on this subject." His class was a burn. All they did was write. Paper after paper after paper. Most kids were failing. Some gave up after the first assignment and spent most of their time baiting Hardin, trying to get him to explode. Leonard was their ringleader.

Lara finally looked at Kelly and said, "What's the plan?"

"I've got inside information on Leonard. A little surprise."

"What is it?"

Kelly shook her head. "Not now. We'll go find Shannon, then talk."

"But how'd you get it?"

Kelly offered a sly grin. "There are perks to being student aide for the counselor. The files get mighty interesting on a slow day when Mrs. Gordon is sick." She reached for her schoolbag and hoisted it to her shoulder. "Let's do some face paint so we can make a stunning entrance."

Lara took her hand and said, "Thou'rt kind, weird sister."

Kelly opened the stall door and smiled, her midnight lipstick absolutely ghoulish. When they stood in front of the mirror, Lara looked at herself and longed to be transformed into someone anonymous and unrecognizable.

"Make me look mean," she said to Kelly. "A real hell-raiser."

"Like a storm threatening on the horizon?"

"Exactly."

Kelly began by covering her face in black. *A mask of night,* Lara thought. *I like it.* Then she added dark purple lipstick and made jagged gold lightning bolts around each of her eyes, followed by tears of blood that dripped down her cheeks.

When she was finished, the makeup mistress took a step back to look at Lara.

"Ready to rock," Kelly announced proudly. "Leonard's gonna take one look and say, 'I'm not messing with her.'"

"Ready for revenge," Lara added.

As they left the restroom and made their entrance into the corridor, they walked arm in arm, a pair of dark twins. Their mouths were expressionless, but their eyes flicked from one student to the next as they strode down the hallway. The doors to the classrooms were decorated with ribbons, tinsel, Christmas tree lights that blinked off and on, wrapping paper, candy canes. As Kelly and Lara passed by the other students, there were whistles and someone shouted, "Check out the lezzies!" A cluster of Snob Hill girls, many of them dressed in their Abercrombie & Bitch shirts, stared in disbelief as if witnessing a procession of aliens from a distant asteroid. *Let 'em look*, thought Lara.

When they moved toward the main entrance, she kept her radar on alert, scanning the passing students for Leonard, secretly hoping that maybe he was cutting today, or that he'd decided to head home and avoid the trouble he was guaranteed to get into. But as they walked past the library, some skaters turned to check out the show, and she saw Leonard's face rise from the crowd. He wore a mask of bruises. His cheeks were swollen, the color of plums. There was a red gash above his eye and his lip was cut. She imagined the rhythm of her brother's fists, a class ring glinting on his right hand, as they rained down on Leonard's face. Leonard stared straight at her, then blew her a kiss with his battered lips. He grinned and she saw the two missing front teeth. She felt Kelly's grip tighten on her arm as they moved away and heard her whisper, "Something wicked this way comes." Then they were past him and she was glad to have her weird sister beside her as she faced the day and all that it would bring.

■ ■ ■

FRIDAY, DECEMBER 19, 1997
7:15 A.M.

S.A.M.

S A.M. Bond (aka Secret Agent Man) lowered his black Ray-Ban sunglasses and studied the red message in foot high letters that greeted him at the entrance to Ravenhill High School: **I RAPED LARA**. He could sense danger in the air and gripped the handle of the black attaché case. It was connected to his arm by a silver chain and a lone steel handcuff that dangled loosely around his bony wrist. *A lie is a poisonous vine whose roots must be ripped away*, he thought. The line came to him so powerfully that he repeated it for emphasis, then filed it away in his mind as material for his memoirs.

He had trained himself for situations such as this, when menace crackled in the moment the way ice crystals snapped under his steel-toed black boots and danger loomed as if it were a scent in the air, something to anticipate, the way a mercenary might smell the aroma of burning petrol fumes a mile away and know the enemy is near. He focused on the crude writing followed by the elegance of her name, *LARA*, a name that had no place in a sentence that belonged etched on a dimly lit bathroom wall. He tried to analyze the letters, even visualize the culprit's

47

hand curled around the can of spray paint as it hissed out a mist of scarlet onto the brick. But whose hand?

S.A.M. knew the victim and her profile. The absence of the u preceding the r in her name was the giveaway. Lara Wright (aka Goddess of the Night). Fifteen years old. A hundred pounds of slim beauty. Snowy skin. Dark hair as black as a raven's wing. Carried a C average in school. Favorite subject: drama. Favorite singer: Sarah McLachlan. Favorite friend: Kelly Mason. Lived with her mother, Teresa, and her father, Ernie.

S.A.M. had studied her from afar ever since he arrived at Ravenhill in late September, *he* the skinny transfer student from Toledo, *she* the hometown beauty he saw standing in the library checkout line, a copy of *Go Ask Alice* tucked neatly under a creamy arm, so luminous against the black tank top she wore. What followed in the weeks to come was strictly undercover. He learned her class schedule, the location of her locker, her home address, her route to school, her friends and rivals, her favorite table in the cafeteria. He knew she didn't have a boyfriend, hadn't dated anyone all year, and that the jocks called her *frigid* and *Lara Lezbo*. All this gleaned while observing from a distance and asking the right questions. In truth, he'd never spoken to her. *My dark, distant beauty,* S.A.M. thought. *I am your guardian, your shadow. No harm shall cross your path.*

He scrutinized the graffiti for a moment longer. No sign of a tag. The writing itself was crude, a rushed scrawl from an unpracticed hand. One that could possibly leave red paint on its fingertips and never think of washing it off after the act. S.A.M. had prepared himself to think outside of the box, to shift the paradigm and examine all the possibilities. This was a skill that could save his life many years from now when working as an antiterrorist operative and finding himself trapped in a rubbish-strewn alley in Damascus, encircled by assassins who lunged at him with knives that flashed in the moonlight, and his only weapon was a jagged shard of glass found in the dust at his feet.

He had embraced the way of the warrior. He had studied the films of John Woo.

S.A.M. needed information and he knew where to find it. If anyone was tuned in to the subterranean web of Ravenhill, then it was the man who had a key to every closet and a combination for every locker; the man who scrubbed and sanded off the latest gossip on the bathroom stalls; the man who scanned the desk of every teacher and administrator while emptying the trash each afternoon. Paul Munn: Head Custodian (aka The Source).

S.A.M. entered the school and headed to the end of the building where Paul had a custodial office on the lower level. He moved with fluid silence, unnoticed by the huddled packs of students who crowded around their lockers. They still stared and occasionally taunted him with names like *Freak Show* and *Dark Man*. There were days when it seemed every eye in the school was trained on him like an infrared sniper scope. But he refused to be a clone for the masses and his "look" had never wavered: jet black hair, slicked back and glistening with mousse; black Ray-Bans that slipped over his eyes like midnight shields; black turtleneck; black pants and steel-toed boots that made him seem taller than he already was. And draped over his thin, wiry frame was the long black raincoat that hung to his knees. London Fog, of course. When he arrived that first day, he made sure they noticed, and he never looked away, never backed off, always stared them down with the unflinching gaze of a special agent licensed to kill.

The attaché case was the finishing touch on his "look," and he took it everywhere with him. Inside were his vital documents and papers, as recommended by the International Undercover Survival Manual: birth certificate, emergency contacts, insurance and medical documents, one hundred dollars in travelers' cheques, passport, and immunization records. If he were to return from school one day after a terrorist attack and find only the bombed-out, flaming skeleton of his home, then at least he'd have a fighting chance. It would be essential to travel light and leave no trail as to one's past history, one's origins. In the face of disaster or an assassination attempt, he'd have to wipe the slate clean and vanish without a trace. He'd have to resurface in a tropical city of his choice.

But on this last day before winter break, the case contained more than just private artifacts. S.A.M. had brought something powerful and mind-bending to school: a top secret project that could alter the future. For months he'd worked carefully on his masterpiece at home and kept it locked away in the fireproof safe at the rear of his closet. It had been the focus of his life's energy, but he'd told no one of his grand plan. Today would be different. Today he'd reveal the passion and splendor of his labor for all to see, and no one, especially Lara Wright, would ever look at him the same way again. As he moved through the halls, he felt the extra weight shift within the black leather interior of the briefcase, a life force of immeasurable power. He would allow nothing to interfere with his calculated plan, even the unexplained message left on the outside wall that threatened to tarnish the name and reputation of Our Lara of Dark Shadows.

When he reached the steps leading to the basement, he moved down two at a time and found Paul at the bottom, mopping up the remains of a 32-ounce Mountain Dew explosion that had splattered on the walls as well as the floor. Paul looked over and saw S.A.M. on the stairs.

"Mountain Dew's the worst," Paul said. "I mop and mop and the floor's *still* sticky. Eats the wax right off. I could always use it as a stripper."

"I never touch the stuff," S.A.M. said. "Rots your teeth. I like the pure adrenaline of Jolt."

"Now there's a healthy drink," Paul said as he stopped to wring out the mop in the metal bucket.

S.A.M. stood next to the green puddle that had ebbed across the floor. "I need some information," he said.

Paul straightened up to his full height and nearly bumped his head against the exposed ceiling pipes. "If you want information from me, then I need some from you. Deal?"

"Deal," S.A.M. answered quickly. He and the head custodian had a business relationship of sorts within the confines of the school. Sometimes he helped Paul out when there was vandalism in the building and he needed a lead. If the heads-up was solid, then Paul might slip a few dollars into his locker. S.A.M. didn't see it as snitching, only justice.

But today the tables had turned. It was Paul who owed S.A.M. the favor. Right before Thanksgiving, a school water line froze and then burst. The library was nearly ruined by the damage, and it was Paul's job to get the place cleaned up during the short break. S.A.M. helped out for $5.15 an hour since his father was out of town for the week at a convention in Las Vegas. He and Paul and Mr. Moore, the ancient librarian, spent two days sucking up water with the Wet-Vac and hauling ruined materials out to the dumpster. In the end, they were able to salvage most of the collection and get the place cleaned up in time for classes to begin.

Paul continued mopping. His tall frame swayed as if dancing to a slow ballad. "So where've you been the last three days?" he asked, smiling. "I haven't seen you at school."

S.A.M. hesitated and gently swung the briefcase back and forth at his side. He thought again of the contents with all of its unseen, unreleased energy. "I've been on a mission," he finally said. End of sentence.

"Mission Impossible stuff, huh?" Paul asked. "What's so impossible?"

"It's top secret," S.A.M. said. "No information available at this time."

"No deal then," Paul said with a shrug. "If you want information from me, then I need straight answers from you. Not this top secret crap." He turned away and wheeled the bucket to the far side of the hall.

S.A.M. looked down and pointed his toe at the dwindling pool of Mountain Dew. "I haven't been officially cutting. They've all been excused absences because Q called them in from Seattle. That's all you need to know, isn't it?"

Q was S.A.M.'s father. He was currently in Seattle on a job. His real name was Quentin, but S.A.M. called him Q after the inventor in all the James Bond movies. S.A.M. and Q were Bond fanatics and had watched all the films from their complete video collection at least ten times. They had elaborate models of all the Bond cars; framed posters from each of the movies; a handsome, leather bound collection of every Ian Fleming book; a photo album that contained 8 x10 glossies of all the Bond girls. They had the rock solid opinion that Sean Connery kicked ass over all the other pseudo-Bond boys, including the current one, Pierce Brosnan. They planned to see *Tomorrow Never Dies* together over the Christmas holidays as kind of a *bonding* experience.

Q was an inventor of sorts, an engineering consultant who specialized in creating high tech security systems for corporate offices, as well as solving computer meltdowns that no one else knew how to fix. He'd worked for all the big companies, including the CIA, and was usually sworn to secrecy at the end of a project. He was always flying off in the middle of the night for a crisis in Atlanta or Albuquerque or Alberta, leaving behind a note that said, "Call you from the hotel," as well as a healthy roll of cash. When Q was gone, S.A.M. was supposed to check in with his elderly neighbors, the Pecks, but he often forgot and no one seemed to notice. He preferred the solo scene anyway.

"*Officially* cutting, huh?" Paul asked. "How do I know you're telling the truth?" He finished mopping up the Mountain Dew, then stepped back to inspect the floor.

"Check the records yourself if you don't believe me. I've been home working on a project." S.A.M. paused, trying to anticipate the next question. "I wanted to get it done before Q gets home tomorrow. This year he's promised we'll have a genuine Merry Christmas, complete with a father in the flesh."

Paul nodded and put an orange plastic sign over the spill area that said *Caution: Wet Floor.* "Okay," he said, "but there's a price for information this time."

"Name it." S.A.M. reached into his pocket and pulled out a wad of bills, the latest generosity from Q before heading out to fly the friendly skies.

"Put it away," Paul said. "That's not what I'm talking about. I don't ever want money from you. But I do need a promise."

"The price of a promise."

"Exactly. I need your butt in class the rest of the day. No slipping out to head home early." Paul held his gaze for a moment. "And I'll check the attendance after eighth hour."

S.A.M. paused, adjusted his shades. "Affirmative on the attendance."

Paul leaned forward, his long neck extended. "If you cut, I'm going straight to Romero. Got it?"

"Got it."

He walked toward S.A.M. and placed his foot on the stairs. "In case you're wondering, it's because I give a damn. I want you to do something with yourself, and you have to be in class for school to count in the long haul." Paul stepped back, tipped his head down and glared at the orange sign. "End of lecture. What information do you need?"

"The message on the wall at the entrance. Any leads?"

Paul laughed. "I'm usually asking you that question."

S.A.M. nodded. "It's important."

"Some cans of red spray paint were stolen from my closet on Tuesday. Bright stuff. I use it to touch up some of the lockers and it's perfect for tagging." Paul leaned on his mop. "I busted Leonard Lamb in the hall on Monday for grabbing Sheri Montrose. I had to pull him off her."

"There's a lot to grab," S.A.M. said, grinning.

"So I figured Leonard would try to pay me back in some way. I don't own a car that he can tag, so he chose the next best thing. My school. He knows who does the cleanup around here. A little gift for the holidays, I guess. He even used my own paint. Nice twist."

"Thanks."

S.A.M. turned to go, but Paul stopped him. "A question before you head out for a day of perfect attendance. Why are you so interested?"

"Let's just say Leonard could interfere with my mission," S.A.M. said. "Time is of the essence."

"I don't think he's going to want the attention," Paul replied.

"Perhaps not." S.A.M. attempted a suave, knowing grin, trying to emulate Bond laughing in the face of peril.

"I'd prefer you didn't get suspended for fighting."

"Live long and prosper," S.A.M. said, making a Vulcan sign. "Thank you O wise and great Master of the Mop."

"Get your wise butt to class," Paul said and S.A.M. was gone, leaping up the stairs and hoping for a glimpse of Lara Wright, the Object of His Protection.

When S.A.M. entered the main hallway, he saw that it was jammed now, a veritable cattle drive of movement. *The masses head for their classes.* He scanned the crowd for any sign of Lara and saw nothing. Perhaps, out of embarrassment, she'd fled for cover and sought the protective shelter of home. He stepped into the steady traffic as some students hustled to beat the bell, while others cruised or hung out. He went past the office and stopped at the intersection of the center stairwell and the main hall, making sure to put his back to the wall while doing a visual probe of the student body. He was located in an excellent defensive position. In a full combat scenario, with an Uzi dangling from his right hand instead of the briefcase, he could cover the entire first floor as well as the stairs. An army of one.

He waited, clicking his headphones into place and letting the roar of the music focus his senses. He was the Prince of Visible Invisibility. He had trained himself to be still, unnoticed, silent. Time meant nothing to him. He could stand for hours like a frozen sentinel and never twitch. *A Master of Menace and Mime.* The minutes seemed to whisper away on a strong undercurrent of tension. Then S.A.M. lowered his Ray-Bans and peered over the rim to spy upon Lara Wright, Her Majesty of Midnight, as she glided down the hall in full gothic splendor a mere twenty feet away. Black was definitely very becoming. She was arm in arm with Kelly Mason (aka The Vamp) and as they approached, S.A.M. reached to his hip and cranked up the decibels on his Walkman so that Cryptogram blasted through to celebrate her procession. He wanted to speak her name, to simply nod in her direction and acknowledge her presence. Instead he lingered in the perfumed wake of her passing and felt a certain radiation of the soul that ripped through him like a Geiger counter clicking to life. It was then, across the hall and behind Lara, that S.A.M. saw one Leonard Lamb (aka The Lurker), his left cheek swollen and purple, as he smiled and blew a kiss to Lara with bruised, puffy lips.

A Judas kiss. A traitorous glance. The kind of giveaway that S.A.M. detected and mentally filed away to be used at a later date. Leonard was the class psycho, notorious for his shrieking "eyegasms" in the hallway whenever an attractive female passed within sniffing distance. He'd often unleash a wolfish howl as he strutted past the lockers, snapping bras and pinching bottoms along the way. He was the master of the unsubtle innuendo, the crude one-liner that could trigger a blush at twenty feet. S.A.M. could think of many titles heard around the school to capture the essence of Leonard: Neanderthal, bottom-feeder, thug, shark, Crip Wannabe. But one thing had always been clear to S.A.M. since he'd first seen Leonard cruising the hallway. He had brains and brawn and was capable of inflicting extreme pain on the weak and less fortunate.

As the bell screamed through the corridor, S.A.M. remained motionless and watched Leonard and his friends move down the hall. He noticed that Leonard was limping, favoring his left leg. Perhaps a bad knee or ankle. Either way, it was a tender target worth remembering. The remaining students dashed off to class while S.A.M. waited at his sentry post. He saw no need to hurry or rush. Being late sent a message. *I'm in control of my fate. I'm on time when I choose to be.* He waited exactly sixty seconds, then took three long strides and slipped through the gymnasium door for PE (aka Punishment Extremis).

■ ■ ■

FRIDAY, DECEMBER 19, 1997
7:20 A.M.

Leonard

At sixteen,
He's heard it *all*.
Been listening to it *all* for years.
All the lies.
All the names,
All the nasties.
One day he just took that shit
and made a rap from the crap
they'd thrown at him.
He sings it to himself
when he's alone,
walking to Raving Hole,
making up a new rhyme
just to pass the time.
Calls it the Crap Rap.

"I'm a psycho,
I'm a killer,
I'm a sicko

in a thriller.
I'm a player,
I'm a dealer.
I'm a loser,
I'm a prick.
Some people call me trouble,
some people call me sick.
One day I'll turn the tables,
I'll buy a big old gun,
I'll strut into that damn school
and watch the teachers run.
You call me a retard,
reject,
pervert,
idiot.
But someday I'll be on TV,
rapping out my game,
and you'll remember Leonard
by a very different name.
Millionaire,
Superman,
Romeo,
Master Lamb..."

WHEN Leonard hit the halls at Ravenhill that morning he was looking for his crew and trying not to limp even though his left knee was on fire from the ambush last night. He thought of Burly Steel, his main man, the World Wrestling Federation champion with the gold lightning bolt tattooed across his forehead. He thought of Burly striding into the ring on Wrestlerama, that smart-ass smile playing across his face cause he knew he was the only stud going to walk out of that ring standing. "You against me!?" Burly would scream at the crowd, the veins bulging out of his neck. "You against me!?" Then he'd jump onto the ropes and unleash his bloodcurdling howl. "I'm gonna make 'em bleed so I get what I need!"

As Leonard walked down Locker Row, he checked out the ladies gliding by and made sure to give them the total body inspection. He especially liked the belly button shirts with the bare midriffs and often imagined his hand sliding over virgin skin and moving south into the panty zone. He saw Sharon Kane, nicknamed Big Kandy, and winked at her, making sure that he scanned the sweet V of cleavage she seductively revealed. She grinned back at him, curling her tongue at the tip, and for a moment Leonard remembered that same tongue sliding into his mouth for a little French action not so long ago.

Been there, done that, he thought, moving quickly past Big Kandy. In November, Ronnie Wilson's parents went out of town, so Ronnie and his older brother Jimbo made the mistake of throwing a little party that got out of control when half the high school showed up. Leonard had gone and after drinking six or seven beers, he saw Big Kandy looking smashed and stumbling around the kitchen. He'd been watching her slam down shooters and knew she was ripped. So when she staggered by, he saw his chance and grabbed her hand, then slipped into a side bedroom, making sure to lock the door behind him. In the darkness he kissed her, then slid his hand under her shirt. Kandy didn't try to stop him, even surprised him when she kissed him back and jammed her tongue into his mouth. It was just like a scene in one of those Triple X movies that Leonard's old man liked to watch after the late shift, the ones Leonard could rewind after Leon had passed out in the EZ-Boy.

Big Kandy had moaned something in his ear, then pulled him onto the bed. He unbuttoned her shirt and spent the next few minutes kissing her breasts before going for the zipper on her jeans. And that's when he glanced up and saw it leap at him in a flash out of the shadows, the tiger stretched tight across its

skin, the red flesh thrusting to strike like some evil snake trying to poison him with its venom.

Leonard jerked back to shield himself from the creature and
fell sideways off the bed, striking the floor with his shoulder. Just
as suddenly as it appeared, the phantom was gone, and he was
left shaking uncontrollably on the floor. He felt ashamed and
wanted to get the hell out of that room, out of that house. Before
he knew it, Kandy was kneeling beside him, her hand on his
shoulder, saying something that he couldn't hear. He pulled away
from her, said he felt sick and needed to go to the bathroom. "It's
just the beer," she said, her voice slurred, her hand trying to rub
his back as she tried to kiss him again. But he pushed her arm
away, stood up, and walked to the bedroom door. His legs trembled as he unlocked it, then stepped out into the hallway. Heavy
metal blared from the next room, and he could hear someone
screaming out the words to the song. He slipped quietly out the
back door and took the alleys, staying in the shadows, laying low,
always on the prowl for the midnight curfew cruisers.

When he got home and climbed into bed and covered himself with a thin blanket, all he could think about was Lara
Wright who lived exactly one block away in a brick house on the
left side of the street. She was probably asleep at this very
moment, her eyes closed, her lips slightly parted, her white
nightgown glistening in the moonlight. She wouldn't see him
slide the bedroom window up and ease inside as if he were some
ghostly visitor. She wouldn't see him as he stood next to her bed
like a sentry and watched her sleep. He might want to hold her
hand or stroke her hair, but he wouldn't. Strictly hands off.
Untouchable. Fragile. He might even lean down and steal a kiss
just to know for sure if her lips felt like warm petals. But he
wouldn't do that either. He'd stand close to the bed, his hand
resting on the pink comforter, and listen to the soft hiss of her
breathing. This was close enough. This was all he needed so he
could sleep. So he could dream.

When Leonard finally saw his crew at the end of the hallway, he unleashed a powerful howl that startled everyone around him. "One more day," he shouted, "and then we're outta The Hole." Rory and Jason and Zeb made room for him near their lockers. They wore black stocking caps that fit snugly around their heads and baggy black jeans and dark T-shirts that hung loosely from their shoulders and hips. The shirts were turned inside out so that the beer or pot symbols on the front didn't show. That way Romero couldn't suspend them for inappropriate attire. They knew their rights. They paid attention in social studies when reading the Constitution, even if it was the *only* thing they paid attention to at school.

"What happened?" Rory asked, nodding at Leonard's face. "You and Leon get into it again?"

Leonard grinned so they could all see the missing teeth.

"Hell no. Leon's too tired from sleeping off the night shift. I'm just changing my image," he said. "I need that Wrestlerama look."

"All you need is a dentist," Jason said. "He can put in some gold teeth. Make you look like a gangster."

"A gangster would be fine," Leonard said, leaning against a locker. "A gangster and a player. Gotta work on my style. Gotta look more intimidating."

"*Gotta work on my thyle,*" Rory mimicked in a feminine voice. "*Gotta look more inthimidating.*"

"Faggot!" Leonard shouted, pushing Rory back against the locker. "What size dress you wear, skank?"

"Go play with yourself," Rory snapped back. "It's all you ever gonna get."

Zeb stepped between them and said, "Don't start nothing. My old man said he'd kill me if I got anywhere near another suspension."

Rory didn't back down. He'd been talking trash at Leonard ever since that Ziploc full of weed mysteriously vanished last week. He didn't accuse Leonard of taking it out of his locker, but Leonard knew he suspected as much. "So what happened to your face?" Rory continued. "You been wrestling with Big Kandy again?"

This time Leonard shoved Zeb out of the way and grabbed Rory by the throat, then pinned him to the locker. It happened lightning quick, before Rory could resist, and Leonard got his face real close this time. "I got jumped last night," he said. "Down by the railroad tracks. Some bum wanted my money. Like I had any to give him."

Leonard could see the fear in Rory's eyes, the way his breath wheezed out. So he squeezed a little tighter.

"I didn't know," Rory gasped.

Leonard eased up, then turned him loose. "Half the time you don't know nothing."

"So what happened with the bum?" Jason asked.

Leonard paused and looked at them. They were eager, wanting a story. So he gave them one, a blow by blow account. One they'd never forget. One they'd be sure and tell their friends. "I was coming home last night when he jumped me. He came out of the trees behind Bo's Tavern down near the underpass. The bastard was huge, bigger than Burly Steel, and there were tattoos covering his arms. He flicked out a switchblade and rushed me. I slowed him down with a kick to the balls. He dropped the knife but kept coming at me. I was just trying to survive. It was close quarters, hand to hand stuff. He'd bust me and I'd bust 'em back. Finally he went down and I kicked him hard and took off. I left a few of my teeth behind, but I was lucky to get home alive."

Leonard paused and looked into their faces. He knew he had them, especially Rory, and knew they were buying it all. He could count on them to spread the story once he was finished. No other way to handle this. After all, he had a reputation.

The real story had been different. Something he'd take care of later when there was time for revenge. The real story was about getting jumped when he let his guard down. Ambush action that required payback, pure and simple. He'd been over at the strip mall until eight last night. He was on a roll playing Night Hunter in the arcade and was kicking some vampire ass. He got to level seven by using the pump action that fired crucifix buckshot. When the Fang Pack jumped him in the Fourth Tower, he obliterated them until their guts were dripping from the chandeliers in the Feast Room and, as a bonus, earned a hundred Blood Rush points.

Afterward, his head still buzzing from the flash and 3-D visuals, he headed home to his old man's place by taking the tracks behind Bo's Tavern. A train was coming down from the north, its yellow engine light shooting ahead like a laser beam. He thought about trying to outrun it at the junction, but then decided he had no chance. Last year some stoned high school kid tried to race the train on foot and got himself cut in half when he slipped in front of the engine. So Leonard waited and counted the boxcars and looked to see if there were any bums hanging out inside the empties. He liked to stand close to the train as it passed and feel the rush of air. The metal wheels were squealing and he counted to forty-six when a sucker punch caught him square on the side of the head and he went down hard on the gravel. He tried to turn and see his attacker, but suddenly he got kicked in the gut and he rolled backward, his ribs on fire. A jolt to the knee followed. In the darkness he saw a shadow looming above him, definitely a wide body who packed a wallop. A heavy boot slammed down on his chest and pinned him to the ground.

"Get off me!" Leonard yelled above the grinding noise of the train. That's when he got hit in the jaw and felt the crack of knuckles and bone against his teeth. The punch rocked him back so hard that his head smashed into the gravel. For a moment the loud clatter of the train seemed far away, almost an echo. He'd never been hit with such force, a shot that stunned him and left him dazed. Suddenly he was wrenched upright by his jacket collar until his toes were the only thing tapping on the ground. Whoever he was, the dude was strong. There was a voice, a mouth inches from his own and screaming above the train sounds.

"You better listen, punk!" the voice shouted. "You better look and listen real good!" By now Leonard had recovered from the punch so he spit in the face of the man and tried to pull off a crotch kick. But he missed and the man hurled him to the ground, then pounced on top and started punching again, the blows flashing at Leonard like the exploding bombs of Night Hunter, his head only inches from the sparking steel rails.

"How 'bout it?" the figure shouted, crouching down close to Leonard's face. "How 'bout I throw you under that train? How 'bout they pick up the pieces tomorrow?" Leonard clawed at the gravel to his right as he tried to pull himself away from the screeching wheels.

"I got nothing!" Leonard cried out. "I'm broke!" The train was suddenly gone, rattling down the tracks, and his voice sounded shrill, hysterical, in the unexpected quiet. "I mean it, man. I spent it at the arcade. I got nothing."

"I don't need your money," said the stranger. "This ain't about money."

Leonard stopped struggling for a moment and stared up at his attacker. "Then what?" he asked.

"You don't know me, do you?" the man said.

Leonard peered closely at him. In the darkness, he could faintly make out his features. There was something familiar, but he couldn't place him.

The man grabbed him by his coat and jerked him to an upright position. Leonard could feel his pulse racing as he stared at him. He tried hard to look tough, to show no fear, but knew he was shaking. "Gary Wright!" the man suddenly shouted, the words spraying into Leonard's face. He was breathing hard, his nostrils flaring, his eyes wired as he glared at Leonard. "Do we have a connection now?" This time Leonard slowly nodded. He could taste blood on the inside of his mouth and felt something loose when he ran his tongue across his teeth.

"Then listen up!" Wright screamed as his strong hands shook Leonard. "And you better listen good! You need to figure out who needs to be left alone so I don't have to pay you another visit. And I believe you know who I'm talking about." Leonard started to say something, but Gary stuck his face close to Leonard's and whispered in a low, threatening voice. "'Cause if I have to pay you another visit, you're going to the ER next time. We're talking broken bones. We're talking fractures and contusions and massive bleeding. I'll leave you in a damn coma, boy. Am I clear?"

Leonard nodded. "You're clear," he said.

"Crystal," Wright said in return.

Leonard exhaled, then relaxed a little and waited to be released. Instead, he felt a sudden, crushing blow to his jaw and dropped to the ground again. His mouth was filled with blood and he spit two front teeth into his hand. When he glanced up, bracing for another punch or kick, he saw that Gary Wright was gone.

Leonard got to his knees and knelt in the gravel for a while. He could feel his jaw swelling and knew it would need ice. Blood dripped from both his mouth and nose. He stayed down a moment longer and looked around for any signs of his attacker. A streetlight gleamed in the distance. He could hear the sounds of traffic. As he knelt, he thought about the handgun Leon kept in a locked case in his closet. He wondered what Gary Wright would have done if Leonard had pulled out that pistol and leveled it at him. *Next time I'll be ready*, Leonard thought. And he knew the key to that gun case was taped to the back of a crucifix his old man kept on the wall above his bed. *Next time will be different.*

There, by the railroad tracks, a plan clicked into place. Tomorrow when people at school asked about the bruises and cuts on his face, he'd just tell them he got jumped by a bum near the tracks. Some railroad hobo hard up for a buck. At least that's what he'd tell his crew and his old man. As for Lara Wright, he didn't give a damn if her brother came after him again. Next time he wouldn't get sucker punched from behind. Next time he'd have his chain with him. Maybe a gun or knife for self-defense. Next time he'd have the sucker begging for mercy and leave *his* blood on the ground.

But first he had to deal with Lara Wright for ratting on him. He'd have to be smart about it and get her attention somehow. Maybe show her a different side and act like he'd changed. Try to soften her up. Make her think she was in the clear, then scare the hell out of her. Set her up so she'd never know what hit her. No clues. No evidence left behind. No chance for Romero to trace it back to him and kick him out of school. *Innocent until proven guilty*, he thought. His new rap would be about revenge. *I'll find a way—to make her pay—*

The five-minute bell sounded in the hallway and Jason slammed his locker shut, then poked Leonard in the arm. "Check it out," he said, pointing up Locker Row. "Check out the Bitches in Black."

Leonard turned and saw Lara Wright and Kelly Mason coming down the corridor like some freak parade, their black dresses twirling around them, their faces painted like vampire queens. He stepped forward so Lara could see him. He waited until she was only a few feet away, then waved her through with a gentlemanly motion of his arm and blew her a kiss, making sure to smile so she could glimpse the gaps in his teeth. *Even a snake can be sweet*, he thought, *before it strikes*.

■ ■ ■

FRIDAY, DECEMBER 19, 1997
7:25 A.M.

Kathie

I TEACH, I touch the future. The words on the faded bumper sticker were only two feet from Kathie Romero's face as she struggled with the car jack and tried to locate exactly where it should go. The left rear tire of the Subaru sagged forlornly onto the pavement like melted wax. The assistant principal of Ravenhill High School was running ten minutes late, and she was dead certain that the halls were erupting in a fiery panic at this very moment, that students were rioting on the last day of classes before winter break. She cursed herself for not getting new tires a month ago when it was written on the "to do" list posted on her fridge, the impossible "to do" list that she scrutinized every Sunday morning after church when she was hopeful and a believer in the possibility of getting things done on time.

But she was not on time this morning. Not even close. Nor was she much of a believer as cars flashed by in a spray of ice and slush. A spasm of coughing, deep and guttural, erupted and she tried to clear away the fluid by spitting into the snow. Her throat was raw from a night of restless flu. She'd been sick for two weeks and hadn't taken a day off to mend and knew deep down this was all catching up to her. When she wasn't hacking and sneezing and finally surrendering to Nyquil for some relief, she fantasized about the luxuries of a long term-illness and a week of R & R at home in bed. Pneumonia would do nicely.

She removed the spare tire from the trunk and set it on the side of the road, then lay the tools out on the pavement: a jack; a jack handle; a screwdriver; a wheel nut wrench. She took the screwdriver and popped off the wheel cover, then located the notch for the jack and snapped it into place. She'd forgotten gloves and her hands stung from the cold steel. With methodical precision, she began to winch the Subaru up and watched it rise slowly from the pavement in an act of mechanized levitation. She had on her best black suit, the only outfit she owned that made her look sleek and corporate, and by the end of this pit stop she was confident that she'd look anything but professional.

It had been a wild morning and the coming day promised more of the same. Last night Kathie packed until 1:00 A.M. so that she and the boys could leave right after school and drive eighteen hours to Chicago to spend Christmas with her parents. Josh and Ben were currently mad at her, even though they tried hard not to show it on the way to their elementary school. She'd forgotten to bake something for each of their class Christmas parties and there had been no time to run to the grocery store for cookies. Ben was the hardest at seven years old with a stormy, unpredictable attitude. He could hold a fierce grudge against her and keep track of all the times she'd let him down, whether it was getting home late from a PTA meeting and not reading him a book, or forgetting to buy Pringles chips on one of her late night shopping assaults on the local Safeway. Josh, who was ten, seemed to be more understanding, but Ben didn't give a damn that she was a single mom in her second year as an administrator in charge of 750 high school students. When she dropped them off at Clark Elementary that morning, Ben didn't give her a kiss or a hug, just that sniper glare, narrow-eyed and deadly, from outside the car.

She started on the wheel nuts, which wouldn't budge, so she pulled a can of WD-40 from under the seat and sprayed each bolt to loosen it up. Then she set the wheel nut wrench at an angle and began to beat on the bar with her boot heel until the nut slowly turned and she was able to grunt each one off. As she did this, her appointment book clicked through her mind with the day's schedule. The flat was definitely going to set her back.

7:45 A.M. — check in with Claudine.
8:00 — meet with Gus to review her
    district evaluation.
9:00 — meet with Mrs. Lomax and her lawyer
    about a potential lawsuit over her son's
    injury in PE.
9:30 — observe Michelle Greene for her first
    year evaluation.
10:00 — talk with Paul about custodial cleaning
    during the holidays.
10:30 — talk to the contractor from Driscoll
    Construction about repairing the leaky
    roof in the gym over the break.
11:00 — lunchroom supervision.
12:00 — ...

A blank space in her mind. She couldn't remember anything after 12:00 and a shot of panic rushed through her. Then, just as suddenly, it came back. The fire marshal wanted to inspect the old alarm system for faulty wiring and needed a tour of the building.

When the wheel nuts had been removed and the tire was loose, Kathie pulled it off the axle and then slid the spare into its place. Suddenly a wave of nausea rose within her and she felt lightheaded and dizzy. She leaned her head against the car for a moment, closed her eyes, and felt the cool metal door against her cheek. Kathie knew she'd been running a fever, but also knew this was no time to be staying home sick. She had a tough day to get through, a long drive to make. She could crash at her parents' home and sleep for days while her dad took the boys to the movies, shopping at the mall, a hockey game. She hadn't slept well for months. When she went to bed, her mind raced with all the school tasks unfinished, all the projects half done, all the lists of phone calls to parents labeled URGENT. On nights like these, she slipped on her bathrobe and went into the boys' room. They were asleep in their bunk beds and she sat and listened to the steady mantra of their breathing. It was all she needed to get her through to the next morning.

Kathie tightened the wheel nuts and thought about the dream she'd had last night when she finally got to sleep. Somehow she was on the space shuttle *Challenger* right before blastoff and strapped into a seat along with the other astronauts. She was wearing a clear plastic helmet and a space suit that puffed out around her like a marshmallow. Suddenly she realized why she was here: the White House had called six months ago and announced that *two* teachers had been chosen to go into space and Christa McAuliffe had selected her from eleven thousand applicants.

She looked over and saw Christa seated next to her. They'd been through weeks of training together and had bonded like sisters. The newspapers and magazines were filled with stories and pictures of the two of them. She had come to know Christa's family and friends, her habits. She knew that her first name was really Sharon and not Christa at all, and that she went to high school and college in Framingham, Massachusetts. She knew that Christa preferred seafood over steak, that she loved to watch Oprah. Her favorite president was Ronald Reagan. Her favorite writer was James Michener. Her favorite movie was *2001: A Space Odyssey*, especially the scenes with HAL, the mad computer, because Christa loved to imitate HAL in a flat monotone when she was in the training module.

At one point, Christa reached over and squeezed her arm and smiled. Somehow Kathie knew what was about to happen and she tried to tell Christa that they had to get off the rocket, tried to scream at her through the plastic bubble of the helmet. But it was too late. Her shouts were lost in the roaring violence of liftoff and she felt the tilt of the huge missile as it began to accelerate into the sky. She turned and found a small window next to her seat, as if on an airplane. She looked down and could see her sons, Josh and Ben, standing on the ground with her parents and waving American flags. They were smiling and looked proud as their image suddenly disintegrated into a billowing eruption of white smoke and fire. It was right then, at the precise moment of leaving her family and the earth forever, that Kathie knew she was not going to touch the future at all, nor would she ever teach again. She was simply going to die.

When she finished changing the tire and placed the flat in the trunk, Kathie wiped the dirt and oil from her hands with some tissues, then noticed the slashes of grime on the front of her suit. She was too tired to even care. *At least I wore black*, she thought. *Grease blends in nicely.* She was still thinking about Christa McAuliffe, her soul sister of social studies, the teacher astronaut who had sat in the space shuttle *Challenger* and gazed down at the blue planet before suddenly being blown to smithereens in front of thousands of students and teachers who were watching on television in their classrooms.

January 28, 1986. At the precise moment of Christa's death, Kathie had been with her seventh grade class at Carlson Middle School having an end of unit celebration, complete with pop and refreshments that the kids provided, while watching the launch of the *Challenger.* They'd spent the last month learning about Christa's life and studying the history of the space program as part of a special unit on exploration. The students created projects to illustrate what they learned, and Kathie's class was crammed with cardboard models, posters, banners, and dioramas.

They even dedicated one corner of the room to recreating the interior of the *Challenger* by using a couple of borrowed reclining chairs, some huge cardboard refrigerator boxes, and plenty of white sheets, which they painted to resemble the control panels of the shuttle.

When the *Challenger* exploded, it all seemed so far away, as if a sparkler had been lit high in the sky and they were watching it sputter and burn before fizzling out. They watched the replay of the explosion again and again on TV and listened to the announcers try to explain what might have gone wrong. A few of the students began to sob, their heads buried in their arms on the desktops. Charlie Barbosa went over to his cardboard model of the *Challenger* and smashed it with his fist, then threw it on the floor. Most of the kids just sat in silence. Kathie wanted to turn the television off, knew that she probably should, but couldn't stop herself from watching. She needed to know the details. And when the bell rang for the end of class, no one budged. The room was as quiet as a tomb and she let them be. Then Danny Trujillo walked up to her with his beautiful, innocent eyes and said, "She's gone, Miss R," and Kathie put a hand on his shoulder and pulled him close for a few seconds before he slipped away and ran into the main hall.

She got into the Subaru, checked her rearview mirror, then eased out onto South Road. Kathie immediately took her cell phone and tried to call Claudine, the secretary at school, once again. She'd been trying to call intermittently for the last ten minutes, but the lines had been busy and she was sure they were jammed with the voices of parents who were threatening lawsuits over the asbestos they knew was hidden in the ceiling above the light panels in every classroom and which, at any moment, might pour down in a cancerous shower on the golden heads of their beloved children.

"Ravenhill High School," answered Claudine, her voice spooky and distant on the other end of the phone, as if she were talking from some far off galaxy.

"Guess who got a flat on South Road?" Kathie said.

"Do you need a tow, honey?" Claudine asked in her Louisiana accent. "I can give Buster's a call right now." Claudine was a bayou transplant who thanked the Almighty each and every day for getting her out of the swamp, as she affectionately referred to her home state.

"No need," said Kathie, "I already changed it. Just tell Gus I'm running late for our meeting."

"I'll tell him you're on the way."

"How are the halls?" Kathie asked.

"I peeked out a few minutes ago. No lewd acts in progress, but a ton of students and not many teachers."

"As usual," Kathie said. "Ask Gus to cruise around until I get there."

"No problem," Claudine said. "But sugar, don't be shocked when you pull into the parking lot. Some angel spray painted a lovely message on the wall right next to the entrance. Paul tried to clean it off, but it's not budging."

"What's it say?"

Claudine's voice became hushed for a moment. Finally she cleared her throat, then said, "'I raped Lara.' Real subtle, don't ya think? Big and red as a billboard."

"Great PR for Ravenhill. Can Paul cover it up with something?"

"I'll check with him."

"Thanks," Kathie said. "And try to give Officer Bradford a call. We'll need his help with this one. I should be there in about ten minutes."

"We'll hold down the fort. Don't hit any porcupines on your way over."

It was a straight shot down South Road, but she ran into the 7:30 traffic and found herself stacked up behind a line of cars at the Lincoln Street light. She had taped a list to her dashboard of all the things she needed to do right after school. The final item on the list, circled in red, was the one that made her pause: *baby gift for Susan.* Susan was her younger sister who lived in St. Louis with her husband Larry, an aerospace engineer. They had five boys who were all homeschooled. Susan was thirty-nine and she called last Sunday to tell Kathie she was pregnant again. "I'm praying for a little girl this time around," she said. Kathie was thinking about buying her some things for the new baby, but she wasn't sure what to get. After five kids, some of the infant clothing must be wearing out, even though Susan would never admit it. "We get by on what the Lord provides," she was fond of saying over the telephone.

They talked almost every week, usually on Sunday evenings. There were times when Kathie was amazed they'd stayed so close, especially considering how different their lives had turned out. Susan had never worked outside the home, was a devout Christian and Republican, and spent most of her time either teaching her sons or volunteering at their family's church, the Blood of Christ Salvation Center.

"Are you worried about having a baby at your age?" Kathie said to her last Sunday on the phone. "You'll be sixty when this one leaves home."

"It's a blessing," Susan told her. "Besides, I'd love to have a daughter around to watch me get old. And guess what?"

"What?"

"If it's a girl, we're going to call her Kathleen. And if it's a boy, he'll be named Wade. Larry wanted something more Biblical, but I put my foot down on this one."

There was a long, awkward pause after she said that. It caught Kathie off guard, her sister's words running clean through her. She didn't cry. She felt too exhausted and sick to cry. She just sat with the two names for a few seconds and let it sink in. This was one of those moments when she knew she could lose it big time. But she hung on. Finally Susan said, "Are you still there, Kath?"

She found the words. "Yeah. Still here."

"You'd be okay with that, wouldn't you? Especially about using Wade's name?"

"I'd be honored," was all she said. "And so would Wade."

Wade had been her husband. He was a construction foreman for the state highway department who'd been killed four years ago in what the papers said was a "senseless and tragic accident." He and three other workers were crushed when a bridge they'd been working on collapsed. It happened about ten miles north of their town and in the months that followed his death, Kathie was haunted by nightmares in which she saw Wade's horror-stricken face, his gentle eyes staring upward as the avalanche of steel and concrete descended in a rush to devour him. They never asked her to identify him. Just showed her the wedding ring they'd taken off his finger. Probably nothing left to ID. She didn't push it and assumed a closed casket would be the norm in a situation like this. To this day, Kathie still couldn't drive by the accident site. She always took a different route whenever she had to go north, which was an additional twenty-minute detour. If the boys were with her, they never asked why she was taking the long way. They knew.

After the phone call on Sunday, Kathie sat at her desk and thought about how simple life would be if she just married a nice dentist or software engineer who would go off to work each day and leave her and the kids and their minivan behind with all the domestic bliss they could handle. It wasn't that she didn't date or that men weren't interested in her. She just didn't have the time or energy. A few months after Wade's death, she made the decision to handle grief by throwing herself into an administrative program at a local junior college to get her Type D certificate. It meant evening classes, but she found a good sitter for the boys. She was even able to do her internship at Ravenhill the following year. And when the assistant principal, Ken Furman, decided to retire early, she was groomed to step into the position with Gus's blessing.

As she turned onto Main at the light, she slowed upon seeing the gleaming white pickup truck parked on the street directly in front of the school. *Dammit,* she thought. *The Prodigal Sons in all their glory.* An enormous wooden crucifix jutted up from the truck bed, and surrounding it were eight men, all dressed in combat fatigues and wielding signs emblazoned with red letters. REPENT! one read. RAVENHELL? read another. The others were similar in tone. DON'T TEACH SIN! IN GOD WE TRUST. LET THE BIBLE INSTRUCT! As Kathie drove past, the men held their signs aloft and stared at her in grim silence. The lone man in the cab, wearing a white baseball cap with the word "JESUS" across the front, smiled and gave her a slow wave and a tip of the hat.

Kathie grimaced as she pulled into the parking lot. She'd nearly forgotten about the Prodigal Sons and it was just her luck that they'd show up today. From her car, she could see the blaze of graffiti on the wall at the front entrance: **I RAPED LARA** it boldly proclaimed. *Great timing,* she thought. Kathie knew that Pastor Rex Reilly was the man behind the wheel of the white pickup. P-Rex, as Claudine liked to call him in the office, was the notorious leader of the Prodigal Sons, a fundamentalist group that saw themselves as warriors for the Lord and used guerilla tactics to get what they wanted. They'd been accused of slashing the car tires of doctors who worked at a local clinic that performed abortions as well as hijacking trucks that distributed pornographic magazines to area stores.

P-Rex's daughter, Rachel, attended Ravenhill and the pastor was currently up in arms over the ninth grade health education program and the fact that birth control, premarital sex, and masturbation were discussion topics in the curriculum. Riley had demanded that his daughter be allowed to take an alternative health class with a Christian perspective, then proclaimed to Gus Gillette, the principal, that he and the Prodigal Sons would picket the school until there was a change in district policy on the health standards. Kathie looked in her rearview mirror at the protesters and imagined the barrel of a semiautomatic rifle emerging from behind one of the posters, its hunting scope aimed directly at her. For a moment she longed to toss a hand grenade under their snow-white truck, then watch as it exploded in a fiery blaze. *That'll give 'em a revelation*, she thought.

Kathie looked at the graffiti again and thought of the Ravenhill parents and how they might react to this. She knew her phone would be ringing off the hook if the red message wasn't quickly cleaned off the wall. At the last school improvement team meeting in November, a pack of angry parents showed up to vent their frustrations on a variety of topics. They were led by Rebecca Cantrell, resident queen of Mountain View Estates and the Apple Valley Country Club, who stood up and read a prepared statement in response to the recent article in the local newspaper about the school's low test scores, which showed a drop of three to five percentage points in both math and reading.

"What I want to know," she said while looking directly at Kathie, "is what you're going to do about it?"

"Well," Kathie said, "I'd like to organize a task force to study the test scores. Any volunteers?"

Only one parent raised her hand, and it was not Rebecca Cantrell.

She'd caught Kathie off guard on a night when she was filling in for Gus, expecting to breeze through the meeting and be home in time to read books with the boys. Afterward, other fired-up parents buried her with a litany of complaints, everything from discipline problems in the halls to teacher competency to an inadequate library collection. They wanted it all and they wanted it now.

I'm sick of this, Kathie thought while sitting in the Subaru. *I could quit and sell Mary Kay Cosmetics from nine to five and cruise around in a pink Cadillac.* She wanted to drive home, climb into bed, pull the covers over her head, and sleep for two weeks. Instead she paused and studied the graffiti a moment longer. She already had a suspect. Leonard Lamb, a ninth grader, was the only one bold enough to do something like this. Unfortunately, he was also the only one smart enough to immediately cover his tracks and lie to her face when confronted. The girl's name on the wall was a different story altogether. Lara. The only girl she knew at Ravenhill with a first name spelled like that was Lara Wright, a nice girl whose mom was involved and came down hard if her daughter stepped out of line.

She hadn't seen Leonard Lamb or Lara Wright anywhere near one another since the beginning of the year but that meant nothing. So much can happen in a single day. A mumbled threat on the basketball court outside. A menacing glare across the classroom. An intercepted note. A raised middle finger. A rock hurled at someone's head. *Welcome to the world of high school justice*, Kathie thought as she grabbed her satchel and purse and got out of the car. There were definitely days when she wanted to borrow a tranquilizer rifle from the nearest zoo and put a few select kids down for a couple of hours. Just so she could catch up on her paperwork.

The final bell shrieked as she came through the main entrance and was nearly leveled by three students sprinting down the hall to get to class. "Walk!" she shouted, and the trio slowed as they turned the corner and disappeared. Within fifteen seconds the halls were empty. No stragglers. No students cruising or ducking into the restroom to avoid her. Kathie liked what she saw. *All quiet on the Ravenhill front.* She closed her eyes for a moment, took a deep breath, then headed for the office to check in with Claudine.

■ ■ ■

FRIDAY, DECEMBER 19, 1997
7:00 A.M.

Hardin

AFTER Kent put on the white shirt and blazer and dark slacks, after he selected the silk tie that a student had given him years ago as a gift, the one with the elegant pattern of gold and silver pens, then he slipped on his new black shoes and went into the kitchen. He was still cold and noticed that his hand trembled from the chill, so he forced himself to sit down and drink a cup of steaming tea before leaving for work.

The doll from the box was still resting on the table where he'd left it. The tiny clown was small, about the size of his hand, and it had been his daughter's favorite toy. *Miss Tickle* was what he always called it. Perhaps it was the sound of the rattle buried under the fabric that made her squeal with laughter, or maybe the bright orange and purple color, or maybe even the fact that it didn't have a face, just simple white cloth where the nose and eyes and mouth should have been. He knew there were pictures of Rachel buried somewhere inside the closet, but it had been months since he'd looked at any of them. As he got up from the table, he took the clown and slipped it into his blazer pocket. He wanted it somewhere close today where he could touch it at a moment's notice. His own personal talisman.

Kent didn't pack a lunch. No time for that. The tea would have to sustain him. He needed to get to school early so he was sure to be prepared. He knew that today would be a grind, but once he'd gotten through it, then he could take himself out to dinner and recover. Maybe even go to The Lighthouse, his favorite restaurant, and order the smoked salmon appetizer, the Caesar salad, the pepper steak with garlic mashed potatoes, a bottle of wine. He grabbed his coat and satchel containing the red grade book, then hesitated. The final stack of damp, smeared essays were on a kitchen chair so he leaned over and tucked them under his arm, then headed out the door to his car.

He took the shortcut down Pin Oak Road, guessing traffic would be light this time of the morning. At a stop sign, he paused to remove the doll from his pocket, then hung it from the mirror by the tiny elastic band on its neck. As it swung back and forth with each bump or curve in the road, it seemed to wave at him with its worn, frayed hands. He was convinced that finding the little clown this morning was a good omen, a reminder of his daughter on a day when he needed strength. *Synchronicity.* He'd never been one to put much stock in fate, but now he looked at the doll and thought of Rachel and her bright, sea-blue eyes. She used to lunge at Miss Tickle with her stubby fingers as he waved it above her, then explode into giggles when the clown swooped down to tickle her belly, her armpit, the soft skin under her neck.

Kent had been away when Rachel died. He'd left Claire and their eight-month-old behind in order to attend an educational institute in New England in July. It was an impressive invitation: a chance to study composition theory with other public school teachers from around the country in a forum taught by Ivy League scholars. His district agreed to pay the tuition, including travel expenses, even though he'd only been at the high school three years. A few months earlier, a student in his Advanced Placement class had won a prestigious writing contest that offered a trip to the capitol and a meeting with the governor. There were pictures taken by the local papers as Kent stood with the student, a gifted young man he'd spent hours with in order to prepare the winning manuscript. He knew that parents were praising his classes and already making special requests to the counselors so their sons and daughters could attend Hardin's courses next year. He was flattered and considered the New England trip a bonus for all the extra work he'd put in. It was understandable that Claire was resistant at first, hesitant to be left alone with the baby for such a long period of time. But Kent persuaded her parents, Phillip and Rosalie, to visit while he was gone, and she agreed for him to go.

The phone call came at three in the morning during the second week of the institute. The shrill ringing startled him awake in his dorm room. As Kent picked up the receiver, he heard Phillip's familiar voice on the other end.

"It's Rachel—" he began. "She's sick. We thought it was just a summer cold, but Claire insisted we take her to the hospital anyway."

"What's wrong?" Kent asked.

Phillip continued, almost ignoring Kent's question. "We took her to the ER. They did a spinal tap and that's how they found the meningitis."

The words stunned Kent, sent him reeling. He'd heard of spinal meningitis and knew it was serious. But was it life threatening? *Could she die?* he wanted to ask, but didn't. Instead, he said, "Where is she now?"

"Children's Hospital," Phillip said. "Intensive care."

"Can I talk to Claire?"

There was a pause at the other end. "Not right now. She's with Rachel and can't come to the phone. She asked me to call you."

Kent hesitated, searching for words, wanting to say the right thing, whatever the hell that was. Then he heard Phillip's voice again, this time almost soothing. "You need to get on a plane, son. You need to be with your daughter. She might not make it."

"I'll be there soon," was all he said. Then he hung up.

The hours that followed were wild-eyed, mad, on the edge, as he raced down a barren highway to Boston and hurled change at the tollbooths. He tore around the traffic circles like a man possessed and thought of Dante's Inferno where the lovers spun aimlessly in the tempestuous whirlwind. When he finally got to the airport and boarded a plane heading west, he tried to close his eyes and sleep, knowing he'd need the rest once they landed.

But he couldn't. He kept seeing Rachel's fluttering eyes as they struggled to stay open, her pulse slowing, her lips pale and still. Questions poured into his mind. *If she survives, what about brain damage, retardation, deafness? And what if she dies?* The word *siege* suddenly popped into his head. *The encirclement of a fortified place by an enemy intending to take it.* He envisioned his wife and daughter in a medieval castle under attack as he came to their rescue. The masked invaders would scale the walls and pound at the drawbridge gate with a battering ram while Claire and Rachel huddled in a locked chamber in the highest tower, the screams of battle and terror echoing outside the heavy wooden door. *I never should have left them*, he thought. *A father's place is at home.*

He listened to the maddening drone of the engines and gazed hypnotically out the window at the landscape far below. When the plane passed over the Midwest, Kent saw the expanses of fields and farmland and thought of it as a vast quilt of earth and shadow that unfurled across the stitched terrain. A shroud. A cloak of mourning. For the first time in many years he began to pray, actually pleading with God and begging Him to intervene and spare his daughter, perhaps spare his marriage as well. *Anything*, he prayed. *I'll give you anything. Just let her live.*

Name your price. There, on the plane in seat M-3, Kent cut a deal with the Lord so to speak, as if God had become this kidnapper who held his daughter hostage in some foreign region so he could barter for her life.

Only Rachel died. He didn't know it at the time while he sat on the plane at 20,000 feet. She died with her mother at her side and her father floating in the air hundreds of miles away. He didn't know she was dead when the plane landed and he rushed from the airport to a taxi, then threw a hundred dollar bill at the driver and shouted that it was urgent he get to Children's Hospital. He didn't know she was dead when he burst into the intensive care unit and grabbed a nurse by the arm and asked for his daughter, Rachel Hardin, who was sick with meningitis, who had arrived last night in an ambulance from a hospital to the north.

But he knew the moment he saw the nurse awkwardly glance away, then mumble something about talking to the doctor. He knew when he turned and saw Phillip and Rosalie, their eyes glazed with shock, sitting on the plastic hospital chairs. He knew when a physician came and tried to speak with him, his voice so distant and artificial in an attempt to be calming, yet the words nearly indecipherable. He knew when the doctor guided him by the elbow into the dimly lit room and he saw Claire on the hospital bed holding their daughter who lay still and quiet in her mother's arms.

He embraced Claire for a long moment, then sat down beside her. He took Rachel's small, creamy hand in his own and held it. When Claire was ready, he took the baby and cradled her in his arms, much the way he'd rocked her to sleep so many nights. She didn't fidget or squirm this time. He wished she was merely sleeping and that if he only put his cheek down close to her mouth and waited for that familiar puff of breath, it would eventually come. He nuzzled her head in the V of his neck and felt that lovely softness, a frail whisper of hair and skin.

He didn't know how long he held Rachel. Seconds. Minutes. But when they came for her, he refused to give her up. Claire had to gently ease the baby out of his arms. And as they took Rachel from the room, Kent turned away and rammed his right fist through one of the plate glass windows. The nurse called security and a pair of muscular guards took him to a pale office with a lone chair and he sat and stared at the white floor and walls with a bandage wrapped around his bloody hand. It took ten stitches to finally close the wound. The scar was still visible on Kent's hand. A jagged pink vein right below the wedding band he wore.

When Kent arrived at Ravenhill, he drove in the back way and parked in a space behind the gym. The faculty lot was toward the front, but he always dreaded running into a parent who might want to pull him aside and ask for a full update on her son or daughter's progress. The back lot suited him just fine, allowed him to slip into the school with a certain amount of privacy and protection. Besides, he knew the Prodigal Sons might be picketing out on the main road near the entrance and the last thing he needed this morning was to stare down a gang of macho Christian militiamen dressed for battle and waving signs telling him he was going to hell for working at Satan's Factory.

He entered the school through a door next to the old furnace, then dropped down a flight of stairs and stood in the hallway near his basement classroom. It was an efficient, quick passageway that allowed him a few extra minutes of solace each day. To the right was the Shop room, where the sounds of electric saws and power tools usually buzzed and rattled the air. He checked his watch and felt relieved it was still early, then straightened up and gripped the handle of his satchel. He vowed that today would be a return to the Mr. Hardin that students once knew, the teacher who was unflinching in his professionalism. Even the staff might notice the sudden change in his demeanor, his attire, the way he carried himself down the hall. *Did you see Hardin?* they'd say in the teacher's lounge at lunch. *Who lit a fire under him?*

Perhaps someone like Kathie Romero might even take notice. Kathie was an attractive widow, as well as his own selection for the Secret Santa gift exchange. Normally he wouldn't have gotten within a hundred miles of a tradition like Secret Santa, but he was trying to fit in with the staff and be less of a newcomer. So during the October faculty meeting, he decided to throw his name in on a whim, then was secretly thrilled when he drew Kathie Romero from the Santa hat. Perhaps this was what he needed to regain a sense of confidence and direction in his life. A little spontaneity. Maybe even a spark of romance.

When Kent came to his classroom, he automatically reached into a pocket for his keys, then hesitated upon seeing that the door was already cracked open. He figured Paul, the custodian, must have left it unlocked by accident after he'd vacuumed and emptied the bins. A simple oversight. After all, it was a crazy time of year and the school was getting trashed on a daily basis. It was understandable to expect a mistake.

Kent nudged the door open, then flipped on the light switch as he stepped inside. The rows of desks were straight and orderly, just the way he'd left them the day before. There was no trash or paper scraps on the floor so the evidence of Paul's work was obvious. The bins had been emptied and replaced with plastic liners and Kent's desk was bare, as always, save for a piece of white paper taped to the center of the clean wooden surface. He walked toward the note until he stood next to it and could read the typed contents. *Hey Hard On*, it said in a jagged, black font. *Missing yer shit? Check The Pit.* He took the paper and ripped it off the desk, started to crumple it in his hand, then stopped. He glanced up quickly, his eyes scanning the room for something missing or out of place. Suddenly, he pivoted and saw the bare space on the wall behind his desk. His quilt from Motu. Gone.

He wheeled around and bolted out the door, making a sharp right turn as he stepped into the hallway. *Check The Pit*, the note said. The Pit was what the students called the basement restroom that was located directly under the stairs. Because of its seclusion from the rest of the school, it was notorious for the vilest graffiti, for the scent of tobacco and occasionally marijuana, and for the worst forms of lavatory terrorism including smoke bombs and torched paper towel rolls. As Hardin pushed open the door labeled "Men" and stepped inside, he was greeted by a bold *FAGGOT* written in black on the far wall. He moved across the tight space to the lone metal stall and saw what he'd been searching for. The quilt was jammed down into the toilet like a plug, then urinated and shit on. The stench was strong enough to force Kent back a step when he first smelled it. Then he slammed his hand against the metal stall and felt a tingling sting as pain shot through his arm.

He knew who was responsible, and it wasn't the first time Leonard Lamb had violated his property. Whether it was raising hell in eighth hour or writing obscenities on the backs of chairs in his classroom or stealing petty items like pens, staple removers, boxes of paper clips and rubber bands from his desk, Hardin knew that Leonard was the culprit. He was also a brilliant liar who could talk his way out of any situation. Leonard had a knack for never being seen as the crime was committed, then slipping away at the last minute. But this time he'd gone too far.

Kent rushed out of The Pit and returned to his room where he quickly pushed the red intercom button on the wall three times, then stepped back and waited. Claudine's voice eventually came over the speaker.

"You're here bright and early, Mr. Hardin," she said.

"Is Paul there?" Kent asked. "I could use his help right now."

"He's speaking with Mr. Gillette, but I believe they're nearly finished," said Claudine.

"Could you ask him to come down to my room when he's done?"

"I surely will."

"And ask him to bring some plastic gloves, a mop, and a bucket."

"I'll tell him right away."

Kent stepped back from the wall and took a deep breath, then slowly exhaled. He needed to stay calm and follow school rules and procedures to the letter. No angry confrontations. No shouting matches or opportunities for Leonard to take advantage of the situation. That's what got him banished to Ravenhill in the first place. *Probationary status* was what district administrators called it. *Pending further review of the classroom performance.* In other words, send him to Principal Gus Gillette with strict instructions to watch his every move.

He'd blown it last year in a basic English class at Eagle Ridge High by letting Jason Clayton get under his skin with all the one-liners, the taunts, always followed by a defiant sneer. *This sucks—This is stupid—This is bullshit—I'm bored—Writing's for fags.* The incident happened in February, the month of cabin fever and deep snows and the long grind until spring break. Jason was being especially mouthy and Kent told him to stop talking to his friends—*When I speak, you don't.* Then he'd momentarily turned his back to the class in order to write the assignment on the whiteboard. Out of the corner of his eye, he saw Jason brazenly give him the finger from his seat in the front row. The students erupted into riotous laughter and Kent whipped around.

"Head to the office," Kent ordered, "and take your finger with you."

Jason sat upright in his seat, a look of dismay on his face. "For what?" he yelled. "I didn't do anything!"

"I'm not blind," Kent said. "I saw it."

"Saw what?" Jason said, his face reddening. He stood up and faced the class. "Did anybody see anything?" he asked. No one said a word. Most of them just looked down at the carpet. Then he turned back to Hardin and casually said, "You got no witnesses. You got nothing. So shut up and teach."

Jason went to sit down, and Kent snapped. He rushed Clayton and gave the student a furious shove that sent him sprawling over an empty desk off to the side. The class was stunned, waiting for the next move as Jason lay silently on the carpet, holding his right shoulder and grimacing in pain. He stared fiercely up at Hardin.

In the seconds that followed, Kent stepped back to the board, his mind racing. "I'm sorry," he finally stammered. He moved toward Jason and offered a hand to help him up, but the student slapped it away, shouting, "Screw you!" Clayton got to his feet and glanced over at the class. Someone in the back yelled, "Sue his ass!" and Jason nodded in agreement.

He turned to Hardin and said, "You're history. My uncle's a lawyer." Then, still holding his shoulder, he walked out of the classroom.

Kent stared at the empty doorway for a moment. When he looked over at the hushed students, he was unsure of what to do next. Finally, he simply said, "Turn to page forty-three and read silently until the end of the period."

Then he sat down at his desk, knowing they'd be coming for him soon, knowing that Jason Clayton was the kind of smart young man who would go straight to the office to report the incident, then call his parents so they could contact the family legal representation. He waited, fully aware that none of the students were reading, that all eyes were staring intensely at the teacher huddled behind his desk. At one point, out of habit, he even rose and wrote the next day's homework assignment on the board. An administrator finally came to relieve him of his teaching duties, and he offered no resistance.

When Paul arrived in the basement with the bucket and gloves, he glanced at Kent and said, "Where's the damage?"

Kent took him to The Pit and showed him the quilt in the toilet. Dismayed, Paul slowly shook his head. "I'm sorry," he said. "It was a beautiful piece of work. I've admired it when I was cleaning your room."

"Yes," Kent said. "It was a gift."

"They sure know how to push our buttons," Paul continued, setting his bucket down. "And they always seem to go for the jugular." Together, they donned yellow plastic gloves, then removed the soaked quilt, unraveling it slowly and trying to scrape as much of the waste off as possible. They didn't speak or look at one another, instead staying focused on the job at hand. After the quilt was extracted and Paul had flushed the remains away, Kent held it above the toilet and saw that the fabric was covered with yellow and brown blemishes.

"I've got some cleaning solution," Paul said. "It's pretty strong stuff. I use it when there's an ugly mess on the carpet. It might get rid of the smell and take out the stains."

Kent nodded and handed Paul the quilt. "Go ahead. It's important to me. It was a gift from the students at my first school."

"I'll see what I can do." Paul folded up the quilt and placed it in his bucket, then carried it out of the stall. They left The Pit and walked into the hallway. Kent expected the janitor to continue up the stairs with his gear, but instead he stopped for a moment.

"It's been a rough year," Paul said, turning to Kent. "Weird group of ninth graders."

"It hasn't been easy, that's for sure."

A long pause followed and Kent put his hands in his pockets and waited. Paul didn't move away, but stood there, holding the mop at his side.

"Are you staying around for the holidays?" Paul asked.

"Yeah," Kent said. "No big plans. I'll catch up on some sleep."

"We could all use some of that," Paul replied, smiling. Then he said, "You got family around? Relatives, wife and kids, that kind of thing?"

Kent hesitated, unsure of how to answer. Finally he said, "No. I've been divorced for a while. We did have a daughter..." He paused, tried to steel himself before his voice could betray him. "But she died." He said it firmly, under control, then stared down at his new black shoes.

At first Paul didn't respond, just let Kent's words linger in the air between them. He seemed comfortable with the silence and in no hurry to rush upstairs to his next task. "I'm sorry for your loss," he said at last. As Kent turned to go, Paul spoke again. "For what it's worth, I think you're a good teacher. You give a damn."

Kent stared intently at him, surprised by the comment. "How do you know what kind of teacher I am?"

"Trust me. When I'm in the hallways and the doors are open, I hear what's going on. I'm a good listener. You push those kids hard and that's what they need."

"Thanks," Kent said. "Tell that to Gillette."

Paul smiled. "Maybe I'll do that." Then he lifted the bucket and went up the stairs, leaving Kent alone in the basement hallway.

He reached into his jacket and felt Miss Tickle nestled deep in the pocket. A sudden thought jolted him—*I wasn't there when she died*—caught him off guard and forced him to lean against a panel of lockers in order to not fall. *I wasn't there*—It had been months since he'd felt this pain, and it rushed at him like an assailant from out of the darkness. *Could I have saved Rachel?*

For a moment Kent remained slumped against the metal panels, his breathing rapid and quick as he panted for air. He loosened the tie at his throat and tried to settle himself. He knew that these ghostly thoughts were partly to blame for the demise of his marriage. In the months that followed Rachel's death, he sought a reason for the tragedy and secretly blamed Claire for not getting their baby to the ER in time, for lingering when the symptoms of meningitis should have been detected earlier. *If I'd been there*—It was never spoken between them, but the question loomed in the rooms they inhabited like a swath of shadow that deepened and grew until it consumed all light. *I could have saved her.* Claire grieved in therapy, then joined a local church and found some peace by attending a contemplative prayer group each week.

Kent, on the other hand, poured himself into his teaching. He spent hundreds of hours reading and critiquing student work, then passing back personalized goal sheets for each individual writer. His lesson plans were masterpieces of organization and creative, unpredictable teaching. His administrative evaluations were flawless, and the principal recommended that other colleagues in the building come and observe him in action as a model of quality instruction. Kent's reputation grew among the parents and his rigorous, demanding courses became legendary in the community. Once, at a Back to School night function, he'd even overheard a parent say, "If you want 'em at Harvard, then send 'em to Hardin."

Kent wrote college recommendations for his advanced students as they marched off to study at Princeton and Stanford and Penn. His office door was always open for conferences before and after school. He spent most weekends hunched over his small desk while trying to stay ahead of the paper load and prepare for future lessons, only sleeping five hours at night, his energy fueled by the gauntlet of responsibility he faced each day in the classroom. When Claire suggested they separate, he quickly found an apartment close to the high school that was only a fifteen minute walk to work. He made sure that the divorce was handled swiftly, professionally, so that his classes would have few disruptions due to his own personal issues.

As for the grief, he dealt with it privately. Never flinched. Looked the problem straight in the eye, then moved on. He didn't have time to deal with marital tragedy, the death of his daughter. He only had time for a legacy to the living, for his students and their futures that he held in the palm of his hand like some luminous pearl. Only one question still haunted him. *What if I had been there for Rachel?* Would he have intervened and noticed the subtle clues, the slight rise in her temperature, the soreness in her neck? If his daughter had survived, then perhaps things might have turned out differently with Claire. *Perhaps. Possibly. Maybe.*

Kent took a deep breath as he leaned against the lockers, then straightened up and checked his watch. Students would be arriving soon enough, their shouting and rowdy clatter announcing their presence in the hallways above his room. He had a Friday to get through no matter how badly it had started, and he knew that Leonard Lamb would be waiting for him in eighth hour at the end of the day. But first things first. There was an act of vandalism to report.

Kent hurried up the steps to the first floor landing, but stopped cold at the top. Two figures, clad in black, were slowly descending the stairs. Their faces were painted with wild, garish makeup. They were an ominous pair, proceeding silently toward him like ghostly messengers sent ahead to warn of impending doom. As they drew close, he shrank back against the wall to let them pass. *A bad omen*, he thought. *Angels of death.* The one on the left suddenly leered at him and hissed, "Show his eyes and grieve his heart, come like shadows, so depart!" The other one cackled, her teeth wicked and white against the black face paint. He suddenly recognized them as Kelly Mason and Lara Wright, two students from eighth hour. They walked past him into the bustling main hall, and Kelly turned to give a sly wink.

"Relax, Mr. Hardin," she said. "Let's have some fun today."

Then they were gone, moving away down the corridor like some dark storm that had passed by, leaving him miraculously unscathed in its wake. He reached into his jacket pocket and felt the comfort of Miss Tickle. He squeezed the doll, thought of Rachel now long dead and how beautiful she might have been, then retreated back down the stairs to his classroom. He could report the vandalism later during his planning period. For now, he had lessons to prepare.

■ ■ ■

FRIDAY, DECEMBER 19, 1997
7:45 A.M.

Lara

SHANNON was waiting for them outside Life Science and her outfit did not disappoint Lara, kind of a Frederick's of Transylvania look. Her bleached blond hair had been replaced by a swirling black wig that flowed over her shoulders in a cascade of sultry locks. Tall and leggy, Shannon was resplendent in dark, fish-net stockings, a hip-hugging leather skirt that revealed plenty of thigh, and a low-cut vest designed to show the deep canyon between her breasts, a view Kelly once christened "The Royal Gorge" when she caught Tommy Olson gawking at Shannon's cleavage. Shannon was physically advanced beyond her years, and Lara knew that this outfit would torch the hormones of most ninth grade boys. Her face was a phantom mask, half black/half white, and she resembled some rock singer about to make her grand entrance on stage.

As Lara and Kelly approached, Shannon slouched against the lockers in a sluttish pose. "When shall we three meet again?" she said with a deep, seductive voice. "In thunder, lightning, or in rain?"

"When the hurlyburly's done," Kelly responded, her voice a low growl, "when the battle's lost and won."

"That will be ere the set of sun," Lara said with a rasp.

"Where the place?" asked Shannon.

"Upon the lab," said Kelly.

"There to meet with Mervar," added Lara.

The girls joined hands and began to circle one another, all the while chanting in unison, "Fair is foul and foul is fair. Hover through the fog and filthy air."

They abruptly disengaged with a squeal and a flourish of hands thrust to the heavens.

"Check out Vicki Vixen," Kelly said, taking a step back to survey the complete Shannon. "You're amazing."

"You're a bad, bad girl," Lara said. "Your parents would be shocked."

Shannon pouted, her lips forming a cherry O of red lipstick, then sighed. "I long for the days of corporal punishment when a girl could get a good spanking."

"We're late," Lara said, interrupting. "We better get to class." She reached for the door to the Life Science room, swung it open, then jumped back upon seeing Stevie Jackson blocking the entrance in a sentry-like pose with the class python, Priscilla, wrapped around his neck so that the reptile's triangular head hung down in front of his crotch.

"All who enter," he said in a squeaky, otherworldly voice, "must pet Priscilla."

Kelly stepped boldly across the threshold and touched the python, then strutted away, saying, "Only in your wet dreams, Snakeman." Lara hesitated, then lightly tapped the brown head with a finger as she quickly slipped into the room.

Life Science was a wild, tumultuous circus, part animal anatomy, part Barnum & Bailey. Today's theme, written on the whiteboard in red marker, was "Christmas for the Critters." In order to celebrate, their teacher Mrs. Mervar had brought an assortment of treats for the pets as well as doughnuts for the students. Most of the class animals had been set free from their cages to run, fly, or crawl around the room. Exotic birds swooped through the air then landed on the still blades of the motionless ceiling fans. Shannon screamed and jumped back as a black and white ferret raced between her feet. A group of students had taken the large tortoise, Darwin, and turned him upside down, his legs dancing in the air in a futile search for solid ground, in order to survey the underside of his massive shell. Lop-eared rabbits scampered under lab tables and white rats perched atop students' shoulders, their snowy heads twitching like tiny sentinels. Mr. Bones, the class skeleton, hung from the ceiling in front of the room and was dressed for the occasion in a top hat and black tux.

Lara scanned the room for Mrs. Mervar and spotted her peaked wizard's cap on the far side near the rat mazes. Mrs. M was Lara's favorite teacher, a tall, pewter-haired grandmother with a PhD in biology who was about to retire after thirty-six years of teaching. She vowed to end her days somewhere in the Galapagos with her husband, Max, so she could ride on the backs of giant sea turtles and sip tropical drinks. Even though science had never been Lara's best subject and Mrs. M gave killer exams, she loved the high energy labs and amazing experiments they conducted in her classroom.

When they approached their teacher to check in for attendance, Mrs. Mervar was intently focused on a rat race with another student in one of the large wooden mazes they'd constructed earlier in the year. She was cheering on her favorite, Algernon, a black and white speckled rat that had been class champion since October.

Suddenly she looked up, saw the girls and shouted above the ruckus, "How now, you midnight hags?" She thrust her wrist at them and they saw she was wearing a Rudolph the Reindeer watch, complete with a glowing red nose at the center. She had a collection of over three hundred watches and wore a new one to school each day. "And how late are we, ladies?" she said, peering down at them through her glasses.

"Only a few minutes, Mrs. M," Kelly pleaded. "And it doesn't look like we missed anything."

Mrs. Mervar's brow furrowed and her mouth scowled. In silence, she glared at them intently as if gazing through a microscope at a cluster of fungus. "What do you mean you didn't miss anything!" she finally bellowed in mock outrage. "You missed the ceremonial freeing of the Christmas Critters! You missed the rampant rampage of the nearly extinct in their last dash for freedom! You missed the stampede!"

Shannon rolled her eyes at Lara and Kelly and the trio knew the punishment that would follow. As eccentric and outlandish as she often was, Mrs. M didn't budge an inch when it came to attendance. She extended a long, bony finger toward the back of the room and said, "I banish you three to the rabbit cages. And let no poop be seen when thou art done."

Grudgingly, the girls picked up the cleaning bucket and supplies and walked to the rear of the class where the rabbits, Galileo, Copernicus, and Einstein were housed. They donned yellow latex gloves and Kelly and Shannon began scooping out the oily mounds of rabbit pellets while Lara held open the green garbage bag.

"What if we got a disease from this?" Shannon asked, dumping a pile of brown waste into the bag.

"Yeah," Kelly said, "what if we got sick and sued the school district for one point eight million dollars? They'd probably do a *Sixty Minutes* episode on our struggle to survive. We'd have some strange virus that invaded our internal organs and turned everything into tomato soup. Like in *The Hot Zone*, when that guy with Ebola barfs all over the plane."

"Enough," Lara said, interrupting her. "Please." The cages had not been cleaned in days and Lara felt dizzy from the acrid smell that stung her nose. She knew that, along with sex, Kelly was obsessed with deadly diseases. She'd read *The Hot Zone* five times. For her scientific research presentation, she'd performed a dramatic recreation of a dying Ebola victim bleeding out, complete with special effects that included ketchup, coffee grounds, maple syrup, and two bottles of chocolate sauce. Mrs. Mervar had called it a tour de force of scientific performance art even though three kids had to run and vomit in the restroom during the presentation.

Lara looked up and saw they weren't the only ones in the back of the classroom. A lone student sat at one of the corner tables wearing a simple, calico dress that hung far below the knees. Her long brown hair was covered with a blue scarf. Someone had taped a sign to the back of her chair that read **Kick me if you love Jesus**.

St. Rachel, thought Lara. *The Martyr of Raving Hell.* It was Rachel Riley, the daughter of one of the town's most controversial figures, Pastor Rex Riley of the Prodigal Son Church. According to Kelly, the queen of school gossip, Rachel had been homeschooled by her mother, like many in the Prodigal Son flock, until this past year. Then her father decided to challenge the board of education regarding the teaching of evolution in science, along with the school's health curriculum. In order to personalize his mission, Pastor Rex chose to have his own daughter subjected to the temptations of the school and all of its evil ideas. So in late August Rachel Riley was seen walking the halls of Ravenhill. Kelly put it best when she saw Rachel during the first week of classes and said, "Now Pastor Rex has his own personal spy here at Raving Hell."

In early September "The Spectacles" began, as Shannon liked to call them, and Rachel Riley transformed her locker into a shrine. On the metal door she affixed a crucifix of Christ hanging on the cross. The interior was covered with pictures and symbols of Jesus, as well as Bible verses written on parchment that were taped to the side panels. In between classes, she knelt in front of the locker and bowed her head before the cross, her arms lifted upward, her eyes closed as she whispered prayers to heaven.

In the ensuing weeks, Rachel became the school outcast and everyone's favorite target. Even though the teachers and staff tried to shield her from the harassment, it was hopeless. When she was kneeling in the hallway, students "accidentally" knocked her over. Some of the stoners even spit in her hair as they passed by while she was in prayer. Obscene drawings and words were written boldly on the outside of her locker. Then a small group of Christian students decided to band together and form a human chain around her as she knelt during passing period. A fight broke out the next day because their barricade caused a riotous traffic jam in the hallway. After that incident, four students were suspended for a week.

A part of Lara felt guilty for never intervening or coming to Rachel's rescue. In a way, she was in awe of her capacity for enduring cruelty. Lara never saw her flinch or hurl an ugly insult in retaliation, as if she were oblivious to the torrent of ridicule showering down upon her. There were days when Lara swore Rachel walked the halls in a trance, her eyes nearly closed as she whispered prayers and made the sign of the cross upon her chest.

"It's almost as if she likes it," Shannon said one day. "Like pain's the name of her game."

"It's all part of her dad's plan," Kelly added. "He's put her up to all this crazy shit." Kelly feigned a look of sweetness and innocence, her eyelids fluttering. "She's a Christian witness to all the heathens. St. Rachel has come to heal the savages." Then she scowled, her face a picture of contempt. "Only one problem. She's about to get fed to the lions."

When they finished cleaning the cages, Lara tied off the garbage bag and dropped it in the trash can. Shannon and Kelly moved to the front of the room to return the gloves and cleaning supplies, but Lara hung back for a moment by the rabbit cages. She glanced over at Rachel, who was still turned away from the class. *Just walk over and say hello*, Lara thought.

What's the harm? So what if Kelly and Shannon see me? Are they my owners or something?

Lara went over to where she sat and first removed the sign that was taped to the back of her chair, proceeding to crumple it up and throw it away. Then she glanced down and saw that Rachel was holding a white rat on the table in front of her. She was gently stroking it with her thumb.

"I've named him Francis," Rachel said, looking up at Lara and acknowledging her for the first time. "Like the saint. He was always kind to animals. I'm trying to keep him hidden so he doesn't become part of Priscilla's holiday feast."

"A good plan," Lara said. She remained standing and rested her hands on the black table's surface, all the while gazing down at the rat.

"You didn't have to take off the sign," Rachel said, without looking up. "I don't really mind. I guess I've gotten used to it."

"But you shouldn't," Lara replied, her voice angry. "It's not right."

"But they know not what they do."

"They know exactly," Lara said, "and it pisses me off."

A long silence followed and they continued to watch the rat as it scurried back and forth across Rachel's arm. *Why did I come over here?* Lara thought to herself. *Why are we talking? What exactly is the point?* By now Kelly and Shannon were shooting twisted glares at her from the middle of the room and waving for her to come over. What they didn't know, what Lara had never spoken about, was that long before she'd ever met either of them, she'd made a secret promise to Rachel Riley.

Suddenly Lara asked, "Would you like a doughnut?" Rachel perked up, surprised. "I'd be glad to get you one," Lara said.

Rachel looked at her. "Are there any left? The boys usually eat most of them."

"Mrs. M bought tons."

Rachel looked down at the rat, which was now crawling up her other arm, then back at Lara. "When I left the house, my dad told me not to partake of Satan's candy today."

Lara waited a moment, then said, "Do you always listen to your dad?"

"No," Rachel said calmly. "Not always."

"So the real question is whether you want glazed or jelly-filled?"

Without hesitation, Rachel answered, "Glazed, please. I like all the frosting." Then, as Lara turned to go, Rachel added, "Have you seen Leonard Lamb today?"

Lara was startled by her question. "Yeah," she answered, "and once was enough."

"Beware of the lamb," Rachel said, an odd grin playing across her face. "Or is the lamb a wolf?" As she spoke, her gaze seemed to look right through Lara with a steely focus that was penetrating, yet also mischievous, as if they were about to set off on some strange adventure and only she held the map. *Some things never change*, Lara thought.

She'd been eight that summer when she first met Rachel at Little Saints. Teresa had been desperate for child care, so she'd taken Lara over to the Prodigal Sons Church because they offered free babysitting to all the working moms. Little Saints was the group for eight-year-olds, and during the span of a few days, she and Rachel became friends and played together on the elaborate jungle gym in the yard behind the church.

In the weeks that followed, Lara's time at Little Saints became a ritual of comfort and security. Rachel would always be waiting at the entrance when she arrived and they spent the day exploring the possibilities of the surrounding yard and the enclosed woods behind the church. Rachel had christened almost every place with a name. The Egyptian Sandbox was where they built mountains out of the desert and buried their toys in deep caverns, only to unearth them later as ancient relics from some lost civilization. The Dreamkeeper's Palace was the dollhouse with its many secret rooms where they hid tiny damsels in distress from sinister men who were trying to kidnap them.

But their favorite places lay in the small forest just beyond the playground where Rachel had created the sacred shrines they would visit each day. Our Lady of Lost Souls was in a wooded glade where she'd taken a dark-haired Barbie dressed as Mary, Mother of Jesus, and nestled her in the sculpted, exposed roots of an enormous tree. The doll was surrounded by the wispy feathers of birds, the bones of small animals, the brittle husks of locusts, even the hollowed shell of a box turtle. They'd scavenge the ground for the remains of anything dead, whether it be animal or insect, then lay it at the feet of Mary in the hope of sending its soul to heaven.

There was the Our Father Tree, where Rachel used grape vines to fasten a crucifix made of two thick branches and mounted it against an old, blackened pine that had once been struck by lightning. Here they would kneel on a bed of soft leaves and give thanks for all plants and living things. Their final stop was always the Sacred Garden where Rachel had placed a framed picture of Jesus, His glowing heart exposed and entwined by thorns, and rested it against a large granite boulder. The picture was encircled with wildflowers and daisies found growing nearby. The first time they visited the shrine, Rachel pulled Lara aside and gazed into her eyes with a frightening intensity as she whispered in a low, reverent voice.

"The Sacred Garden was where the apostles fell asleep and betrayed our Lord at His hour of greatest need," she explained. "Let us promise to never be asleep when Jesus comes on the final day."

"I promise," Lara murmured quietly

Then they knelt in front of the picture and bowed forward until their heads touched the ground. They prayed for minutes on end as if whispering secret vows to the earth that would never be broken. And when they finally rose and left the shrine, Rachel took Lara's hand in her own and led her quietly through the woods and back to the Little Saints playground.

One morning near the end of summer, Teresa announced over breakfast that Lara wouldn't be going back to the Prodigal Sons Church anymore, that she wanted to try a new place closer to their home. Lara threw a fit and went to her room, locked the door and refused to come out until her mom told her why they had to leave. It was only then that Teresa confessed the real reason: Pastor Rex was secretly matching up all the single moms with his Prodigal Sons for required dates each week and there was no way she was going to support such a vile practice. After that, she and Rachel only saw each other a few times over the ensuing years. Once at a birthday party. Another at the town's Fourth of July picnic. Occasionally she'd catch a glimpse of her amidst the shelves at the public library or in the checkout line at the Shop'N'Save. But they never spoke and never once acknowledged each other's presence.

Suddenly she heard Mrs. M squawk out her name, "Lara Wright!" over the noisy tumult. She turned to the front of the room and saw Mrs. Knight, the office secretary, standing next to her teacher by the door. Lara walked up the aisle to where they stood, and as she approached, Mrs. M said in her deepest, most sonorous voice, "I'm afraid you have a date with destiny, my dear. Mrs. Romero has called you to her chamber."

"For what?" Lara asked, her voice suddenly defensive.

"Just come along, honey," Mrs. Knight said. "You're not in trouble. She just needs to ask a few questions."

Before Lara could even turn and glance back at Rachel, she was led outside the classroom as the door snapped shut behind them and she found herself in the quiet hallway with Mrs. Knight heading to Romero's office.

■ ■ ■

FRIDAY, DECEMBER 19, 1997
7:50 A.M.

Kathie

WHEN Kathie first entered the main office that morning she saw Jackie Hull sitting on the visitor's bench to the left. Mrs. Hull, a successful local attorney and city council-woman, was a tall, imposing figure with striking red hair. She was also a frequent visitor to the office, primarily due to the chronic problems of her only son Blair, who was twelve. According to his mother, Blair was a *gifted* child who had tested out at the upper level in his core subjects and was currently placed in all ninth grade classes so he would be challenged aca-demically. Jackie Hull was immaculately dressed in high heels and a jade pants suit with padded shoulders that made her look like a chic linebacker. Kathie quickly estimated that one sleeve of her expensive outfit probably cost more than the total of her own mud-spattered black suit.

Claudine stood up from behind her desk and said, "Mrs. Hull stopped by right after you called. I explained that you were hav-ing car trouble, but she said she could wait."

Kathie smiled and extended her hand. "Nice to see you, Mrs. Hull."

Jackie Hull shook hands, then said, "I need to speak to you privately about an emergency concerning Blair."

Kathie gestured to her office and said, "Of course. Please go in and have a seat. I'll be with you as soon as I speak with Mrs. Knight about a scheduling issue."

Without another word, Jackie strode into the office while Kathie moved toward Claudine, who stood up from behind her desk. Claudine was a small woman in her fifties who wore her iron gray hair in a tight bun. As usual, she was neatly dressed in denim jeans and a western shirt complete with turquoise buttons and a silver eagle bolo around her neck. Claudine had gone western a few years ago after she and her husband Earl started taking country swing dance classes at the school. Kathie leaned close to Claudine and whispered, "Pray this'll only take a few minutes." She'd already dealt with numerous episodes involving Blair Hull and on each occasion his mother had attempted to muscle the outcome with sly legal threats. In the main office she was known as "The Incredible Hull."

With an exasperated look, Claudine said, "I tried to get her to reschedule until after the holidays, but she wouldn't hear of it. She insisted on seeing you right away."

"We're public servants," Kathie said, grinning, "at the mercy of the taxpayers."

"I'd like to show Ms. Malpractice a little mercy."

"I'll take care of it. Could you cancel my appointments until eleven? I need to deal with this graffiti situation right away."

"Fine," Claudine said. "But what about Driscoll Construction? The leaks in the gym ceiling are getting worse. We're going to be in trouble if it snows any more. The whole damn roof could cave in."

"See if they might come by today and give us an estimate on patching it up." Kathie started to leave, but hesitated and turned back. "Could you find out what class Lara Wright's in and call her down so we can chat."

She went into her office and closed the door. Mrs. Hull was already sitting so Kathie pulled up a chair across from her and said, "I'm sure you saw the vandalism on the front of the school. We're in the process of getting it cleaned up and finding out who's responsible."

Mrs. Hull looked directly at her and said, "I hope that justice, as well as the cleanup, will be swift. It's a disgrace to have that kind of a message desecrating public property."

"I agree," Kathie said. "Now, what's the emergency with Blair?"

Jackie Hull stared down at the coffee table between them for a moment as if pondering the question, then said, "It's about Blair's penis."

Kathie was silent at first. As the sudden image of Blair Hull's penis flashed through her mind, she had to stomp down a giggle. She knew that it wouldn't be wise to laugh at the penis of a city councilwoman's adolescent son, especially in the presence of the city councilwoman herself.

"Is there a health problem?" she asked calmly.

"No, it's not that at all. Blair may look frail, but he's in excellent health."

"Then what is it?"

"His penis is rather small."

I'm sure it'll grow, Kathie thought. Instead she asked, "Shall I contact the school nurse?"

"Unnecessary," said Mrs. Hull. "It's strictly a discipline issue, which is why I came to see you."

"It is?" said Kathie, genuinely curious.

"Well," Mrs. Hull continued, "since Blair is scheduled in ninth grade PE with the older boys, they always have to change together in the locker room."

"Yes."

"Some of the boys have been making fun of him and he is deeply disturbed by it. They point at him while he's dressing

105

and..." Her voice quavered as she looked down at the table. Kathie began to say something, but instead chose to nod silently. "Blair is seeing a therapist right now who specializes in penile trauma," added Mrs. Hull.

"Well that's good," Kathie said. "Is Blair getting teased outside the locker room as well?"

Mrs. Hull's face snapped up and she said, "It's beyond teasing. It's harassment. It's grounds for legal action."

"What kind of teasing?"

"The older boys have a name for Blair. They used to taunt him in the shower, but now they've started hounding him in the halls and on the playground and shouting it out loud. I want this stopped right now. He's being persecuted by these bullies."

"What exactly do they call him?"

Mrs. Hull paused, an uncomfortable frown creasing her mouth. "They call him TP."

"Which stands for?"

In a hushed voice, she said, "Tiny pecker, I believe." Mrs. Hull then leaned forward and said, "I'm concerned about how this might affect the self-esteem of a gifted child like Blair. He's at a very sensitive age right now. And we all know that the heart and soul of a man flows through his penis."

Kathie said, "I'll do some follow-up on the name calling. In the meantime, would you like for me to talk with Blair about this?"

"No offense, but is there a male on the staff that he might confide in?"

"Coach Zupanci also teaches health. I'm sure he'd be glad to talk with Blair."

Jackie Hull looked up at Kathie and smiled uncomfortably. Then she reached across the table to shake her hand and said, "I'm so glad we were able to discuss this incident and come up with a plan without having to get legal. Both of Blair's grandparents attended Ravenhill and I'd like to see him continue with the family tradition. We'd hate to have to consider other educational options."

"We'd hate to lose a fine student like Blair," Kathie said as they rose and walked to the door.

She knew, of course, that when Jackie Hull said "other educational options" she was alluding to The Academy, a charter school that opened two years ago and had been flooded with wealthy refugees from the public schools. Funded by state tax dollars, as well as generous donations from its affluent parents, The Academy had a waiting list of three hundred names. According to the school's headmaster, Griffin St. Clair, they were merely providing a service for parents who wanted their sons and daughters to benefit from small classes with strict academic expectations in preparation for the university experience. In other words, The Academy provided what parents of the upper echelon considered the critical edge. "And of course," Mr. St. Clair was quoted as saying in the local newspaper, "scholarships are available for those less fortunate students." *Like my own sons*, Kathie was thinking as she watched Jackie Hull strut out of her office. *All my less fortunate, middle-class sons.*

Before leaving, Mrs. Hull turned and smiled. "Have a wonderful Christmas," she said. "And I hope you'll be prompt in apprehending the person responsible for the graffiti on the wall. It is a shameful display in the public eye."

"I'll get right on it," Kathie said in return. Then Mrs. Hull was out the door with a whirl of her fashionable black cape.

Kathie walked over to Claudine, who looked up from the computer terminal where she was working on the morning attendance. "What is it this time?" Claudine asked.

"Blair is suffering from penile trauma. I'll fill you in later."

"Hell," Claudine said, "maybe he and Earl should get together and compare notes." She motioned with her hand to the front of the office, then whispered, "I went and got Lara for you. She's here in all her glory."

Kathie turned and saw that Lara Wright, in full costume, was seated on the bench. "Nice outfit," Kathie said, "quite stunning." Lara shrugged and looked away. Kathie waved her into the small office. "Let's talk."

They went in and she closed the door. Lara sat down, folded her arms, then looked up at the ceiling as if expecting to see a bare bulb hanging down for the interrogation about to begin. Kathie sat across from her.

"It's my job to ask this first question," she began. "It's the law and we have to get it out of the way. Have you been assaulted by anyone?"

"No," Lara said, exasperated.

"I'm sorry about the graffiti," Kathie continued. "We're hoping to get it cleaned off. Spray paint on brick is hard to remove." Lara scratched at her leg and remained silent. "I'm sure it was the last thing you wanted to see when you came to school this morning. Any idea who wrote it?"

More silence. Kathie swore she saw a small tear forming in one of Lara's eyes, but she quickly wiped it away.

"No," Lara finally said. "Just some jerk trying to be funny."

"Do you think it's funny?"

"Am I laughing?" Lara said with a sneer.

A concrete cookie, Kathie thought. *Tough on the outside, soft on the inside.* "I know you're not laughing. I'd just like to catch whoever did it so it won't happen again. It's against the law. Whoever did it has no right to humiliate you."

"I'm not humiliated," Lara said. "I could care less what some idiot writes."

"It's still harassment and it needs to stop."

Lara was silent. She hadn't yet looked Kathie in the eye.

"Are you being threatened?" Kathie asked. "Are you scared to tell me who it is?"

"I'm not scared. Somebody's gonna have to do a lot more than that to scare me."

"It's okay to tell. If you're being threatened or harassed, I can make sure it stops. I just need a name."

For the first time Lara looked at her and held her gaze.

"I got a name for you," Lara said. "Leonard Lamb."

"Has he threatened or hurt you?"

"He threatens everyone. That's how he is."

Kathie leaned forward. She knew there Lara was holding back something. She'd been too quick to offer his name. Too eager.

"Are you scared of Leonard?" Kathie asked.

"Most people are."

"Why did he choose your name for the wall?" No answer. Lara stared at the small window behind the desk. "Why did he pick you, Lara?" Kathie continued, pressing. Lara's arms and legs were still crossed and she glared out the window with a fierce intensity. "Did something happen between you and Leonard? Something sexual?"

Lara looked at Kathie, her face suddenly agitated, disbelieving. "God, Mrs. Romero. I'm not that far gone," she said.

"I mean has he hurt or threatened you?"

Lara paused, her hand coming up to rub her lip. "I can't talk about that right now," she said, her voice cracking.

"If I'm going to deal with Leonard and make sure he can't hurt other students, then I need you to talk."

"Not now. Maybe later. I just need some time to think about it."

"Later in the day?"

"Yeah," Lara said, unfolding her arms. "Eighth hour. I'll be in Hardin's class."

Kathie stood up and moved to the door. "I'll come and get you during last period. Deal?"

Slowly Lara nodded, then rose to leave.

Kathie put a hand on her shoulder and Lara waited. "It's not right for him to hurt people or make them scared. It's my job to stop him if he is."

"I know," Lara said.

Kathie smiled at her, gave her shoulder a squeeze. "Shakespeare would have loved the outfit."

A brief smile flickered across Lara's face as she headed out the door on her way back to Life Science.

Before checking in with Gus Gillette, Kathie paused at Claudine's desk and said, "Could you pull Leonard Lamb's schedule for me?"

"Sure thing. And before I forget, Officer Bradford called back. He'll be here as soon as he can."

"Thanks," Kathie said. "I think I'm going to need all the help I can get today." Officer James Bradford had been assigned by the city police to help out at the school. He also assisted Kathie when it came to dealing with a few of the tougher students.

She walked over to Gus Gillette's office and stopped outside his door. She could see through the window that he was at his desk on the phone, so she tapped lightly on the glass to get his attention. He looked up and waved and she stepped inside, closing the door behind her. Gus was almost sixty, bald, with a neatly trimmed silver beard and gold-frame glasses. He was a short, compact man who liked to strut through the halls at a bulldog pace; some of the kids had nicknamed him the "Human Bowling Ball." Today he was dressed in a white shirt and scarlet tie with his sleeves rolled up to the elbows. He was being dramatic on the phone, his free hand gesturing in the air as he spoke.

"Dammit Rob, I just want Rex Riley off my street. I don't like waking up in the morning at six A.M. and seeing him out there in his truck with that big cross. It gives Marilyn the creeps, and that's the last thing she needs right now. Something else to get her all shook up." Kathie knew that Rob was Robert Gibson, chief of police. Gus paused to listen for a moment, then nodded vigorously. "I know it's a free country but isn't there some law that says you can't consistently park in a residential area where you don't live?"

Gus looked at Kathie and rolled his eyes as he held the phone to his ear. She knew Gus's mannerisms, his trigger points. He had a short fuse and came from a different generation of disciplinarians who once ruled the school hallways with an iron fist. When it came to working with kids like Leonard, Gus would often try to muscle them and it backfired when they didn't show any fear.

Gus could be a screamer, but Kathie also knew his other side. Ever since Wade's death, he'd been like a second father to her boys. A week after the funeral, when they were all still paralyzed from the shock, Gus and Marilyn drove over to their house unannounced and came in and sat with them at the kitchen table. "Whether you like it or not, we're here to help out." Marilyn brought some boxes and talked with Kathie while she packed up Wade's things. Gus took the boys to a local park and played some football. When they left that night after dinner, Gus gave her a hug and said, "We're going to drop by and check on you every week. You can count on it." And true to their word, they did just that.

Gus had been the principal at Ravenhill for twenty-five years, and for three of them, Kathie had taught social studies just down the hall from the main office. They'd been a good administrative team since she was hired as the AP, and Gus had gone out of his way to show her the "ropes" as he liked to call them. When she first began, they reached an agreement and split up the workload. Gus liked the business end of being a principal and agreed to handle all the district administrative issues, half the staff evaluations, as well as any major facility maintenance problems. Kathie would work directly with the students, staff, and parents in taking care of discipline issues and serve as the facilitator for any committee meetings.

"Could you at least send a patrol car by to scare him off?" Gus said in an exasperated tone. A long pause. "That would be great, Rob. Both Marilyn and I would appreciate it."

After he hung up, Kathie smiled and said, "Sounds like Pastor Rex has been trying to convert you."

Gus frowned. "Every morning for the last week I go out to get the paper, and he's waiting on the other side of the driveway in his white truck with that big crucifix sticking up in the air. He's got this sign that he flashes at me that says TEACH JESUS in big letters."

"He's out there praying for you bright and early," Kathie said.

Gus yawned and stretched his arms overhead. He looked exhausted and his cheeks were red and mottled. "I don't mind the prayers," he said, "but it gets Marilyn upset and she doesn't need the stress of having some guy lurking outside our house."

Marilyn was Gus's wife of thirty years. She'd been pushing him to take an early retirement package from the district and do some traveling. They were going to Mexico over Christmas to unwind.

"How is Marilyn?" Kathie asked.

"Hanging in there," Gus said. "Anxious to get someplace warm."

"I'll think of you both on my way to Chicago."

"Just stay awake at the wheel."

"I'll have Ben pinch me if I start to doze off."

"He'd enjoy inflicting a little pain on his dear mother."

There was a lull in the conversation and Kathie sat back, took a deep breath. She knew the rest of the day was going to be a wild race, an all-out assault on her schedule and her patience. But here in Gus's office she could sit for a moment. He understood the frenetic pace and knew this was her lone sanctuary of calm. Kathie stared at the wooden baseball bat mounted on the wall, a Louisville Slugger autographed by Ernie Banks of the Chicago Cubs. Gus was a baseball fanatic, especially when it came to his beloved Cubs. Every spring on the opening day of the season, he got on the intercom and sang, "Take me out to the ballgame" to the whole school and the students howled and covered their ears.

"Sorry I'm running so late," she said. "Bad time for a blowout on South Road."

Gus smiled. "Not a problem. Just sit and catch your breath. It's madness as usual on the last day before break."

"My evaluation meeting is going to have to wait," Kathie said. "I've got some damage control this morning."

"We'll get to it after the holidays. But you better be ready," Gus said with a sly grin. "I'm going to be a hard-ass this time. You're not getting off easy like before."

Kathie feigned a hurt look. "I guess I better look for a job over the break."

"Damn right," Gus said. "Oh, by the way, did you see the lovely holiday greeting on the wall as you came in?"

"Yeah. That's the damage control I was referring to. I've already spoken with Lara Wright and she said it was just some prank. I'll talk to Paul about getting it cleaned up."

Gus didn't respond. He was searching for something on his desk, which was piled high with papers and file folders. His face was knotted in concentration, and Kathie thought that he'd aged a great deal over the last year. She worried about his health and had been pushing him to go in for a physical. "Quit bugging me!" he'd snapped at her last week. "You're as bad as Marilyn!" When he saw the hurt look on her face, he'd apologized. She appreciated the gesture. He'd been a good friend to her over the years, guiding her through extension courses so she could get her administrative certificate, even advising her on financial matters when Wade had died. He and Marilyn never had children of their own. They tried for years, then gave up. Gus never talked about the complications, but once he'd said to her, "Why would I need a kid of my own? I've got seven hundred and fifty right here."

Suddenly he glanced up and saw Kathie staring at him.

"You look wiped," she said. "Are you okay?"

"I'm buried alive like everyone else around here," he said. "I was at the school board meeting last night until two in the morning. They were hammering the principals again with the same crap. Low test scores, high dropout rates, our failure to meet the community's expectations. Nobody said a thing about the budget cutbacks and overcrowding. Now they want an action plan from us by February." He leaned back, removed his glasses, then rubbed his eyes. "I wish I could give you a hand with this graffiti, but I've got to deal with Hardin today. I've got a post-evaluation meeting with him today."

"How's it going?"

Gus rubbed his jaw, then winced. "Not well. He doesn't listen. The students push his buttons and he goes off. He's burned out and needs to move on." Then Gus paused abruptly, and tapped his fingers on the oak desk with a flourish. "But I'll be damned if there aren't days when I stop by and see a completely different teacher. It's like Jekyll and Hyde. He can be amazing, especially when he's teaching writing." Gus leaned over his desk and rested his elbows on the surface. "But those days are few and far between. Most of the time it's a mess in his classroom. A real war. If I don't get him out of there by the end of the year, I swear the kids and parents are going to kill him."

Kathie knew Kent Hardin all too well. He'd once been a high school teacher who was widely respected in the neighboring community of Eagle Ridge. A veteran English instructor and department chair, Hardin was forced to transfer to Ravenhill after an incident last year at his old school. According to the local newspaper, a male student had insulted Hardin in front of the class and he'd shoved the young man onto the floor. The student accused Hardin of taunting him, but nothing was ever proven. The superintendent had placed Hardin on leave for the rest of the term, then transferred him to Ravenhill with the understanding that Gus, the senior principal in the district, would smooth over the situation and get things back to normal.

But after Hardin's arrival at Ravenhill, nothing had gone smoothly. During the first quarter of school, parental complaints had flooded Gus's mailbox. According to the notes and letters, Hardin was a tyrant and intimidated the kids in his classes. He gave inappropriately complex assignments and ridiculous amounts of homework. He wrote condescending, insensitive comments on student papers. When Hardin submitted his first quarter grades, he listed F's for 65 percent of his students.

By mid-October, Kathie realized what was going on: Gus had been appointed the hit man by the superintendent. His job was to take Hardin out of the system. He could've looked at it as a compliment that the central office was entrusting him with this delicate situation, but Kathie knew Gus didn't see it that way. He didn't like having to take care of the district's dirty laundry, especially when there were highly paid administrators sitting on their asses out at headquarters. It meant a mountain of extra paperwork for Gus, including weekly classroom visitations to document any problems, as well as a written record of any parental or student or staff complaints that could be used in court if Hardin decided to countersue the district.

And Kathie knew that Gus had deliberately kept her out of the loop. She knew he was trying to shield her in case things got ugly. It was messy, complicated work to fire a teacher who was a union member, but Kathie knew that the day of reckoning was coming for Hardin. March would be perfect. Hardin could leave quietly over spring break, and the district wouldn't need to hassle with the union reps. The week off would allow some time to find a replacement, and if Kathie knew Gus, he'd already cut an under-the-table deal to bring an old friend out of retirement, a veteran who needed some extra money and could step in and finish out the year in a professional manner. Gus knew how to keep the parents happy, especially taxpayers like Jackie Hull who could make any principal's life miserable with a single phone call.

Kathie stood up to leave. "Good luck with Hardin. I hope he listens to what you have to say. I'd offer to buy you a beer after work, but I have to get on the road to Chicago."

"I'll drink one for you in Cozumel," Gus said with a wink.

"I'm jealous. You get the sun and I get the snow."

"Senior citizens deserve a break now and then."

As Kathie stepped out of Gus's office, Claudine was waiting for her.

"Just so you know," she said, "Leonard Lamb is in social studies with Macon during second period." She paused, then spoke in a low, conspiratorial whisper, "Would you like me to fetch him. I love yanking 'em out of class and watching 'em squirm. Kind of a power trip, I guess."

"No, I'll do the honors this time," Kathie said with a smile. "I want to take him to the scene of the crime for a little interrogation."

"Sounds like a good plan," Claudine said. "I believe that boy could use a glimpse of the afterlife right about now. In other words, give him a little hell."

"I'll do my best," she said before heading out into the hall to search for Paul Munn, the Ravenhill custodian. She had a mess to clean up and something was telling her that it wouldn't be the last before the day was over.

■ ■ ■

FRIDAY, DECEMBER 19, 1997
7:50 A.M.

S.A.M.

FIRST hour coed PE was taught by Coach Tony Zupanci, and S.A.M. was currently getting a D-. He was getting a D- or F in every class except art, where he was earning an A from Miss Healy. In art he did every homework assignment, met every deadline, completed every project. Art mattered. It fed the soul and spirit. In his other classes he did nothing. Zero. He didn't raise his hand. Ever. He was a mystery to many of his teachers, and that's the way he liked it. A mystery. They deserved nothing more. It wasn't that he couldn't do the work. He listened and was mostly attentive while soaking up any useful information. It was just that he chose *not* to do the work because he was managing his energy. He knew the game. They'd pass him on because he wasn't a behavior problem. The school counselor would write on his file: *loner; socially isolated; may be depressed.* But S.A.M. knew that depression had nothing to do with it. It was simply his way of being. *The Zen of the Secret Agent.*

As he entered the gym, he saw Coach Zupanci standing at center court in his gold Ravenhill jacket. His hair was silver, slicked back like a Mafia don, and he stood erect, a tall figure surrounded by volleyballs that encircled him in an orbit of white spheres. The gym was empty, except for Coach Z, while the other students changed into their PE uniforms.

"Any chance of you dressing out today?" Coach Z yelled.

S.A.M. shrugged, squeezed the briefcase handle, and gestured toward the bleachers. "The usual," he said.

"Then assume the position," Coach Z said and S.A.M. took his regular seat in row D, seat 3. The other students soon began filing out of the locker room, dressed in the standard white T-shirt and black shorts, and lined up for attendance. He and Coach Z had reached an agreement in October after extensive negotiations. As long as S.A.M. showed up, sat in the gym or on the sidelines of the athletic field, didn't cause trouble, and participated in the testing that occurred once a month, then he'd receive a D- for the quarter and semester. Passing. Tolerable.

It wasn't the exercise that S.A.M. hated. Back in Toledo at his martial arts academy, Master Yang put S.A.M. and the other students through a hellish evening regime that would have broken most teenagers. It was the control game that he hated as Coach Z ran the students through his silly drills and exercises, always barking orders, always screaming lame slogans like "Put some muscle in your hustle!" S.A.M. couldn't imagine James Bond ever dressing out in black gym shorts and taking orders from some redneck ex-Marine with a phallic whistle hanging around his neck. Bond might tell the old fart to screw off, then head home to practice karate with his nubile, martial arts instructor who was always impeccably dressed in her tight leather outfit. Think Pussy Galore from *Goldfinger.* A flick of the zipper and it could peel off like a thin layer of skin.

As S.A.M. sat in the bleachers, he knew that today was different from the previous classes when he played the waiting game. There was little time to waste if he was to accomplish his mission. Escape was on his mind. If Coach Z noticed his absence, then he'd probably administer one of his infamous "Scrub the showers with a toothbrush" detentions. If the price of protecting Lara Wright was the skin off one's knees, then so be it.

S.A.M. waited the obligatory minutes until the gym resounded with the smack of volleyballs sailing through the air. As soon as Coach Z turned to scream directions at one of the teams, which seemed to misunderstand the concept of the ball going *over* the net, S.A.M. was gone, easing silently out the door. The hallway was empty, the only noise echoing from within the gym. He needed information about Leonard in order to intercept, interrogate, detain. Specific locations. Schedule for the day. To proceed, he needed to infiltrate central intelligence. He started to move toward the main office, but first removed his glasses. *A lie is best delivered by looking the victim directly in the eye and never breaking the visual connection. No artificial barriers. Establish trust and never crack the mask of falsehood.*

For S.A.M. the lie was an offensive weapon designed to throw the victim off track, a mental monkey wrench tossed into an adult's linear brain. He was an artist when it came to the lie and Ravenhill had been his training ground. He practiced at home in front of the mirror in order to experiment with technique, eventually removing all facial nuances and tics that could betray him. S.A.M. knew that a future in espionage, law enforcement, and antiterrorist activities would require psychologically enhanced skills to defend against interrogation. *A lie can be a thing of beauty.*

He had imagined the scene a hundred times before: the shadowy room with the single bulb swaying overhead, suspended by a frayed cord from the cracked plaster ceiling; his skin dripping with perspiration from the jungle humidity and heat; the two-way mirror on the far wall; the three men, their shirts stained with sweat, each of their forearms tattooed with a black scorpion. They leaned toward him, their breath foul, their accents thick as they flung curses at him in broken English. "I vant answers," one hissed. S.A.M. gave them nothing but deception: false codes, untraceable phone numbers, phantom agents who existed only in the impenetrable vault of his imagination. And when they reached for the electric cables connected to the portable battery, he braced himself for the surge of current soon to follow. He was immune to pain. His body was a fortress of stone.

But S.A.M. had concluded there were certain people in his life who deserved the truth, while others deserved a lie. Miss Healy (aka Mona Lisa) got the truth. The jury was still out on Mrs. Romero. There were times when she seemed capable of trust, but then he'd see her with Mr. Gillette (aka Odd Job), principal of Raving Hell, with his shiny dome of a head, and he was sure they were evil twins of deceit. Coach Z got a lie whenever possible, whether it was a question about the whereabouts of his PE uniform or the last time he took a genuine shower.

There were variations on the lie in his repertoire, all delivered with the same earnest, shy tone that implied sincerity. When a teacher would ask him to remove his Ray-Bans in class, he'd simply reply, "They're prescription glasses to protect my eyes from the harsh daylight. I'm going blind, you know. No surgery can correct the disease. No known cure. The doctors have tried everything, but I've accepted the outcome, as well as the darkness. Next year all my books will be in Braille."

He hesitated outside the main office window, first checking to see that Mrs. Romero and Mr. Gillette were nowhere in the vicinity. Then he boldly entered and went straight to Mrs. Claudine Knight , the head secretary. She looked up from her computer terminal and saw him waiting by her desk.

"Good morning Mrs. Knight," S.A.M. said, even though he took one look at her gaudy silver necklace and was tempted to say, *Good morning, Miss Cow Patty.* But he held back, instead offering, "Stunning pendant. Is it an Apache design by chance?"

Mrs. Knight reached down and touched the silver eagle at her throat. "Why yes," she said, "thank you." He detected a slight blush rising through her cheeks. "It *is* authentic. It came straight from an Apache reservation and was handcrafted by one of their master artists."

"May I?" he asked, coming around the side of her desk. He didn't give her time to answer, but instead leaned down to inspect the item that dangled only inches above her bosom. "A beautiful specimen," he said. "Clearly one of the artist's finest achievements."

"It did cost a pretty penny. It was an anniversary gift from my husband Earl."

"My mother had one just like it," S.A.M. said. "It was a gift from an Apache shaman. In fact, she was wearing it the morning she passed away." He hesitated, making sure the last sentence had time to achieve its desired effect as his eyes collapsed to the floor.

"I'm so sorry," Mrs. Knight said. "When did she die?"

"Last year. It was quick, thank God. A rare, flesh-eating disease: necrotizing fasciitis."

"Flesh eating," she gasped as a look of horror came over her face. "How awful."

"Yes, it was an ordeal," S.A.M. said. He dropped his head and stared intently down at the carpet as if studying an insect trapped in the weave of the rug.

"You poor dear," Mrs. Knight finally said after a prolonged silence.

S.A.M. let the quiet linger a moment longer to establish a climate of honesty and trust, a place where strangers could share even their most intimate secrets. "I'm sorry," he said, moving back to the other side of the desk. "I don't usually talk about Mom. She's gone now and my father and I need to carry on."

"Of course you do," she answered.

"Anyway," S.A.M. said, his voice snapping to attention, "I'm here on a simple errand for Coach Z. He's busy officiating volleyball and asked me to get some information on a student and *hustle* it back to the gym *pronto*."

Nice touch, S.A.M. thought. *Hustle and pronto.* Two of the coach's favorite words. They gave the request a certain validity.

"And who might this student be?" Mrs. Knight asked.

"Leonard Lamb. Coach Zupanci needs to know his schedule for the next two periods."

Claudine scanned her computer screen. "And what sin did Leonard commit this time?" she asked without looking up at him.

"I'm not exactly sure, but I believe the coach wants Leonard to identify the origin of some complex pictographs depicting various stages of the *Kama Sutra.*"

Mrs. Knight pulled away from the screen and said in a flat monotone, "Honey, could you give me that in plain English?"

"Coach wants to see Leonard about some dirty pictures on the locker room wall."

"Gotcha," she said. "Thou shalt not draw porn in the potty." She glanced back at the screen for a moment. "Leonard's in math with Mr. Baker right now."

"And what about second hour?" S.A.M. asked. "Just in case he can't get to him right away."

"Second hour he's with Mr. Macon for social studies."

"Thank you Mrs. Knight." He was sure to smile. *Do not linger after the lie,* he thought. *Hit and run.* He put the Ray-Bans on, pivoted to go, but was stopped cold in his tracks. To his right, the door to the assistant principal's office had opened and Lara Wright was walking his way. She looked at him for a moment and he saw that her face was cool, emotionless, staring straight ahead. Mrs. Romero followed closely behind. S.A.M. didn't need an electronic surveillance device to understand the topic of their conversation.

Lara walked past him out the door and never once glanced his way. S.A.M. followed, keeping a safe distance behind.

He paused outside the office, then moved toward the gym, a slow fadeout, all the while looking over his shoulder as she moved the opposite way down the hall. The click of her heels stopped suddenly and he turned to see her standing at her locker, the slim curve of her profile so alluring. The inside panel of the locker door was garishly decorated with magazine glossies of rock stars and hunky underwear models and some photographs of Lara and friends. She turned her back to S.A.M. and gazed into a mirror glued to the metal and began to brush her dark veil of hair.

He pivoted toward her and approached with the briefcase firmly in his grasp, his secret lying securely inside the case. She was twenty feet away and he glimpsed her eyes in the mirror and could already smell the clean scent of apricot lotion on her skin. *Is it destiny?* he wondered, *our paths crossing like this? Should I reveal my power?*

Like a slap, he suddenly realized he'd never actually spoken to her. In fact, he wasn't sure if she'd ever heard his voice. He approached quietly, careful not to startle her, and stopped a few feet away. Her eyes looked red and tired in the small circle of mirror, and he was tempted to offer comfort by kissing the ivory nape of her neck. Suddenly her shoulders tightened, and he knew she'd spotted him in the mirror.

Before she could turn and face him, he said, "There's no need to be afraid," in his deepest, most masculine voice. He delivered the line as smooth as bourbon and thought of Bond in *Thunderball* as he reassured a bikini-clad beauty in peril.

She stopped brushing her hair and turned and S.A.M. saw the Jockey underwear models above her shoulder with their gleaming smiles and hairless, muscular chests.

"And what, exactly, do you think I'm afraid of?" she asked, looking at him with those killer eyes. His breath caught for a moment and he tried to respond to her question, but for once he was speechless.

He recovered by imagining Bond, the master of suave, in just such a dilemma. Then he said, "Let's not play this game, shall we?" even though he was clueless as to exactly what game he was referring to.

"Why not?" she asked, her voice sharp. "Isn't that what everyone does at Raving Hell? Play games?"

"I don't." He let the words stand alone like a soloist on a bare stage confronting his critics.

Her lips parted for a moment, as if to snap out another question, but she stopped. She placed her hand on the locker door and nervously swung it back and forth. "And who exactly are you supposed to be?"

"Your defender," he said. "Your protector."

She smiled. "My terminator?" She started to giggle, then stopped. "This isn't some weird sci-fi movie, is it? You're not some alien warrior from another dimension?"

"No," he said. "I'm from Toledo." He waited, expecting a response. Then he added, "In Ohio."

"I know where Toledo is. I took geography."

"My name's Bond. S.A.M. Bond. I'm in your eighth hour language arts class with Hardin. I sit on the aisle in the back."

"Aren't you new?" she asked.

"Sort of," he said. "I moved here in mid-September. My old man decided to relocate."

"That must be hard. Moving to a new school, I mean."

"I've relocated many times. You get used to it."

A long silence followed. He realized they were completely alone in the hall. *The school has never been this quiet before. Ever.*

"So I shouldn't be afraid," she said. "That's what you were saying at first, right? And that I need protection?"

"Exactly."

"From what?"

"Leonard Lamb."

"And why should I be afraid of Leonard?"

"The writing on the wall. He did it. It's classic Leonard."

"But you're assuming it's about me. I know a lot of girls named Lara."

"Maybe L-a-u-r-a," he said, "but not L-a-r-a. And not at Ravenhill. You're it."

She looked away, then stared at the precarious stack of books on the shelf in her locker and bit her lip. The tips of her fingers were red and swollen as they tapped against the metal.

"You can be straight with me," he said.

"And how do I know..." She stopped in mid-sentence. Her eyes were suddenly electric, darting around as if cornered and looking for an exit. "I should've gone home sick," she said. "I should've known the minute I walked into school. I never should've stayed." She put a hand over her eyes and momentarily hid them. Her cheeks were flushed with panic.

"You still could," he said. "There's time to get away." He took a step closer, wanting to reach out and take her hand, touch her hair. "I won't let him hurt you."

Lara looked up at S.A.M. and said, "Nobody raped me."

"I know."

"How do you know that?" she asked, her voice edgy, breaking. "You don't know me."

"I know you," he said, leaning toward her.

"So what am I like then, Mr. Defender?" she snapped.

S.A.M. stopped, his mind faltering. The question loomed in front of him like a great wave. He momentarily retreated, stepped back, then gazed at the turquoise and silver ring on her finger. He was probing for a detour, an end around lie, some bridge to another topic. *Stunning ring*, he could say. *Is it Apache silver by chance?* But then she looked at him and he began. "You're different," he said quietly. "It's the little things. You save a place for your friends in the cafeteria and don't mind picking up their trays after lunch. You decorate their lockers for birthdays. You wait with a friend after school until the last bus has arrived. In art you draw portraits of people. Mostly an older

125

woman. Maybe it's your grandmother. You like to sing when you walk to school, especially when nobody's around. A lot of Sarah McLachlan songs. You've got a nice voice, but I bet you'd never admit it. You love drama, especially doing Shakespeare on the stage. But your favorite times are the days when your father drives you to school in his red truck. You're bright as a torch when he drops you off and you come into the hall." He stopped and waited. Her face was stone-cold sober. Perhaps she was imagining that he was some bizarre creature from the *X-Files*.

"Go on," she said.

"You don't have a boyfriend. You could if you wanted one. A lot of guys want to take you out. But you're waiting for something."

She glanced into her locker again and tentatively ran a finger down the spines of the textbooks.

Without looking at him, she said, "I've heard the others talk about you. No offense, but they think you're creepy. Serial killer stuff. Maybe it's just the black coat and glasses and all."

"The price one pays for individuality," he said crisply.

"Whatever," she said. "But you're not like that, are you?"

"Not even close."

"And how'd you know those things about me?"

He took a breath, waited a beat, then said, "I know you could use a friend right now. Someone to count on during dangerous times."

"And I can count on you, right?" she asked, stepping toward him.

"Absolutely."

Her hand slowly rose, as if she were about to straighten his collar or remove a piece of lint from his coat. Instead, she reached up and carefully slid his glasses off with a certainty that S.A.M. found genuinely erotic as the plastic frames eased across his temples. "I've been standing here wondering what your eyes look like," she said.

"Now you know," he said, gazing at her through an untinted world.

"Your eyes aren't so dangerous," she said. "They're nice. Eyes are the windows to the soul. My grandma used to say that."

She handed the glasses back to him. He didn't put them on. She asked, "How do I know it wasn't you that put the writing on the wall?"

"You have to trust me," he said.

Suddenly he remembered the briefcase in his right hand and the secret it contained. A part of him wanted to share it with her, wanted to say, *Can I show you something?* But he held back, uncertain if she could handle the power of his creation. *She's so vulnerable, so raw. The timing must be perfect.* He knew an impulsive, rash act could backfire and his hours of work would be obliterated by a simple lack of discipline and self-control. He needed to be patient, especially when the time of revelation was so close. He needed to stick to the original plan and wait for eighth hour when the truth of his intentions would be made clear.

Lara swung the door shut on her locker. "I need to get back to class."

"Can I walk you?" he asked.

"Don't *you* have a class?"

"When I want to be there," he said confidently.

They went down the corridor together and he wondered if she would've agreed to walk with him if the halls had been full and the other kids were there to see them together. When they reached her classroom, she stopped and said, "So I have nothing to be afraid of, right?"

"Steer clear of Leonard."

"What are you gonna do to him?"

"Try a little reasonable persuasion."

"He's not the most reasonable person."

"Everyone is capable of reason when the timing is right."

She smiled and her teeth were radiantly white. "Thanks for the escort. I never knew I had a bodyguard."

"Just a friend." He slipped the glasses back on and smiled. "I'll see you in eighth with Hardin."

She laughed. "Right. How could I forget Hard On."

"Later," he said.

"See you."

Then S.A.M. turned away and started back down the hall. *Until fate intercedes*, he thought. *Until our paths cross again.*

■ ■ ■

FRIDAY, DECEMBER 19, 1997
8:30 A.M.

Lara

BEFORE Lara returned to Life Science, she waited outside the door, her hand resting lightly on the knob. There was a place at the nape of her neck that was tingling and warm and she felt dizzy for a moment, even reaching out her other hand and bracing it against the wooden frame for balance. She was still seeing S.A.M. Bond looking at her through those mirrored glasses and, in a hushed voice, saying things that no one else knew about her. For a moment she'd wanted him to grab her hand and say, "Let's get out of here," then whisk her away to the front of the school where a Harley with polished chrome was waiting to roar out of the parking lot in a flurry of speed and deafening noise. When she removed S.A.M.'s glasses, his eyes had been so blue it startled her. She expected brown or green, but not the soft blue that was the same color as the turquoise blouse she sometimes wore when she wanted to feel sexy, and hoped the guys would notice her. She wondered what Kelly and Shannon might say if they knew she'd talked with him in the hall, if they knew she'd had this moment when she wanted to reach up and kiss him as if her life depended on it and whisper, *Where have you been hiding?*

And what if she didn't tell them? What if she kept the moment all to herself for the rest of the day, her secret, and never said a word to anyone, just carried it around within her like some mysterious tattoo engraved on the inside of her thigh? It felt powerful to know what they didn't know, what no one else knew. It gave her the same little rush as when she reached up and slowly removed Sam's glasses and stared into his eyes and felt her breath quicken. She'd read somewhere that a famous Indian guru could meditate and then slow his pulse down until his heart was hardly beating and he was medically dead. She wanted that kind of control right now, to slow everything down and close her eyes and freeze that moment in the hallway so she could stay with it all day.

When Lara entered the classroom, she saw that the lights were off and students were watching a video that Mrs. M had started yesterday, a movie called *The Lucifer Plague* about a deadly virus that erupts in Washington, D.C. and threatens to destroy the planet. Shannon and Kelly were sitting on the far side of the classroom at one of the lab tables.

She saw Rachel Riley at the back of the room and remembered that she'd promised her a doughnut. She went to Mrs. M's desk in the front and studied the contents of the white pastry boxes, then selected two glazed doughnuts from the few that remained. As she headed down the side aisle, she passed Kelly and Shannon.

"What did Romero want?" Kelly asked, her voice eager for information.

"No big deal," Lara said. "A few questions. That's all."

"Was it about the graffiti?" Shannon said.

Lara nodded, then held up the doughnuts. "I need to deliver these, but I'll come back and fill you in on all the gory details."

Kelly held out an arm and stopped her progress down the aisle. "And you told her about Leonard?"

"Not exactly," Lara said, "but his name came up."

"Maybe she'll haul *his* ass out of class too," said Shannon.

Kelly pouted, then gestured at Rachel Riley. "Are you gonna dump us for the saint?"

"Or is she trying to save your soul?" Shannon asked.

"It's nothing like that," Lara said. "We're just talking."

"Well, let me know if she starts praying in tongues," Kelly said. "I love to translate all that weird Latin stuff. I've watched *The Exorcist* until I've practically got it memorized."

Lara went to the back where Rachel was still sitting. She slipped onto a stool and set the doughnuts on the lab table in front of them.

"Sorry that took so long," Lara said as she slid one over to Rachel. "Romero wanted to see me."

"What about?" Rachel asked.

Lara hesitated as she looked at the doughnut in front of her and picked at the thick layer of frosting with her finger. "She needed to ask me some questions."

"About the writing on the front of the school?" Rachel said, her eyes locked on Lara.

"Yeah, about that." Lara waited a moment as she brushed some crumbs off the table. Then she said, "Why'd you ask me about Leonard earlier?"

"Because I pay attention to details," Rachel said. "More than you know. And Leonard isn't exactly subtle when it comes to his intentions. Just be careful around him."

"I will," Lara said.

A long silence followed as they ate and watched Francis the Rat scurry back and forth across the table. At one point, Lara raised the doughnut in front of her as if she were making a toast and said, "Well, Merry Christmas."

Rachel took a bite, then broke off a few crumbs with her finger for Francis to munch on. "It's not too merry around our house right now," she said. "Christmas never is. My father thinks Christmas is a pagan holiday that promotes Satanic materialism so we don't do much celebrating."

"Do you open gifts or anything like that?" Lara asked.

"My mother gets us a few things," Rachel said. "But she has to sneak them behind Dad's back. I think he knows but chooses to look the other way." She took another bite and chewed it slowly. "After all, if anyone in the church found out we actually celebrated Christmas, it would ruin Captain Macho's image." Lara saw a sly grin play across Rachel's face. "That's what my sisters and I call him when he's not around. Captain Macho. He used to be in the National Guard and he's always strutting around the house while planning some mission for the Prodigal Sons."

They finished their doughnuts as the sounds from the movie continued behind them. Francis scurried around, devouring the feast of sugary morsels that fell onto the black surface. The rat looked up at them, his nose twitching, ready to scavenge for more.

"Do you ever want to switch places with someone?" Rachel asked.

Lara glanced over at her, a bit startled by the question. "Like forever?"

"I mean just for a little while. So you can feel what it's like to be in someone else's life."

Lara thought for a moment, then took the last tiny circle of doughnut and slipped it over her finger like a ring. "Maybe. I guess that's why I like drama. You get to be someone else when you're playing a character. Somebody new."

"I'd like to switch with you," Rachel said.

Lara laughed softly, then stared at her. "Why me? I can't imagine anyone wanting my life."

"Because you're pretty and everyone likes you." Rachel didn't look up as she spoke, kept her eyes focused on the table in a dreamy way as if she saw something in the scratched surface. "You're decent to others. Even to me. You always have been. You're the only person in the hall who smiles when you see me coming."

Suddenly Mrs. M hustled by their table, holding a squirming ferret in her hands. She flipped open a cage with her elbow, thrust the animal inside with a flourish, then slammed the gate shut and snapped the lock. She turned to the girls, sucked in a deep breath, then exhaled. "That's one less pesky varmint I got to run down later," she said with a Western drawl. "Catching Ol' Jackaroo is like trying to pin down greased lightning." She smiled, then spoke in her normal voice. "I've been observing you two for the last few minutes and assume this conversation is far more important than the science fiction masterpiece the rest of the class is watching." Her shaggy left eyebrow arched up toward her forehead and Lara knew she was waiting for a response.

"It is important, Mrs. M," Rachel said. "Very."

"Could we please have a few more minutes?" Lara asked. "We were about to discuss the origin of the universe."

Mrs. M gave them her best evil glare, eyebrows slanting down until she resembled some ancient owl. "Do me a favor?" she said. "When the two of you win the Nobel Prize in science, don't forget to mention your lovely old teacher in the acceptance speech. I'd also like a cut of the prize money."

"It's a deal," Lara said with a smile.

"Please hurry," Mrs. Mervar said, "or you'll miss the end where the plague infects Washington, D.C. and the president turns into a zombie." Then she was off again, scurrying after a floppy-eared rabbit named Alice who was scrambling up the center aisle.

After she left, Rachel smiled and rested her chin on her hand. "Can you keep a secret?"

Lara nodded. "Absolutely."

"I'm going away," Rachel said quietly. "Today. This afternoon."

"For the holidays?" Lara asked.

Rachel reached into her dress pocket and pulled out a bus ticket, which she slid onto the black tabletop. "For good," she said. "And you're the only person who knows."

"You're running away?" Lara asked.

"Not exactly."

"Then where are you going?"

"To this place in the mountains," Rachel said. " I read about it in a Christian newsletter my mom gets. It's an abbey."

"What's that?"

"It's like a monastery."

"But that's where monks live."

"True, but this is different. It's only for women. They call it The Sanctuary because it's for anyone who hears God's calling. I wrote to them and they sent me the information."

"Are you gonna be a nun?" Lara asked.

"It's not a convent," Rachel said. "But it is a place for women who want to give everything to God. And they've agreed to take me in."

"Do they know how old you are?"

Rachel smiled. "I estimated my age in spiritual years, which makes me around eighteen."

Lara glanced down at the white bus ticket. The movie had ended and she was aware of movement behind her as the lights flickered on. Students were sliding desks back into place and the hum of conversation was filling the room again.

"Your dad is gonna be pissed," Lara said.

"He'll be upset I'm gone. But I have a letter for my mom telling her why I'm leaving. I think she'll help him understand."

"I won't tell anyone," Lara said.

"Thanks. I appreciate that."

"Do you have enough money? I could loan you some if you need it."

"No, I have enough to get me there. I've been saving for a year from babysitting at Little Saints so I'm using what I've earned. After that, who knows? I'll leave that part to God."

Lara couldn't think of anything to say so she just sat there as the class came back to life behind her. A few animals were still on the loose and an exotic bird swooped by, nearly clipping the tops of their heads.

"I admire you," Lara finally said. "I always have."

"For what?" Rachel asked.

"For believing in something and sticking with it. No matter what the cost. And now for having the guts to leave."

Rachel smiled. "Thanks," she said.

"Will you write me once you're settled in?" Lara asked. "I'd like to know you got there safely."

"Sure. I'll send you a letter after I arrive."

Suddenly they heard Mrs. Mervar's voice booming through the classroom. "Gather round!" she shouted. "We only have a few minutes left. Gather round, I say!" Lara and Rachel turned and saw that the students were clustered together in the center of the room. Kelly and Shannon stood on the outer rim to the right so Lara walked over and joined them.

Mrs. Mervar was wearing a red Santa Claus hat with a bell at the end of the tassel. "Lights," she yelled to Steve Jackson, who was standing by the door. He flipped the switches and for a moment they were all bathed in shadow, the only illumination coming from the side windows. Mrs. M suddenly vanished into the prep closet at the front of the room, and when she reappeared, she was holding a large sheet cake with candles glowing on top. The students moved aside and cleared a path for her as she walked to the center of the room and placed the cake on a table. In the light from the candles, Lara could see that the chocolate surface was decorated with white-frosted symbols that covered the top.

"It's a white blood cell cake," Mrs. M said. "And not just any white blood cells." With a flourish, she waved her hand through the air and said, "These are Killer T cells and we know they can kick some butt when it comes to disease." She then turned to a student who was seated in a chair next to her, his baseball cap turned backward, a pair of crutches at his side. Lara recognized him as Gary Gerard. In the dim light his face seemed sunken and gaunt, yet he smiled when he saw the cake. Gary had been fighting leukemia since the fifth grade and most students knew his story. Over Thanksgiving break he'd flown to a big amusement park in California where he got to ride on roller coasters with an ex-Super Bowl quarterback. There were even rumors around school that his parents let him smoke pot to ease the nausea after chemotherapy.

Mrs. M took Gary's hand in hers, then looked out at the class. "Gary is going in for another round of chemo after the holidays, and we all know how tough that is after having studied diseases." The room was terribly quiet now, the only sounds coming from the animals. "But we also know how strong Gary is," Mrs. M. continued, "and we're sending him off with a thousand good thoughts so he'll come back to us soon." Lara watched as Gary leaned forward to blow out the candles. He suddenly paused, as if trying to catch his breath, then glanced up.

Someone was coming forward through the pack of students, breaking the circle, and people were stepping aside. Lara looked away from the glowing cake and saw Rachel walking toward Gary. Nobody said anything, nor did anyone stand in her way as she went to where he sat. She stopped next to him and looked down and smiled, then raised her hand and slowly removed his baseball cap. Even in the faint light, Lara could see the barren, white scalp with the web of veins threaded across the skin. Rachel took her palm and placed it on his head, then closed her eyes and Lara knew she was praying, her body motionless and still. Gary did not resist, allowed her to touch him as the quiet grew. There were no insults shouted at her, no ridicule. More of an understanding now. An acceptance of the possibilities she had to offer. And when she was finished, she opened her eyes, then leaned down and kissed his forehead.

There was a hush in the room, as if everyone held their breath together, waiting for the right time to exhale. Then

Mrs. M broke the silence. "Thank you Rachel," she said softly. "Thank you for that."

As Gary blew out the candles, the room erupted into applause and shouts of encouragement. "This is a cancer-kicking cake!" Mrs. M shouted above the noise. "Let's eat!"

■ ■ ■

FRIDAY, DECEMBER 19, 1997
8:50 A.M.

Leonard

AFTER Leonard busted out of math, he headed down the hall for second hour social studies, the one class he actually looked forward to. And it wasn't just because of the teacher, Mr. Macon, or the stuff about the First Amendment or the Supreme Court that he droned on about. All that was boring as hell. This was the lone period where he got to hang out with his Crew. The counselor at Raving Hell must have been smashed the day she scheduled all four of them together in the same class. Since Macon didn't use a seating chart, Leonard and his friends took over the back section of desks next to the windows and made it their turf. They called it Ripper's Row because of what they threatened to do to anybody who actually had the guts to try and sit there.

As Leonard zigzagged down the jammed hallway, he slowed when he saw his sister, Jenna, as she stood next to her locker. She stayed with Leonard's mother up on Snob Hill. Ever since his parents split up two years ago, his mom had worked as a live-in housekeeper for a rich lawyer who gave her a basement apartment in his mansion so that she and Jenna had a place to stay.

Leonard didn't get to see his sister very often because each time their parents got within shouting distance, it usually ended in an ugly fight. Still, Leonard tried to look out for her at school.

Now Jenna was opening her locker while some older jock stood behind and poked at her with his finger. She was wearing a skimpy top with a plunging neckline and as she turned to mess with her combination, the jock tried to snap her bra. With a laugh, she whirled around and slapped at him. Leonard knew she looked older than ninth grade, especially with her makeup and hip-hugging jeans. She'd developed quickly and her full breasts and sleek curves were causing a lot of heads to turn in the hallway when she passed by. He also knew what the older guys were thinking when they spotted her. *Check out the fresh flesh. Juicy.*

Leonard walked quickly toward them and got up a head of steam, then rammed into the jock's blindside with a firm shoulder that sent him sprawling onto the floor and knocked his baseball cap off. The guy leaped up and started to make a move, but then Leonard gave him a menacing smile and he scrambled quickly down the hall.

"Leave Robbie alone!" Jenna yelled. "He was just joking around. He was only teasing."

"I'm the only joker around here," Leonard said, moving on past her. "And next time I'll tease his head with my fist." He needed to have a little chat with her about coming to school dressed like some trick slut. Maybe over the holidays. After all, she was his sister and the last thing he needed to hear about was some pretty boy jock getting into her pants.

His friends were waiting for him outside Macon's class and they entered together. Social studies was always rowdy and today was no exception. Most of the kids in second hour were repeats, meaning they'd failed once already, and the decibels could get cranked. But Mr. Macon was okay, at least by their standards. As Leonard made his way to the back row, he raised a fist at the teacher and said, "What's shaking Macon?" The teacher turned away from the board where he was writing the class agenda and waved in response. He was colorfully dressed in a white shirt and Christmas tie complete with flashing red and green lights that flicked off and on.

Even though Leonard had hated social studies last year with Mrs. Stone, he'd given Macon a chance in the beginning. During the first week, the teacher cut a deal with Leonard and his crew. "The back row's yours," he said to them. "If you don't want to do the homework, that's fine. But you have to give me something in return. I want you in class on time. All of you. No cutting what-soever. I want you participating in all the activities, no questions asked. And no disruptions. This includes all tests. If you can do this, I'll consider giving you a pass." They looked at each other and nodded in agreement. Then Macon leaned forward and said, "But if you burn me even once," he paused and stared straight at them, "then the deal's off. And I don't like to get burned."

There were other things Leonard liked about the class. Macon didn't lecture or teach straight from some textbook with a bunch of worksheets. At least once a week, he had them do a game, a "historical simulation" as he called it. Leonard's favorite was the one called *Collision* about the Plains Indians Wars. For two days they moved all the desks to the outside of the room and created a huge map of the western United States on the floor. Leonard was assigned to be Geronimo, one of the Apache Indian chiefs, and he got to make surprise attacks on the Great White Father's soldiers. In the end, his tribe lost the game and they found themselves crammed into the "reservation" corner of the classroom where they howled in rebellion at their misfortune.

Leonard slipped into a desk and immediately propped his feet up on the seat next to him. Today they were finishing up the expert speeches. Macon had asked them to research the history of a topic they were interested in being an expert on. He didn't care what it was as long as they were dedicated to learning more about the subject and willing to share their information with the class. Leonard's choice was easy: the history of the Ford Mustang. He used some of his old man's *Car and Driver* magazines for research, even finding one entire issue completely devoted to the subject. But his greatest resource was the 1972 midnight blue Mustang sitting in Leon's garage that was waiting for Leonard when he got his driver's license. He and his old man had worked on it for years and it was a beauty. Leon was a part-time auto mechanic and he bought the car dirt-cheap from the wrecking yard after some punk was killed when he rolled it out on the interstate during a blizzard. They hammered out any dents and sanded and painted the exterior so that it looked like an expensive classic at one of those big auto shows, then put in leather seats, new brakes, flashy doors, even a slick engine that gleamed silver in the light from the overhead garage lamp,

Sometimes Leonard dreamed about that car. Leon had promised it to him and there were nights when he imagined quitting school and becoming one of those stock car racers who stand in the winner's circle with the screwdriver chicks draped all over him. He knew some of the high school boys raced on the weekends out on the interstate long after midnight, and once he and Zeb had slipped out of the house and rode their bikes all the way up to Cemetery Hill just so they could watch the races. It was a full moon night and they sat on the slope overlooking the highway and watched as the cars roared by, their tires squealing and burning against the asphalt. Leonard knew that someday he wanted to drive his Mustang on the Interstate with Zeb riding shotgun as they left some Camaro or Firebird or Trans Am in the dust, a small figure in the rearview mirror growing smaller each time he gunned the accelerator.

Mr. Macon wrote the names of the final presenters on the board. Leonard had done his presentation three days ago just to get it over with. He'd received a 75 percent and Mr. Macon had said he was passionate about his subject. First up today was Chuckie Meek, otherwise known as Meek the Geek, a dark-haired little guy with prominent ears and an enormous nose. He'd brought a big poster as a visual aid and when he put it face-down on Macon's desk, somebody in the front yelled, "Suck up points!" and Chuckie scowled at them.

Macon yelled for the class to settle down and Chuckie began by holding up the poster. At the top was written "The Rottweiler" in enormous letters, while underneath was a large drawing of the imposing black dog, its fangs bared. Leonard bristled when he saw the picture.

"My presentation is on the Rottweiler, one of man's least understood friends," said Chuckie Meek. "My family owns three of them and this is a drawing of Spike, one of my favorites."

Leonard hated dogs, especially Rottweilers. Hated their glossy black coats and drooping jowls. Hated their jagged teeth and vice-like jaws. Give him a rifle and he'd shoot every one of them to extinction. Then he'd burn the carcasses until there was nothing left but charred flesh and bone.

He had reason to hate them. He was nine the summer it happened. They were living in the trailer park, over near the VFW, and his parents were always gone trying to make ends meet. Leon was working for the towing company and doing a lot of double shifts because they were short-staffed and everybody kept quitting. His mom had taken a job as a cashier at the Gas'N'Go three blocks away in Old Town. She left in the morning to go to work and Leonard was supposed to watch Jenna until she got home at 6:00 P.M. Her phone number was on the fridge in case of an emergency and she always left some bread and cold cuts for lunch. On Fridays she slipped Leonard a dollar for the ice cream truck that would come in the afternoon. Every week she gave him the same lecture until he got sick of hearing it.

"Don't be running off and leaving your sister alone," she would say. "You're responsible for her. Stay in the house or the yard. You're the big man when your dad ain't here."

He hated the trailer park. There weren't any kids around his age to hang out with, and it seemed full of old people who looked like they were about to die. No swing sets or monkey bars or teeter-totters. So he did what he could for his sister. She played with her dolls in the morning while he watched cartoons and the old shows on TV. After lunch, when the stupid soap operas came on and the metal roof of the trailer started to sizzle under the hot sun, he put out the plastic swimming pool in the backyard, then used the hose to fill it up so they could splash in the water and cool off.

On most afternoons he sat in the shade of the trailer awning and watched the new neighbor build a deck and wooden fence in the yard next door. He was a tan, muscular guy with a head as bald as an egg who often worked with his shirt off and Leonard could see the tattoos covering his chest and back. Sometimes they turned different colors in the bright sun and Leonard was fascinated by the changes. The man's dark skin made him look like an Indian. One night Leonard overheard his parents saying that the new neighbor was living there for a couple of weeks and doing some home improvements in exchange for rent.

"Nice enough fella," Leon said, "but he's got his work cut out for him. That old place is a mess."

At first Leonard said nothing to the man when he and Jenna were in the back. *Don't talk to strangers.* But one day he ambled over to the edge of the yard and watched as the tattoo man cut up some two-by-fours in a spray of sawdust. Leonard was curious and figured this was as good a time as any to ask his question. So when the man looked up for a moment, Leonard said, "Are you an Indian?"

The man smiled, unplugged his saw, then set it on the ground. Sweat was running down his face, and he took out a bandanna and wiped it away.

"What do you think?" he asked Leonard.

"I think you're an Indian," Leonard said. "You look like one. We studied 'em in school and you look like the pictures I seen."

The man grinned at him again and Leonard saw he had two gold teeth right in the front. "So I guess I'm an Indian," he said.

"And I bet your tribe painted all those tattoos on your skin."

"That's one way of looking at it."

"What tribe are you from?" Leonard asked.

The man rubbed his head for a moment, then said, "I'm from the Whatchamacallit tribe. Did you read about them in school?"

"No," Leonard answered. "Never heard of 'em."

"We're the oldest tribe around. Older than the Apache."

"I read about those Apaches. They were good fighters."

"Yeah, but we're better. We kick their butt all the time."

A long pause followed. Leonard could feel the hot sun on his neck and arms, and he turned to go back into the shade.

"So who are you?" the tattoo man asked.

Leonard stepped back. "I'm no Indian," he said.

"But what's your name?"

"Leonard." Then he pointed over at the pool. "And that's Jenna, my little sister. I take care of her during the day."

"I'm Skin," the man said, reaching out to shake Leonard's hand. As they shook, Leonard was amazed at the size of his palm, which seemed as big as a catcher's mitt.

"I've been noticing something," Skin said.

"What's that?" Leonard asked.

"That you look pretty bored just sitting over there."

"I guess I am."

"Then come on over and learn something."

"Learn what?"

"How to use your hands to make a living."

So Leonard did. For the rest of the week, while Jenna played in the pool, he helped Skin work on the fence and deck. He taught Leonard how to use a hammer and only drive the nail part way down at first, just in case you screwed up and needed to yank it out with the claw end. He showed him how to use the tape measure, the level, the handsaw, and even gave him his own hammer and a nail apron to wear around his waist. Skin showed him the design he'd drawn on a piece of scratch paper of the deck and fence. He seemed pretty sharp at figuring out what materials they needed, almost down to the nail. He taught Leonard how to use the circular saw and Leonard loved how it ripped through a board, the way the sawdust shot into the air and he could feel the heat radiating off the steel teeth.

When Leonard went over to help Skin the following week, he saw a huge black dog sitting in the shade by the tools. The animal wasn't chained up, nor did it seem to notice Leonard as he stood at the edge of the yard. Suddenly Skin appeared from out of the trailer. "Hey Lenny," he said, pointing at the dog. "This is Bonnie. She's been with some relatives until just yesterday. I had to drive up north to get her."

Leonard stayed put, hands in his pockets, hesitant to move any closer. "What kind of dog is she?"

"A Rottweiler," Skin said. "Best damn guard dog there is. I usually take Bonnie on all my jobs and just leave her on the site. Trust me. Nobody messes with my tools when Bonnie's around."

The dog was mean looking and Leonard didn't want to get any closer. "How long have you had her?" he asked.

"A few years. I stole her from a neighbor who used to beat the hell out of her with a belt when he got drunk. Old guy was a security guard who taught her to attack on command. She used to have those killer instincts. I saw her get into a fight once with a big husky across the street. Wasn't a thing anyone could do. She killed that dog in nothing flat. Had to get a crowbar to pry her jaws open. You can imagine what she'd do to a man's face."

Skin went over and started petting Bonnie. She licked his hand and then rolled around in the grass while he scratched her stomach. "I've trained her different since I rescued her," he said. "No need to be afraid. I took her to my sister's house up north and she was giving all the kids rides on her back. She wouldn't hurt a fly." Then he beckoned to Leonard. "C'mon over and say hello."

Leonard slowly approached, his hand outstretched. The dog sniffed at his fingers, then licked them with her warm tongue. "You see," Skin said, "she likes you. She'll be your best friend before you know it." Leonard reached out and stroked her smooth, black coat. "You've got the right touch, Lenny, and now you'll have a buddy for life."

For the rest of the week, Leonard worked mostly as the "gofer," the guy who brings things to the construction boss and hands him tools and supplies. He didn't mind getting ordered around because he was learning something and it was more interesting than watching his little sister play in the pool. Once Skin even let him take a sip of ice cold beer from one of the cans he kept in a blue cooler on the back step. Bonnie stayed put under the tree and didn't move around much. Skin's story about the husky still gave Leonard the shivers and he made sure to walk slowly around the Rottweiler whenever he had to move the extension cord for the electric saw.

Sometimes they talked while working, and Skin told Leonard personal stories about his life. How he'd been drifting across the country living in his van, working when he needed to, and trying to get to California where he had a girlfriend. He showed Leonard a snapshot of Doreen. She was a slim, long-legged blond in a tiny bikini standing on a beach. "She's my honey pie," Skin would say, "and she's been waiting a long time for me. I just need to save up some money so we can get married."

Skin was funny. Sometimes he told Leonard jokes he'd heard on the late night talk shows. Most of the time Leonard didn't understand them, but he laughed anyway because he didn't want him to think he was stupid. Skin was funny looking too. Not just the tattoos and the bald head. Most of his teeth were crooked and bent like he'd been in an accident or something.

One day Skin was hammering in some nails on the main floor of the deck. Suddenly he cursed and hurled the hammer down on the wooden planks with a loud bang, then held his jaw as he winced in pain.

"Dammit," he moaned. "Hammer popped up and hit me in the mouth." Skin extended his hand and Leonard could see two gold teeth in his palm. He opened his mouth wide, exposing a big gap in the top row, then said, "I hate when this happens."

Leonard didn't know what to say or do. "Should I call a doctor?" he finally asked.

Skin started to laugh so hard he had to lean against one of the sawhorses. "Little joke," he finally said. He popped the two teeth back into his mouth and Leonard could see that the top row was now intact. "When I was younger I got kicked in the mouth by a mule," Skin said. "Had to get some falsies." He grinned and the two gold teeth gleamed. "At least they're good for a few laughs now and then."

Another time Skin told him stories about how he'd come to acquire all the tattoos. "I picked 'em up all over the world," Skin said. "I used to be in the Merchant Marine and sailed on all the big oceans. Went to Hong Kong, India, Australia, Borneo. I fought pirates in the South China Sea and survived a trip around Cape Horn with fifty foot waves. I been everywhere. Some people bring back souvenirs from their travels. I bring back my tattoos."

He pointed at the huge tiger emblazoned across his belly with the piercing green eyes and the sweeping tail. "Got this one in Thailand." Then he stretched out his left arm and Leonard could see a menacing red snake coiled around his wrist, its glistening fangs dripping with poison. "This one's from Bombay." Each tattoo was different and colorful and Leonard had never seen anything quite like it. "It's time for a geography lesson, Lenny."

Skin explained each of the tattoos and took him around the word on the map of his skin. Leonard heard the names of places he never even knew existed: Sri Lanka, Bangladesh, Patagonia, Copenhagen, Calcutta. The names danced through his mind like an exotic parade of animals at the circus and he longed to follow Skin on more adventures and leave the trailer park far behind.

Mid-July brought a heat wave and in the morning Leonard put out Jenna's little pool so she could have a swim party in the shade with her dolls. Skin was nearly finished with the deck and fence so he was pushing hard in the hot sun, drinking a lot of beer and talking about Doreen. At the end of the week they were taking a little siesta after lunch when Skin handed Leonard a full can of Budweiser and said, "Drink up, Lenny. You deserve it. Besides, it's hot as hell and you don't want to get dehydrated." The beer tasted bitter at first, but it was ice cold and felt good as Leonard drank it down. He forced himself to finish the can, and afterward he and Skin exchanged loud burps and laughed.

"Hey," Skin said, "you want to see a naked South American beauty named Lolita?"

Leonard had seen naked women before, but only in quick glimpses when his old man had one of those girly videos on the TV late at night. "Do you have a picture?" Leonard asked.

"Yeah," Skin said. Then he lowered his voice. "It's in a secret place and it's only for us guys to see." He winked at Leonard and grinned. "But once you've seen her, you'll never forget her."

"Sure," Leonard said.

Then Skin gestured at Jenna who was still playing in her little pool. "After all, this is something private. It's for men like us, and not little girls. Right?"

Leonard looked over at his sister and nodded his head in agreement.

"Let's step into my office," Skin said.

The trailer had a walkout screen door and they slipped inside. It was dark and stuffy in the room and it took Leonard's eyes a moment to adjust after being in the bright sunlight. He could smell something bad, like a toilet that hadn't been flushed in a long time. The room was a mess of pizza boxes, beer cans, a few sawhorses, and some broken pieces of furniture. Leonard stayed close to the door where he could keep an eye on Jenna in case she noticed he was gone and got scared.

"Lolita's my little secret," Skin said. "Got her in Jamaica and I keep her in a special place." He turned around so that his back was to Leonard and started to unbutton his jeans. "Now don't get freaked, Lenny," he said. "I'm not some weirdo. I have to do this to show her off." Leonard saw that Skin didn't have any underwear on. His bottom was white as snow under the jeans and he slid them down so that his rear was facing Leonard. "Do you see her?" Skin asked. "You have to look real close."

Leonard bent down and saw a small figure tattooed on his butt. It was a naked woman with pointy nipples and long black hair. "Watch this," Skin said and he flexed a muscle and it looked as if Lolita was actually moving.

Suddenly he turned around and grabbed Leonard by the shoulders and pulled him close, like he wanted to dance.

"Come here," he said. His voice was different now. Strange and faraway. Almost a whisper. "I got something else to show you."

Leonard smelled the beer on Skin's breath and saw the tattooed tiger glaring at him from Skin's belly, its green eyes all spooky, ready to pounce. They were standing close to the screen door, and Skin twisted Leonard around so he could look at the yard.

"Do you see Bonnie out there?" Skin said, pointing at the dog, his voice louder than usual. Leonard saw the black animal under the tree, her head alert and attentive. "Do you know what Bonnie would do if I yelled 'Attack!'?"

Leonard said nothing. He could see Jenna standing twenty feet away in the small pool's shallow water with her Barbie.

"What I said about Bonnie, about her being all nice and everything. Well, that's bull." His mouth was right next to Leonard's ear and his breath was hot. "She'll attack on my command. Her jaws are like a steel trap. They'd probably tear a little girl's face clean off." Skin placed one of his big hands on

150

Leonard's shoulder and started stroking him there. "I know you care about your pretty sister," he said. "So you'll do what's best for her. Whatever it takes."

Leonard remained silent. He didn't nod or try to look at Skin. He kept thinking about his parents, hoping they'd somehow show up and help him out, but he knew it was hours before they were due home. He kept staring at Jenna in the pool, at Bonnie under the tree.

"And what's best," said Skin, "is that you grab that sawhorse next to you with both hands." Leonard thought about trying to make a break for the yard. Maybe he'd turn and kick Skin in the privates. But then he saw Bonnie and his little sister and knew if the dog attacked, he could never reach her in time. So he did what he was told and grabbed the splintered wood of the sawhorse.

Skin was messing with Leonard's pants, his hands rough and quick as he yanked them down. The can of beer made Leonard feel wobbly and slow, like a bad dream, like he was underwater at the big city pool and watching all the swimmers move around him. He needed to go to the bathroom.

"This is what men do for each other, Lenny," Skin said. "They help each other out. And now you're gonna help me." Leonard bit his lip so he wouldn't yell and the dog wouldn't hear him cry out. He was so scared, didn't really understand what was happening behind him but knew it was bad. Skin's hands gripped him, held him firm. "You're my little helper, aren't you?" Skin whispered.

Leonard started to scream so many times from the pain, felt the tears on his cheeks, and wanted to yell out, but he bit down hard on his lip until it bled and kept staring at that black dog and his sister and knew what had to be done. *Take it like a man,* Leon always said when he whipped him with the yardstick. *Take it like a man.* And he did. *Like a man.* It seemed to go on and on. Forever.

When Skin finally backed away, his breathing heavy and erratic, Leonard's knees buckled and he fell to the floor. He looked up and saw that Skin was buttoning his jeans. "You need to stay real quiet about this, Lenny, or Bonnie and me are gonna pay little Jenna a visit. Besides, if you tell, everyone's gonna know you're a faggot."

So Leonard never said a word. Never yelled out. Never screamed. Not once. Not when he pulled up his pants and stumbled out into the yard. Not when he got Jenna out of the pool, all the while keeping an eye on Bonnie, then took her by the hand and rushed into the house. Not when he dead bolted the doors and sat her in front of some TV cartoons while he went to his room and crawled into bed. Not when his mom came home and asked him what was wrong and he told her he didn't feel good, something he ate at lunch, and he lay in bed all that night and dreamed of killing Skin and Bonnie with that electric saw, cutting them both into bloody scraps. Not when he got up in the dark and went to Jenna's room and stood guard by the window, a butcher knife in his hand, watching the bedroom door, making sure that if Skin broke in he'd be ready. Not the next morning when he saw the dried blood on his underwear and secretly threw them out with the trash. Not when his mom asked him why he was walking funny and he just said he was still feeling sick, a stomach ache, and having trouble going to the bathroom. Not when Skin cleared out, packed up his tools and truck and vanished in the night, leaving behind a wooden deck without a railing, an unfinished fence, a pile of scrap wood. Leonard never said a thing because he was a good brother and he'd done what needed to be done, he'd saved his sister's life, and now he had a secret he must never tell. That was the price he had to pay. And he never told a soul about what Skin did to him. Not a soul. Ever.

"*Leonard*," a voice said. It wasn't Chuckie Meek or one of his friends. It was Mr. Macon calling to him from the front of the room.

"Yeah," he said, sliding his feet off the chair and straightening up.

"Mrs. Romero is in the hall," Macon said. "She'd like to speak with you."

Leonard looked at his crew and rolled his eyes in mock disgust. Then he rose from the desk and walked across the room to the door where Mrs. Kathie Romero was waiting for him.

■ ■ ■

FRIDAY, DECEMBER 19, 1997
8:55 A.M.

Hardin

WHEN first hour ended, Kent quickly organized his desk, then locked the classroom door and headed up the steps, his stride assured and confident. During his planning period, he had a meeting scheduled at 9:00 with Gus Gillette, but was hoping to catch Kathie Romero in her office so he could report the incident with the quilt. Since Kathie was the assistant principal, she handled most of the disciplinary issues. He also knew that she worked closely with Leonard Lamb.

Kent walked rapidly down the hallway, pausing only to weave around a few students as they made their way to class. When he entered the main office, he saw Claudine at her desk.

"Good morning," he said briskly as he moved toward her.

"And good morning to you, Kent," she said. "I hope you and Paul were able to clean up the mess in The Pit. Forgive me for not asking about the details, but my stomach's a little tender this morning. I can only imagine."

"Yes, we got it cleaned up. But I need to see Kathie about an urgent matter." He saw that Kathie's office door was closed.

"She's in a meeting right now. I'm not sure how long she'll be, but you're welcome to leave a message or talk to Gus. He's expecting you this morning."

Kent hesitated in front of her desk, uncertain about what to say next. The last person he wanted to report the incident to was Gus Gillette. Ever since he'd arrived at Ravenhill, Gillette had been in his face, reminding him in closed-door meetings that he was on probation and that he better watch his step. Once a week Kent submitted his lesson plans to Gillette so the principal could peruse them for any "glaring inconsistencies." There were surprise visits to his classroom in which Gus would stand in the back corner, a look of intense scrutiny on his face as he studied Kent's every move. There were also the innumerable memos left in his mailbox reminding him to be visible in the basement hall-way during passing period, that the trashed out Pit area was his responsibility to supervise, that parents were complaining about his homework assignments being too lengthy and rigorous, and that he was four minutes late on Wednesday for bus duty in front of the school.

Kent understood the firing game and had watched it happen to other less competent colleagues over the years. He knew that Gillette was trying to rattle him by turning up the heat with the hope that he'd resign by Christmas. There was a time when he considered contacting the teacher's union about administrative harassment, but he decided to let it go. He didn't have the energy for a fight and vowed to stick it out. Besides, in April he could fill out a transfer request to move to a new school for the following year.

"Just tell Kathie that I need to report a theft from my room," Kent said. "I believe it involves Leonard Lamb."

"That'll get her attention," Claudine said. "Leonard's already in the hot seat around here. I'll make sure she gets the message."

"Thanks. Is Gus waiting for me?"

"Yep," she said. "Go right on in."

He walked back to the office and could see Gus Gillette standing behind his desk, his head lowered as he perused a stack of file folders. Kent rapped lightly on the wooden door frame and Gus looked up.

"Good morning, Mr. Hardin," he said. "Please come in." It bothered Kent that Gus was always so formal when addressing him. It was never, "Good morning, Kent," one of those upbeat, first name greetings he reserved for the rest of the staff. It was always, "...*Mr. Hardin.*" Gillette kept him at a distance, keeping their relationship professional, impersonal, by the book. And even though it angered Kent, he understood the strategy. If Gillette ever tried to force a resignation from him or even push an incompetence hearing with the school board, it would be easier if there were no personal strings attached. Strictly business.

Kent stepped into the office and said, "I know we have an appointment to talk about my evaluation, but I need to report a theft. Someone broke into the classroom and stole my personal property. I believe it was Leonard Lamb and I'd like him brought in and questioned."

Gus set the files aside and came out from behind the desk. He rested a hand on the wooden edge and said calmly, "Have a seat and let's talk this one through."

"I don't want to talk it through," Kent snapped. "I want Leonard brought in and dealt with this time."

"What do you mean 'this time'?" Gus asked.

"I want him held accountable for his actions. Not just a reprimand or a few days of in-school suspension. This incident is grounds for expulsion."

"Slow down," Gus said. "What the hell happened?"

"When I got to school this morning, my door was open," Kent answered. "Either Paul forgot to lock it, which he's never done before, or somebody broke in."

"Everybody slips up," Gus said, "especially this time of year. Paul's got a lot on his mind. Mistakes are going to happen."

"Anyway," Kent continued, "when I got in the classroom, I saw that my quilt was missing from the wall."

"I've seen it during my observations. It's beautiful."

"It was a gift from my students when I was in the Peace Corps."

"And you think Leonard stole it?"

"When I came in the room, there was a note on my desk telling me to look in The Pit. So I went in and found the quilt stuffed down the toilet. You can imagine the condition it was in."

Gus scowled, then looked at the floor and shook his head in disbelief. "I swear these damn kids get meaner every year. I'm sorry."

"I know it's Leonard Lamb," Kent said. "It's exactly the kind of thing he'd do to get back at me."

"Could you tell it was his handwriting on the note?"

Kent hesitated. "The note was typed. But I'm sure it was Leonard."

"How do you know?"

"Because he's stolen other things off my desk."

"But have you ever caught him? Have you ever reported him for stealing?"

Kent stared out the office window for a moment. "No, I haven't. I've had things missing and I always suspected him. But no, I've never actually reported it."

"Have you contacted his father about your suspicions?"

"No, I haven't done that either. When I tried to get a hold of Mr. Lamb about Leonard's grade at the beginning of the year, he never returned my phone calls. So I figured it wasn't worth the time."

Gus Gillette motioned to a chair. "Sit down for a minute," he said. At first Kent ignored him and remained standing. Finally, he relented and sat in one of the black, cushioned chairs directly across from the desk.

"More than anyone," Gus said, "I know that Leonard Lamb is a pain. Kathie and I have spent hours dealing with him and we know he's trouble. But he's also smart. He knows the rules. You're not the first teacher he's retaliated against and you probably won't be the last." Gus leaned forward and ran a hand over his bare scalp. "But until you have evidence that he's the one who stole your quilt, there's not much I can do except haul him in here and read him the riot act. He'll just give me that smart-ass smile, shrug his shoulders, and say he didn't do it." Gus leaned back in his chair. "When Leonard Lamb graduates from Ravenhill, I'll be the first to escort him off school grounds. But until then, we're stuck with him and there's not much we can do except watch him like a hawk and try to catch him in the act. Period."

Gus rose slowly from the chair and walked to the other side of the desk. "I'm sorry for the damage that's been done. I'm sure the quilt was important to you. My only suggestion is to not keep personal items at school where students can get at them."

Kent grimaced and stood up. He started toward the door, but then stopped and turned around. "Is that it?" he said firmly. "You're not even going to question him about this?"

"Sure, I can question him, but I don't think I'll get anywhere. I've been through it before. Ask Mrs. Callahan about the purse stolen from her desk. Or Mr. Bradley about the stereo taken from the band room. Or Ms. Carlson about her new Jeep Cherokee that got the broken window. There's not much I can do without evidence. And I'm certainly not going to get any help from his father. Leon Lamb backs his kid up on everything."

"What if I solicited some evidence," Kent said firmly.

"And how would you go about doing that?"

"The police department pays for information related to crimes."

Gus shook his head. "We don't have any money in our budget to pay student informers. Parents would be outraged. I can hardly buy enough textbooks for the classrooms."

"Maybe I'm willing to put up a little money of my own," Kent said. "It's important to me. It's personal."

Gus was silent for a moment. He peered intently at Kent, studying him. "Look," he finally said, "it's the last day before the holidays. Why not deal with this when we come back in January?"

"I'd prefer not to wait," Kent said, vigorously shaking his head. "This needs to be dealt with now. Who knows what he's going to do next?"

"Let Kathie and I deal with it this morning," Gus said. "We'll haul Leonard in and give him the third degree. If he talks back, we'll suspend him and send him home. Then after the holidays we'll follow up on the quilt. That's a promise."

Kent looked at Gus and shook his head, perplexed. "And if he doesn't get suspended, then I get the privilege of spending eighth hour today with a thief who got away with a crime and damn well knows it."

"If you don't want him in class during eighth, just send him to me. I'll take care of it."

"And what kind of a message is that?" Kent asked. "That I can't handle him? That I need you to step in and take over?"

Gus leaned back in his chair, checked his watch, then said, "That's not what I meant."

"Then what did you mean? Why don't you spell it out for me."

Gus paused and rested his chin in his hand, all the while staring at Hardin. "We're not going to agree on how to handle this," he finally said. "That's a given. I'm sorry about the quilt. If we can get some evidence that Leonard did it, then he'll be punished." Gus tapped the watch on his wrist. "But we have some other things to discuss this morning."

"Such as?" Kent asked. "Another classroom visit? Or do you need to see more of my lesson plans?"

"No. I've seen all I need to see." Gus picked up a file folder and handed it to Kent. "Your midyear evaluation is inside. I've been very honest about your performance based on district criteria. You need to read it sometime today. Then we'll have a conversation about your future at Ravenhill. I'd like to meet with you again after school in my office at three-thirty. The executive director of human resources will be present as well as the deputy superintendent."

"I see," Kent said. "You're bringing in the heavies from Central Office."

"I can't say anything more. Just be in my office at three-thirty. Sharp."

"I want someone from the teacher's union there."

"You have that right."

Kent glared at Gus. "I can't believe you're pulling this right before Christmas," Kent said.

"There's never a good time," Gus replied.

"At least give me until spring break. I need to make some arrangements."

"We'll talk more at three-thirty."

"Jesus, look at my résumé, at my years in the district. I've been busting my ass to make this transfer work. This is my damn career we're talking about."

"Three-thirty," Gus repeated. "Call the union if you need someone to advise you."

There was more that Kent wanted to say, but he held back, afraid it would spill over like flame erupting from an oil fire. His hands were trembling. *Keep a lid on it*, he thought. Gus came forward to escort him out, but Kent pivoted and left on his own without saying a word.

As he emerged from Gillette's office, he saw that Kathie Romero and Officer Bradford were talking in front of Claudine's desk. Bradford was the policeman assigned as liaison to the school and he was frequently in the hallways and classrooms of Ravenhill chatting with students and teachers. He was a big man and he loomed over Kathie and Claudine as he spoke with them. Kent hesitated when he drew close and waited on the periphery until he sensed there was a break in the conversation.

"Excuse me, Kathie," he finally said, "but I need to speak with you."

Kathie smiled and turned to face him. "Claudine told me you stopped by," she said. "Why don't you wait in my office until I'm finished with Officer Bradford and I'll be right with you."

She went to turn away, but Kent stepped closer and said, "This really can't wait. It's urgent. We need to talk *now*." His voice was abrupt and emphatic. She took a step back and looked at him again.

"What exactly is so urgent that it can't wait a few minutes?" she said impatiently.

"Something was stolen from my classroom this morning."

"Well," she said, "you know the process. Write up what happened on a discipline referral and put it in my mailbox. I'll get to it as soon as I can."

Hardin could feel the trembling in his hands again. He was suddenly cold, as if he were at home in the trailer. "That's it?" Hardin said, his voice quavering. "That's all you're going to do?"

Kathie sighed. "Yes, that's it for now. My plate is full today and it's going to have to wait."

"Well, it *can't* wait," Kent said adamantly. "It needs to be handled immediately."

"It's going to have to wait, Kent. I've got other problems to address that take priority."

Hardin was aware that Bradford and Claudine were staring at him, perhaps wondering why he didn't relent and just walk away. But he couldn't. That's what Leonard would want. Hardin could see him jamming the quilt into the toilet, then squatting over it. Leonard would want him to walk away and never look back. Leonard was counting on his cowardice, his inaction.

"It's interesting," Kent said. "You and Gus have your administrative priorities so clear. You've got time to stand around and chat with the police, but when a thief steals my personal property, it can wait. And when it's time to fire a teacher right before Christmas, that takes priority and gets moved to the front burner."

Kathie turned completely around to face him. "What are you talking about?"

"My three-thirty appointment with Central Office."

"I don't know anything about that."

"Right," Kent said, "it's always easier to look the other way when the goddamn axe is falling."

Suddenly Officer Bradford stepped toward him, his face threatening. "You need to watch your language in front of the ladies," he said sternly.

"And you need to stick to handing out speeding tickets and parking fines," Hardin said. "Stay the hell out of this."

Kathie moved quickly between them. "Gentlemen, I have enough to deal with today without having a staff member hauled off to the police station." She turned to Kent and said, "Look, I can't deal with your situation this very moment. But write it up and give it to Claudine and I'll try and get to it this afternoon. Okay?"

Kent took a step back. "I would appreciate that," he said. Bradford was still glaring at him from behind Kathie.

"And I don't know anything about a meeting at three-thirty," Kathie said. "Sometimes Gus schedules administrative functions and I'm not involved or invited. Honest."

"Okay," Kent said, moving toward the main office door. He paused, uncertain of what to say next. "I'm sorry."

"Let's talk later," Kathie said.

"Yes."

Kent opened the office door and went into the empty hallway. Before returning to his classroom, he stopped off at the faculty lounge to check his mailbox. The handle of a coffee mug jutted out of his compartment. He removed it and saw the profile of a jolly Santa Claus painted on the side. It was filled with gourmet coffee beans covered in chocolate and the attached note simply said, "From your Secret Santa." He looked at the mug and for a moment envisioned it exploding on his fence when a bullet pierced the white enamel and shattered the exterior.

From his own jacket pocket he removed an elegant, cream-colored envelope with the words *The Lighthouse* engraved on the front. It was his Secret Santa gift for Kathie Romero, and he hesitated before slipping it into her box. He hadn't meant to be so confrontational in the office but felt he had to stand firm on this situation. Surely she'd forgive him upon discovering that he was her Secret Santa. Over time, and perhaps dinner, she might even come to admire his hard-line stance when it came to Leonard. For now Kent had other pressing matters to consider. He had "reward" signs to make and a bounty to offer for information regarding the vandalism that occurred in Room 222. One hundred dollars should do nicely.

■ ■ ■

FRIDAY, DECEMBER 19, 1997
9:25 A.M.

Kathie

AFTER Hardin left the office, James Bradford turned to Kathie and said, "What's his problem?"

She shook her head. "Hardin is new to our school this year. He was a forced transfer from Eagle Ridge after he hit a student. He's had some difficulties adjusting."

"He'll get adjusted all right if he talks to a police officer like that again," Claudine said before going back to her desk.

"I've seen him around," Bradford said, "but I've never spoken to him before. What's he got against the police?"

"Don't take it personal," Kathie replied. She moved closer to the officer and lowered her voice. "I'm not trying to make excuses for him, but he might be losing his job today. He's under a lot of pressure from the district. He's also has some emotional problems."

"Maybe he just needs a break from teaching."

"Maybe so. He's not real stable. Gus and I have wondered if he can handle the stress." They were silent for a few moments before Kathie spoke again. "I really appreciate your coming in. I knew you'd want to be informed if Leonard might be involved."

"Absolutely. I've invested too much time in that young man just to let him screw up like this."

Bradford had taken a personal interest in Leonard Lamb after Kathie had asked him to intervene in mid-November. She figured that an older male, especially an authority figure in the community, might be able to talk with him. So the officer had scheduled weekly meetings with Leonard in order to reach out to him and offer advice. On a number of occasions after school, he'd even invited Leonard to ride in the squad car in the front as he drove his patrol route around town. For a while it seemed to be making a difference in Leonard's behavior and attitude. Until the graffiti incident, he hadn't been involved in any altercations in the classrooms or hallways for almost three weeks.

"I'm sorry I can't stay longer this morning," Bradford said. "I have to get back to the station."

"I understand. Just so you know, I'm going to pull Leonard out of class and ask him a few questions about the writing on the wall."

"Good idea. If he's involved, hold him accountable. I'll try and stop by again later in the day and you can fill me in."

"I'd appreciate that."

After Bradford was gone, Kathie returned to her office and grabbed a small paper bag from the desktop, then walked over to the staff lounge. Upon entering, she saw the teacher mailboxes lining the right wall in alphabetical order. From the paper bag, she pulled out a gift wrapped in shiny red paper with a small white bow. Even though it felt as if she'd been forgetting everything lately, she had remembered to buy her final Secret Santa gift. It was a faculty tradition at Ravenhill and Kathie had helped organize it this past year in order to keep up staff morale.

This time she'd intentionally drawn a new faculty member, Michelle Greene, a first-year special education teacher fresh out of college. Michelle had a tough case load, so ever since Thanksgiving Kathie had been slipping anonymous gifts into her mailbox each week. A tin of fragrant herbal tea. A gift certificate for a local coffee shop. A book on managing stress. A coupon for a free massage at a local health club. She'd saved her favorite gift for today: a pair of turquoise earrings she'd bought for herself in New Mexico over the summer, but then decided to give to Michelle. She'd attached a small note that said, *Santa can't keep a secret so have a great Christmas. Kathie.*

After slipping the gift into Michelle's box, Kathie checked her own and found an envelope with engraved lettering on the front. She hesitated before opening it. She also had a Secret Santa, but the items left for her over the last month had been oddly extravagant. Pro football tickets for her and the boys. A bouquet of roses delivered to the office. A costly box of chocolates. A gift coupon to a plush, local spa for a weekend stay. She'd become increasingly uneasy about the expensive gifts, as well as curious to find out the identity of her Secret Santa.

She quickly picked up the envelope and tore it open. Inside was a gift certificate to The Lighthouse, easily the most elegant restaurant in the area. Kathie had never been there before, only heard people talk about it. A note was attached that simply said: *Dinner for two? If you're willing, please make a reservation. They'll contact me when you call. It would be a treat—to finally meet.* The note was unsigned.

She heard the door to the lounge open and turned, casually sliding the envelope into her jacket. She saw Paul, the head custodian, standing in the doorway. "There you are," he said. "Have you got a minute?"

"Sure," she said. "This is good timing. I was going to look for you this morning."

"Then I'll save you a trip." He ambled into the room and stood next to the mailboxes. The ex-priest was tall and thin and wore his trademark denim shirt and corduroy pants while holding a brown grocery bag in his right hand. Kathie often imagined him standing in the pulpit and towering over his congregation.

The students affectionately called him "Tall Paul" because of his height and gangly stride as he moved down the corridor during passing period. He'd been on the Ravenhill staff for three years, and Kathie knew how fortunate they were to have him. When she attended the district administrative meetings and listened to the others complain about their unreliable custodians, Kathie was thankful for having someone as dependable as Paul.

"It's about the graffiti on the wall," he said. "I stopped by the office first thing this morning, but you weren't in yet."

"I had a flat on the way to school."

"Would you call that a tire tardy?"

Kathie smiled and said, "Something like that."

Paul continued. "I wanted to tell you that I had a can of red spray paint stolen from my closet on Wednesday. I checked and it's a match with the paint on the wall. I'm pretty sure it was Leonard. Probably revenge against me because I broke up one of his hallway romances the other day."

Kathie leaned against the mailboxes. "I can search his locker, but I don't think it will lead to anything. Leonard's too smart to leave it there."

"I tried to get the paint off the wall but nothing worked," Paul said. "I may have to order a special cleaner from the district warehouse."

Kathie closed her eyes for a moment and warily shook her head. "In the meantime, could you cover it up with something?" she asked. "It's not exactly the kind of welcome message I had in mind for visitors to our school."

"Sure."

Paul reached into his grocery bag and pulled out a small gift wrapped in white tissue paper and tied with red yarn. It looked tiny in his large hand as he extended it to her. "On a more positive note, I wanted to give you this."

Kathie took the present. "You shouldn't have." She held it for a moment as if cupping a flower in her palm.

"Something for your Christmas tree," Paul said. "I made it."

She carefully peeled away the paper to find a wooden ornament, an angel, about the size of a chess piece. The angel had long, flowing hair and golden wings that were outstretched as if in flight.

"It's lovely," she said.

He nodded. "It's a guardian angel. When I carved it, I thought of you because you're always watching out for everyone around here."

His comment caught her off guard. She was dead tired and stared down at the angel, nervously rubbing her thumb over the intricate carvings. She couldn't look up at him, couldn't allow herself this moment. Her throat burned with infection and her head ached. The angel was so smooth to the touch, so light and perfect. She could hold it forever.

"Thank you," Kathie finally said. "It's the best thing I'll see all day." Then she reached out and put her hand on his forearm and let it rest there. Without hesitation, he slowly lifted his other hand and momentarily placed it against her forehead, something her mother had always done when she was a little girl. His palm was cool to the touch, like a damp washcloth on a fevered brow.

"You're burning up," he said. "You should go see a doctor."

"I know," she said. "One more day and I can crash and recover." She leaned closer, still holding on to his arm. Right then she wasn't thinking about the door opening and a teacher walking in or whether it was professional to be standing in the lounge holding onto the custodian's arm. She was thinking instead of his kindness and how comforting it felt to stand close enough to smell the soap and wax of his daily work and not feel the need to pull away to a safe distance.

Then Paul was stepping back, whispering, "Merry Christmas," in a hushed tone, and he was suddenly gone through the door, leaving her alone in the lounge with the guardian angel. *Did I embarrass him?* she wondered.

She sat down for a few seconds to gather herself. *A momentary letdown. Pull it together now. This is no time for a breakdown, a meltdown.* She took a deep breath, then rose from the chair and moved out into the hallway, her steps feeling short, compact, confident. *The showdown strut.* It was time to pay Leonard a little visit. She had the cell phone on her hip and knew she was packing the only kind of heat Leonard would understand this morning, the kind that could reach out to the police on a moment's notice. The heels of her boots made a steady, rhythmic click in the empty hallway as she headed toward the social studies class where Leonard Lamb was waiting.

When she reached room 108, she opened the door and eased in. The class was in the middle of transitioning between presentations. She waved to Mr. Macon, the teacher, then spotted Leonard in the back row, slumped low, trying to hide from the action. When Macon came over, she simply said, "Sorry to interrupt, but I need to see Leonard immediately."

"No problem," he said with a grin. "Keep him as long as you need him." Then Macon called Leonard's name aloud and motioned for him to come to the front as Kathie stepped out into the hallway to wait. When Leonard joined her, he had a sullen, annoyed look on his face. He wore a pair of enormous, baggy jeans that swayed around his legs and dragged on the ground as he moved.

"You know the routine," she said to him. "Let's go to my office and talk."

"Right away, Miz Romeo," he said. His head was covered with a black stocking cap, while his dark shirt hung low to his knees. He walked in a combination strut and shuffle and took his own sweet time moving out.

"What happened to your face?" Kathie asked him.

He grinned, then said, "I fell off my skateboard, Miz Romeo."

"Must have been a long fall."

"Wicked fall," he said. "Monster fall." He made a soft whistling sound that ended in an abrupt explosion.

"You're a pretty lucky kid to survive a fall like that."

"I'm always lucky," Leonard answered. "Lucky with *every-thing.*"

"How fast were you going?"

"Warp speed," he said, suddenly adopting a skater stance in the hallway, his body poised atop an imaginary board. "It was a killer ride."

When they neared the office, Kathie suddenly said, "Detour," and abruptly veered to the left at the main entrance.

Leonard followed her out the front door where she stopped and turned on him, her face only inches away. She pointed at the graffiti sprayed on the wall and said, "I'm ticked, Leonard. I'm angry. In fact, I'm pissed off about this."

Leonard took a step back. "Miz Romeo's *cussing,*" he said. "Talking like that could get you fired."

She could feel the heat rising in her, but knew his style, knew that for thirteen years he'd been homeschooled by a drunk father on avoiding the truth. So she didn't bite. Didn't even nibble. *Stay cool,* she told herself. *Don't play his game.*

"Someone must be after Lara," Leonard said, pointing at the wall. "That's nasty talk."

"I'm going to find that someone," Kathie said, "and then I'm going to call his favorite police officer and ask him to get involved."

Leonard stepped back, a hurt look on his face. "What are you bringing me here for? I'm not messing with that girl."

She scanned his fingers for signs of paint. Clean as a whistle.

He turned his back on her, swaggered a few steps, then pivoted around and got into her face. "You got nothing on me," he said, spitting the words out contemptuously. "Nothing at all. And I'm sick of being harassed. I get accused of every punk thing that goes down in this damn school. Gonna get me a lawyer and sue your ass."

Kathie held her ground and waited until he was finished. "Some red spray paint was stolen from the custodian's closet," she said. "Do you know anything about that?"

"See!" he said, jumping back. "See! You out to get me, lady! Buncha crap! I get accused of every damn thing that happens. Some little dude trips on his jock in the locker room and I get the blame."

"Do you know anything about the missing paint?" Kathie repeated.

"No!" he shouted.

She took a step closer and calmly said, "It's very simple, Leonard. I'm going to find out who did this sooner or later. If it's you, I'm going to call Officer Bradford and he's taking you to Juvenile Hall for the holidays."

"Do it!" he yelled. "Call the police! You still got nothing 'cause I'm innocent."

"Right," she said. "Innocent until proven guilty. But if you know anything about this and want to cooperate with me now, I might let you do some community service over the break to clean it up. And Officer Bradford never gets called."

"You got nothing to call about."

"You've got a day to think about it."

"I don't need to. I'm innocent."

"Enough talk," Kathie said. "You know the situation. Now head back to class."

They entered the building again and Leonard only got a few feet down the hall before he turned to her and said, "Is it true what I heard? Your old man got squashed under a bridge?"

Kathie glared at Leonard. "My husband's death is none of your business," she said coldly.

Leonard continued backing away from her in a slow shuffle. He suddenly slapped his hands together with a loud whack that echoed in the corridor. "Man, all that concrete coming down," he said. "I'll bet he was flat as a tortilla when they found him."

Then Leonard gracefully spun a 360 and vanished around a corner as he headed back to class. Kathie did not pursue him or even attempt to call him back. *Guerilla tactic,* she thought. *Let it go.* She stood motionless in the quiet hallway and thought about Wade, saw his weathered, tan features, his brown eyes.

Then Kathie realized she was gripping something in her left hand, crushing something as it dug into her skin. She opened her fingers and saw the angel resting in her palm. One of the wings had snapped off and it looked small and frail against her skin like a gold petal. The break looked clean. *Nothing a little superglue couldn't fix.* She decided to keep the angel in her pocket for the rest of the day, then take it with her on the drive to Chicago. She'd place it on the Subaru dashboard where she could see it while she drove. It would be her good luck charm. A little boost for the day ahead. A little grace for the long haul.

■ ■ ■

FRIDAY, DECEMBER 19, 1997
8:45 A.M.

S.A.M.

BY the time S.A.M. returned to the gym, he saw that the other students had already gone to change and realized that first period was nearly over. Suddenly he heard the roar of Coach Z from across the floor.

"Bond!" he screamed, "so nice of you to return. Did you take a little cruise around the school?" S.A.M. didn't even try to duck back into the hall, but instead headed straight at him.

"Back up!" the coach yelled. "Don't come onto this court with those boots. I just got this thing waxed and the last thing I want is a bunch of black marks messing up my floor." *My floor,* S.A.M. repeated in his head. *King Kong's court.*

S.A.M. retreated and waited at the blue out-of-bounds line. Coach Z gave a laundry cart brimming with volleyballs a powerful shove and sent it squealing toward the bleachers.

"I thought we had a deal," Coach Z said. "A D- as long as you kept your butt in class."

"I had to go to the main office. It was an emergency."

"An emergency? What kind? Did your gym uniform arrive UPS?"

S.A.M. held out a trembling hand. "I had to get my medicine. I forgot to take it this morning at home. I keep some extra
pills in the office just in case."

"Medicine for what?" Coach Z asked.

S.A.M. brought up the other hand, which was also quivering
as if a tiny electric current was pulsing through his veins. He
had practiced the tremor to perfection in front of the mirror at
home. "My nerves," S.A.M. said. "If I don't take my medicine, I
get the shakes. It starts in my hands and then moves through my
whole body. Once the medicine kicks in, I'll be fine."

Coach Z looked concerned. "Are you going to a doctor,
Bond? You should get this thing checked out. My brother started
getting headaches and finally went to the hospital. Then bam!"
The coach slapped his hands together. "They found a brain
tumor the size of a baseball and he was dead within a week. It
can happen to anyone, anytime."

S.A.M. slipped his hands into his coat pockets. "My doctor
gives me a weekly prescription to take care of it."

He stared down at the polished floor to avoid eye contact.
Look hurt, he thought. *Look embarrassed. Tug at his heart-
strings a little.*

"Well, it's okay this time," Coach Z said. "But you need to
tell me about these things."

"I'll try. I was too embarrassed. I didn't want anyone to know."

Coach Z took an awkward step back and studied S.A.M. as if
he were some rare and exotic lizard trapped behind glass at the
zoo. "Son, you should keep taking that medicine."

S.A.M. nodded, his head bowed.

"If you ever need to see a counselor, I'd be glad to write you
a pass. Mrs. Gordon helps all kinds of kids with their problems."

"I'll be fine," S.A.M. said. Then he turned and headed out
the exit leading into the hallway. The corridor was packed as he
knifed through the human traffic to get to the stairs. Art was on
the second floor and he leaped nimbly up the steps, two at a

time, all the while thinking about Lara Wright and their brief exchange in the hall. "And I can count on you, right?" she'd asked before removing his glasses and staring into his eyes. At the end of the hall he glimpsed Miss Healy standing outside her door and talking to a student. She was the youngest teacher on the Ravenhill staff, probably in her mid-twenties, and today she looked especially fetching in an embroidered denim skirt and white turtleneck. She usually dressed like some hippie from Woodstock and S.A.M. thought she was the spitting image of Janis Joplin on a windy day. She was a broad-shouldered woman with wild, wavy hair that floated down her back in copper ripples. Upon seeing S.A.M. she smiled and said, "Merry X-mas, Darkman. You're looking festive."

S.A.M. grinned and said, "Santa Claus is dead. I dressed for the occasion."

"Aren't you the sensitive soul." She smiled, then leaned close and whispered, "I'd ask what you're doing over the holidays, but I'm sure it's top secret."

"Classified and confidential."

S.A.M. walked into the classroom and went to his usual seat in the far corner of the studio. The room was a wild catastrophe of posters and prints and photographs plastered on the walls and ceiling, all hung at tilted, odd angles. *Dali on drugs* was what S.A.M. had thought when he'd first entered Miss Healy's room. The tabletops and floor were splattered with dried paint and clay. Whatever space that might be left on the walls was covered with student artwork, each drawing or watercolor labeled with a title and the name of the artist. It was the only class in the school that was even more of a wreck than his own room at home and S.A.M. loved the mad, off kilter, out-of-sync way it made him feel. "Art is nonlinear," Miss Healy was fond of telling her students. "Anything can happen. An explosion of color. A burst of creativity. Be ready for the surprise so you can trap the inspiration and hold it hostage."

TIMOTHY HILLMER

They were working on their final projects for the end-of-semester show in January and the room hummed with rock music from four gigantic speakers that perched in the corners. At his desk S.A.M. found a small package wrapped in shiny green foil. It was the size of a postcard and his name was blazed across the front in gold letters. He opened it and found an outrageous caricature of himself, his exaggerated face and slicked-back hair nearly filling the portrait. In the drawing he stood against a backdrop of an atomic mushroom cloud and held a long paintbrush like a spear while using his palette as a shield. The picture was labeled "Darkman" in jagged, lightning bolt letters that streaked across the top of the page. S.A.M. knew that Miss Healy once worked as a caricature artist at an amusement park. It was a tradition in her class for each student to receive a Christmas portrait done in her own unique style.

"It's definitely you," a voice said from behind him. He turned and saw Miss Healy standing there with her assignment chart. "I hope you like the nuclear landscape."

"Thanks," S.A.M. said. "I'll add it to my private collection."

"I'm honored." She placed her chart on the table. "Now, let's see what you're working on." Every week Miss Healy tried to have a conference with each student to discuss their progress on an individual project. Today was Sam's turn and he was prepared. He opened his classroom portfolio and placed it in front of her. Inside was a single drawing. The paper was thick, like parchment, and he loved the rough texture and how the ink soaked into the page to create something permanent.

Miss Healy studied the picture, entitled "The Goddess Awakens." It was carefully done in pen and ink with an intricate border surrounding the page that revealed a dark menagerie of ghostly animals and spectral phantoms half-hidden in shadow. The border itself served as an audience, all eyes trained on the striking central figure. A young woman was rising from a clear lake, her sleek form clothed in a watery sheen, her hands

178

thrust skyward as a brilliant full moon loomed in the night sky. The woman's features and flowing hair all belonged to Lara Wright. At the bottom of the page was a caption written in swirling calligraphy:

When a crimson moon lingers on the horizon,
the goddess stirs from slumber, a pale cheek
rising from the midnight pillow.
The evening is her refuge,
a nocturnal sanctuary, and she listens
to the flutter of bat's wings,
the owl's cry lost in the wind,
the chorus of wolf howl
as a dark kingdom awakens
to do her bidding.

"Impressive," Miss Healy said. "Rich details. Next time, ease up on the shading in the border. Some of the images get lost."

"I think it's finished," S.A.M. said.

She scrutinized it a moment longer, then nodded her head in agreement. "I think you're right this time," she said. "And I wonder how Lara Wright's going to feel when she sees this."

S.A.M. didn't respond and continued staring at the drawing.

"Every artist has his muse," Miss Healy continued, "and Lara Wright seems to be yours." She placed the picture back into the portfolio. "But just because she's your inspiration doesn't mean she'll want to be your girlfriend."

"But there's a chance," S.A.M. said. "Let fate decide."

"Perhaps," Miss Healy said. "I just don't want you to get hurt."

"No artistic strings attached, but I did talk with her this morning."

Miss Healy feigned surprise, then placed a hand over her mouth. "The Darkman speaks to his beloved?"

"She was at her locker and I saw my chance."

"Did you show her this?" Miss Healy asked, pointing at the drawing.

"No. There wasn't time. Maybe after the holidays."

S.A.M. closed the portfolio. He knew she needed to meet with other students, but he caught her eye and said, "Since I'm done, I was wondering if I could slip out and take care of something."

"What exactly do you need to take care of?"

"Some personal business. Let's just call it closure."

"I don't like the sound of this."

"A simple conversation with an acquaintance."

"And is this acquaintance cutting class?"

"Not technically."

"And is this acquaintance Lara Wright?"

"Some things cannot be revealed."

Miss Healy rolled her eyes.

"Trust me," he said. "I could just as easily have asked to go to the restroom and you'd never even know. I'm trying to be honest."

"Trust," she said, "is a fragile thing. Once broken, it takes a long time to mend."

"Point taken," he said.

"Happy holidays. Hustle it up."

Once in the hallway, he moved quickly to the steps and descended to the first floor. He stopped and removed a yellow pass from his pocket. It was blank, but when seen at a distance, it created the illusion that he was officially on his way to the library or nurse or counselor. He turned the corner and immediately saw Mrs. Romero heading his way. He didn't look down or make any attempt to avoid her. She, however, looked distracted and hardly noticed his presence. He made sure the pass was visible and walked straight by her as she turned into the office. Mr. Macon's room was at the far end of the school and he hurried toward his destination.

S.A.M. turned a corner and abruptly stopped. Leonard Lamb was ambling down the empty hall, tapping the lockers with his fist. He suddenly cut to the left and disappeared into the boy's bathroom in C-Wing. *Seize the moment*, S.A.M. thought. *Strike first before the serpent awakens.*

He walked rapidly to the restroom and paused outside the door to pull a key from his pants and unlock the handcuff so it dangled free. He removed his Ray-Bans and slipped them into a coat pocket, then opened the door with a hiss and slid the attaché case against the cinderblock wall that separated the bathroom from the entrance. He crept forward and peered around the corner where he spied Leonard at one of the urinals. Quickly, S.A.M. scanned the perimeter. Two bathroom stalls. A sink and mirror. A slender, high window against the far wall that nearly touched the ceiling. He memorized the scene, then silently entered.

There was no hesitation in S.A.M.'s movements. Master Yang had taught him to be swift, deliberate, and to exploit an opponent's human frailties. He'd taught him the weaknesses of the body, the key points where a lethal foot or hand could inflict the most damage, and S.A.M. was well versed in the anatomy of pain. Leonard was turning away from the urinal when S.A.M. struck, his black boot flicking out like a switchblade and finding its target, the fragile left knee, as the heel caved in the joint. Leonard howled with pain, then collapsed on the tile in front of the urinals.

S.A.M. stood over his victim. His heart was pounding, his breath quick. *In battle, adrenaline is the potion of the gods.* As Leonard lay writhing on the floor, S.A.M. crouched down and took his fist and held it in Leonard's face.

"I could break your nose," S.A.M. whispered, his knuckles only inches away. "But then the janitor would have all that blood to mop up." Leonard's eyes rolled back in pain, his breathing deep and guttural. "I have a message for you," S.A.M. said. "Leave Lara Wright alone."

"And why would I mess with her?" Leonard asked, wincing.

"I saw the writing on the wall." S.A.M. paused as he stared into Leonard's eyes, his fist cocked. He savored the power he felt in the moment. *Finish the job* was what a combat-hardened mercenary might order. But he was a disciplined warrior, capable of both rage and compassion for the enemy. "Will you do this?" he asked.

"I didn't write anything on the damn wall," Leonard gasped.

"Will you leave her alone?" S.A.M. said persistently.

Leonard nodded, then whispered, "Yeah."

S.A.M. rose and turned to go. Suddenly he heard a metallic rustling from behind. He whirled around, tried to raise an arm to fend off the blow, but it was too late. The length of chain hurtled through the air like a steel whip and cracked him full in the face. He fell backward, clutching his eye as the world flashed white, his head smacking hard on the tile. Leonard popped himself up on his right knee and was upon him in seconds. He straddled S.A.M., pinning him to the floor, then slammed a fist into his nose. The blow detonated and exploded inside his skull and he could taste the blood as it poured from his nostrils. Suddenly, he felt himself jerked upward, his neck wrenched under a burly arm. Before he could gather himself to resist, his head was rammed into one of the metal stalls and his vision blurred, the pain shooting through his forehead like a spike.

"*I could break your nose,*" he heard Leonard say, his voice a girlish mimic. " I know what you need, asshole." Suddenly he felt the chain wrapped tightly around his throat like a garrote. He was being dragged now, his neck locked in a steel vise. He wanted to fight, try to unleash a kick to the groin, but he couldn't see, couldn't breathe. "You look thirsty," Leonard said, strangling him with the chain. "How 'bout a little drink?" S.A.M.'s face was suddenly thrust into a stinking pool, the water fetid and reeking of urine as his hands flailed at Leonard's torso. He tried not to swallow, but did anyway, the salty taste choking him. He gripped the porcelain sides and tried to push himself away, but Leonard's enormous bulk pinned him down. He started to gag when he smelled the acrid scent and was sure he would vomit at any moment as Leonard twisted the chain even tighter and sent him down again. He braced his elbows against the toilet's rim and grasped for anything that might keep his head out of the foul stench.

Suddenly the pressure lifted and S.A.M. whipped his head up, gasping for air. He crashed into a side panel and dropped to the floor, clawing at the metal as he tried in vain to pull himself up. He could hear laughter and covered himself, recoiling for the next blow. Then he saw Leonard standing in the entrance to the stall, the chain hanging from his clenched fist like a limp snake. "Don't mess with me," Leonard said, "or I'll drown you next time." S.A.M. closed his eyes and stayed on the wet tile until he heard the door open, followed by Leonard's voice again. "As for Lara Wright," he said, "she's mine."

S.A.M. waited until he was sure Leonard was gone, then tried to stand up. His head was pounding and blood dripped from his nose, forming small puddles on the white floor. He slid an arm overhead and gripped the top of the stall and hoisted himself upright. There wasn't time to do an inventory of his injuries. *A concussion*, he thought, *perhaps a fractured skull.* No time to even look in the mirror and witness the horror of his face. His left eye stung when he touched it and he could feel the swelling from where the chain had struck him. He visualized James Bond strapped to the table in *Goldfinger* as the laser beam moved dangerously, inevitably toward his abdomen where it could slice him in half. There was only time to retreat and plan a course of action. *Every action deserves a reaction* was what Q always said.

S.A.M. stumbled out of the stall to the door. He suddenly remembered the attaché case and turned for it, only to see an empty space next to the wall. He imagined Leonard limping from the bathroom and picking up the case like some trophy, his gap-toothed smile wide and menacing. *To the victors go the spoils.* A surge of panic overcame him, a sense of powerlessness, and he ripped open the door to enter the hall. But he stopped, as if standing on the edge of a vast precipice, and forced himself to retreat into the bathroom. He waited until his breathing had settled, then grabbed a wad of paper towels and pressed it to his face to stop the flow of blood. He looked at his watch and saw that the next bell would ring in exactly three minutes. He needed a refuge, a temporary hideout to recover and regroup.

He checked the hall, saw that it was vacant, then moved out, staying close to the lockers. He took the first set of stairs to the basement and soon reached the door labeled *Head Custodian: Mr. Munn,* where he turned the doorknob and found it locked. He fumbled in his pocket for his keys, then located the Triple o, the same Triple o that he'd lifted from Coach Z's key ring one October morning for exactly two hours, just long enough to ditch his dentist appointment, get to the hardware store where he slipped the locksmith an extra twenty so a duplicate could be made, then return the original to the Coach's desk by lunchtime. The lock clicked open with the key and S.A.M. slid into the little office, quickly shutting the door as the shriek of the bell erupted behind him in the hallway.

S.A.M. turned on the light and sat in a folding chair. He was shaking as he heard the clamor of the students outside and imagined Leonard flashing the black case to his friends as he strutted to class. *At least he doesn't have the combination,* S.A.M. thought, knowing that the Executive Attaché, a handsome gift from Q, would take time and tools to break into. *I must retrieve what is mine.* He was thankful for the powerful scent of ammonia and cleaning fluid and wax stripper in the closet, anything to overwhelm the foul odor that emanated from his clothing.

He walked to the far end of the tiny corridor that made up the office. Tucked behind some lockers was a makeshift shower with a crude tin floor and an overhead nozzle. To his right was a dilapidated cardboard box labeled *Lost and Found.* S.A.M. had seen Paul drag the box down to the main entrance once every month so students could claim any items left behind. He dug around and found a pair of jeans, a white T-shirt, a faded denim jacket with the sleeve ripped. No time to be picky. He set the clothing aside and began to strip off his own bloody coat, shirt, and pants. When he turned the shower on, the water was icy cold, a shock to his naked skin. He forced his body under the nozzle and began to scrub away the dried blood that was caked to his face and hair. *A cleansing, a sacrifice of blood.* He imagined Lara Wright walking the halls at this very moment, unaware of Leonard's cruel intentions. "I never knew I had a bodyguard," she'd said to him at her locker. *I am your defender, your protector, your guardian*, he thought to himself, repeating this vow like a prayer in the shadows of the closet.

■ ■ ■

FRIDAY, DECEMBER 19, 1997
10:00 A.M.

Paul

WHEN he found the mess in the C-wing restroom, Paul knew right away it had been a fight. The huge dent in one of the panels. The bloody handprints on the metal door. The blood on the floor. If a parent had walked in, they might have been shocked at the scene. But Paul was used to the savagery of high school and its sporadic, yet furious, scenes of combat. Ninth graders could be the worst, especially the small ones who were spit on and kicked and humiliated until they blew up. Like Peter Fisk, a little redhead who brought an aluminum baseball bat to school one day. He jumped Jason White in the parking lot and proceeded to bash him in the head. He would've crushed his skull if Mr. Friedman, a bus driver who saw it all go down, hadn't stepped into the line of fire and taken a blow to the chops, then ripped the bat from his hands.

Paul decided to wait until after the passing period to report the damage to Kathie Romero so she could follow up. He slapped an orange CLOSED sign on the restroom door and hurried down to his office to get the bucket and mop. Paul knew that if he hustled, he might be able to get it cleaned before any students saw the damage and started talking it up around the school.

When he reached the closet, Paul hesitated before going in. Ever since the paint theft, he'd been extra careful about making sure the little room stayed locked. But he saw a slice of light gleaming under the sill and heard running water. So he quickly unlocked the door and went in. At first he didn't recognize the dripping figure standing under the bare light bulb next to the lockers. Then the intruder saw him and grabbed something from the lost and found box to cover up with. By then Paul had already glimpsed the naked body and recognized the jet black hair, the rail thin arms and bony shoulders. But there was something unfamiliar and foreign as well. The small breasts, the blond V of pubic hair that illuminated her groin. And he knew why she covered up, told him to get out, her sobs echoing in the closet.

Paul turned to go so she could dress in private, but he hesitated, his back to her. He suddenly remembered the voices of those who had come to him in confession when he had been a priest, all those who whispered to him from behind the thin screen, their voices often hushed with shame. And he knew what needed to be done.

"I won't tell," Paul said to her. "Not a soul." Then he left the closet, making sure the door locked tightly behind him.

■ ■ ■

FRIDAY, DECEMBER 19, 1997
11:45 A.M.

Hardin

$100.00 REWARD
IF YOU HAVE INFORMATION
ABOUT THE VANDALISM AND THEFT
THAT OCCURRED IN ROOM 222,
THEN PLEASE SEE MR. HARDIN.
<u>DEADLINE: 3:15 TODAY!</u>

ONCE Kent had finished preparing the reward sign over the lunch hour, he dashed to the teacher's workroom and ran off thirty copies on bright yellow paper. Then, with a roll of masking tape in hand, he went through the main hallway and posted the signs. He even taped one on the door leading into the office just so Gus and Kathie would know he meant business. He hoped that a bold student, perhaps someone who had been harassed or threatened by Leonard in the past, might appear at his door with the kind of hard information that could be used to nail Lamb to the wall.

When he had finished hanging them, he hustled back to his room. The morning classes had gone well, even better than he'd expected. The students were giddy with all the possibilities of a two-week vacation away from school. Nothing seemed to faze them. When he handed back the *Christmas Carol* essays, they glanced momentarily at the grade, then either tucked the papers away in their folders or immediately trashed them in the bin. No angry retorts. No threatening challenges. No scowling looks. It was often like this in the morning when they were still half asleep or dreamily trudging to class like obedient soldiers following the cadence of commands. Sit down. Pay attention. Open your books. Raise your hand. Copy it down. Pass it in. And Hardin knew the drill better than anyone, knew how to march them through the grammar lessons, the textbook exercises, the vocabulary worksheets, the comprehension questions. At least it went well on days like this when he was organized and prepared and ready for the challenge. So far so good.

He knew the afternoon would be different. Especially eighth hour. A class loaded with outcasts and rebels. At the end of the day they were usually cranked up and angry, which was a nasty combination for any teacher. But not all of them were losers. Lara Wright and Kelly Mason had potential, if they could only tear themselves away from their makeup and compact mirrors long enough to pay attention to the notes he'd written on the board. Leonard Lamb was simply there to raise hell and try to con others into joining his war on authority.

When Kent reached the bottom of the stairs, he was surprised to find a young, thin girl waiting for him just outside his door. At first he didn't recognize her, but then she turned around and he saw that it was Rachel Riley from eighth hour. There was something different about her, and at first Kent couldn't put his finger on it. But then it hit him. He was accustomed to seeing her in the formal attire that the Prodigal Sons demanded of their women. She usually wore a simple denim dress with the hem dropping far below the knees, a long-sleeved white blouse with the top button neatly closed at the throat, and her hair always pinned up in a bun at the back of the head.

Today, however, Rachel wore blue jeans, and it was the first time he'd ever seen her in anything but a dress. She had on a yellow T-shirt under a camouflage vest. Her long brown hair was loose and draped over her shoulders so that it flowed down her back, and she wore a pair of brown hiking boots with thick soles.

The basement was empty now and as he moved toward her, he pulled his keys out and went to unlock the door.

"Hello Rachel," he said. "I hope you haven't been waiting too long." Kent figured that he'd probably made an appointment with her earlier in the week to retake a test or quiz over lunch and he'd forgotten. She'd been absent a great deal over the last month.

"No," she replied, "not too long."

"And what do you need to make up?" he asked.

"Nothing," she said. "I don't have an appointment or anything. I just stopped by to talk for a moment."

"No problem," Kent said as he swung the door open. "Please come in."

Even though Rachel Riley was a member of the "eighth hour outcasts," she was a different story altogether. From the first time Kent called her name on his attendance roster and she looked up and said, "Yes sir," he knew there was something familiar about her. On that opening day she'd been sitting in the front row in a long dress and, for a split second, Kent was sure he knew her from somewhere. A church picnic. A block party. Then the name hit him—*Rachel*—and he gazed at her long after he should have moved onto the next name on the roster.

It wasn't until after class, when he'd gone into the men's restroom and locked the door and splashed cold water on his face, that he could accept it. He had witnessed a ghostly vision of his daughter if she had lived. The young woman that he saw today could easily have been a girl named Rachel Hardin, age fifteen, daughter of Kent and Claire Hardin, born at St. Luke's

Hospital in late October on the first snowy day of the year. Only she had died a long time ago.

During those early weeks of school, he'd gone to the counselor and requested some background information on her. He learned about her father and his connection with the Prodigal Sons, then saw in the file that she'd been homeschooled for most of her life. In his class, she was withdrawn and quiet, often sitting by herself in a corner desk in the front row. She hardly ever raised her hand and seldom spoke to anyone, unless she was called on to answer a question.

One day during the second week of school, she stayed after for a moment while the other students filed out. She was copying something into her notebook, although Hardin couldn't imagine what it was since he hadn't given any homework. She waited until the room was completely empty, then rose from her seat and paused next to Hardin's desk for a brief moment. He was busy recording daily attendance onto his green scan sheets and when he looked up, she quickly slid a wrinkled manila envelope onto the wooden surface. Then she was gone before he could even call her back and inquire about the contents.

The envelope had his name, *Mr. Hardin*, written in blue ink on the front. At first he didn't know what to make of it. Was it her secret diary? Her collected poems, all written with passion and verve since the age of seven? But when he opened it, he found something quite different. A typed manuscript with precise margins and spacing. A story. There was a handwritten note attached that said, *Please don't share this with anyone. I'm giving this to you because I think you'll understand it. Rachel Riley. P.S. Sorry if there are mistakes.* For a moment, he held it in his hands and admired the care with which it had been put together. Neatly stapled; pages numbered; even a proper heading on the front with her name, date, and the title of the piece. So he began to read.

Scars

Even now I can still see the scars on his hands and remember the rough edges of his fingers. His name was Roy and he'd been a cowboy all his life. He worked on a ranch in Wyoming and is probably still working there to this day. Once I asked him about the scars and how he'd gotten them. He paused, looked down at his palms, shrugged, then told me about his father, a rancher named Buddy. "He was a tough old coot and prided himself on being mean. Guess he wanted his son to be just as strong so he never let me wear gloves. Not once. No matter what the job, no matter how cold it got. No son of mines gonna wear sissy gloves he said to me. None of that girly stuff. Most of the time I got used to it. But mending fences was the worst. The barbed wire just rippd my hands up. Got so I'd stick them in the snow or the creek just so they'd stop hurting."

I met Roy when my father sent me to this place in Wyoming for teenagers in trouble. I guess he thought I was being to sinful for a young woman my age. It was called the Resurection Ranch and most of the other kids were potheads and gang members and juvenile delinquents. That first week they tried to break us all down. From sun up to sundown, all we did was work. Feeding animals, cleaning the stable, baling hay, fixing fences. The chores went on and on. No slacking. Just hard, hot work. A bunch of the others couldn't cut it and skippd out one night to catch a bus back to wherever they came from. I knew better. I knew if I tried to leave that my dad would track me down like one of the animals he loved to hunt and send me right back. No chance for escape.

I was in the Apostle Posse which was Roy's work crew. He was in charge of us and we rode in the back of his truck and helped him with whatever needed doing around the ranch. He was about twenty years older than the rest of us and was a straight-shooter. First day he told us he wouldn't take any atitude. "Do your work and we'll get along just fine. If you dont do your work, I'll just tie you to the back of my pickup and drag you through Rattlesnake Ravine." Then he grinned and winkd at me. He had this thick, black mustach that made him look like one of those gunslingers you see on the old westerns on TV. Wyat Earp. Maybe even The Sundance Kid.

On the second day, some big guy from Houston decided to take Roy on. We'd driven the truck out about five miles to drop some hay. When the bales were unloaded off the trailer, Houston turned on Roy and said, "I'll take them keys if you dont mind. I need to borrow your truck for a little drive back to Texas." Then he flickd out a big switchblade and flashed it at Roy. All I really saw was the glint of that steel in the sun before Roy took him down. Within seconds Houston was flat on his back, his arm bent behind him, the blade pointing straight at the sky as Roy said, "In Wyoming, we call this a toothpick son. He pluckd the knife out of his hand and flippd the blade down, then let Houston get up. Roy grinned at him and said, "Be careful now. I know cowboy karate. Got me a first degree black buckle." The rest of us laughed and then got back to work. Houston never messed with Roy again.

I'll be honest: I wanted to cut out during those early weeks. My muscles had never been so sore. It hurt just to roll over in my sleep. But I'm no quitter and I hung in there. To tell the truth, by the end of the third week I kind of liked going to bed dead tired. No time to think or talk back or even worry about all the problems at home. I was too exhausted to even pray.

It actually felt good to be far away from my dad, to not be wearing dresses and always have to look and act like a proper Christian lady. It was just hard work, plain and simple. And I liked hanging out with Roy. I liked his funny stories, his quiet ways. Sometimes after dinner and the evening Bible study, he and I would go out to see the horses in the stable. Roy told me there names, showed me how to brush and wipe them down, how to clean out there hooves with a pick, and how to put on a saddle so it stayed tight around their bellys. Sometimes he even let me ride one of my favorites, an Apaloosa named Sundown around the practice ring.

One night we stayed at the stable later than usual. I remember the lantern hanging overhead and how it swung back and forth in the wind and cast little rays of light up in the rafters. It was a warm night and Roy said there might be a thunderstorm coming from the west and they could use the rain. I was stroking one of the horses with a brush when Roy just reachd over and slid his hands around my hips and came up behind me and pressd his face against the back of my neck. I could smell the sweat and tobacco smoke on his skin and I waited to see if he'd pull away. And when he did I just kept brushing that horse like nothing had hapened. But after that, I knew something was diferent between us.

Thats how it started. We never talked about it. We workd hard all day and every now and then he'd look at me when no one was around and smile. Roy wasnt a talker. I don't think he cared that I was fifteen. We just liked hanging out together in the stable at night. Pretty soon we got past the hugs and he took me over to a clean pile of straw and a blanket in one of the far corners. I kept waiting for him to say something to me but he never did. He was shy when it came to making conversation. He'd look at me and smile and nod like he was agreeing with something I'd said, even though I hadnt spoken a word.

The first time he kissed me I never even thought about wether it was right or wrong or sinful. His lips were soft and gentle, but the whiskers on his mustach tickld my lip and I wanted to giggle. I felt far away from that place where God's judgment ruled with an iron fist and Hell was always right around the corner. I just thought about how Roy's scarred hands would gently stroke my back, my legs, all the rest of my body. He taught me to feel things that I never thought were posible and showed me how to love in return. And when I went back to my bunk, it was like I had this glowing ember inside my chest all night, a warm piece of fire that would never go out. I wonderd if this was part of God's plan. Maybe this was His blessing on me. It felt truthful and honest and absolutly right. Like a prayer.

When summer came to an end and the time was drawing near to leave Resurection Ranch, I kept waiting for Roy to say something about my going home, about what might happen to us in the future. But he never did. And then one night when we were in the stable and kissing on the blanket, the side door flew open and one of the Resurection directors came in, an old guy named Pastor Laroot. He was looking for Roy, yelling something about playing poker. I scrambld up from the straw, but it was to late. He'd already seen me. He turned away while I buttoned up my shirt, then said to me with a snort, "I think you'd better get on up to the bunkhouse, missy."

So I left the stable, then waited just outside the door so I could hear them talking. I was woried for Roy about what might happen now that we'd been discovered, and I heard Pastor Laroot yelling at him. "Are you pulling this again? Damn, Roy, I've warned you before not to mess with the girls. I thought we were clear about this. What is she? Barely fifteen? Why don't you get yourself a woman from town your own damn age? Do you think I want to end up in court?"

I listend for a while longer until I couldnt stand to hear anymore, then went back to my bunk. I did not sleep that night, nor any of the other nights I was to spend at Resurection Ranch. From that day forward, I did not look Roy in the eye or return any of his glances. I would not speak to him. More than anything, I understood that what had happened in that stable between us was a lie, that I'd been used, and I was not the first.

On the day before we were scheduld to leave, Roy slipped a note under my pillow. His handwriting was crude, like that of a child. All the note said was, Meet me in the stable tonight. We need to talk. He didn't even sign it. I guess he expected me to show up as if I were some filly being whistled in from the meadow for a feeding.

So I went. I waited until it was night, then slipped across the yard. There was no lantern in the stable this time. Only the moon to guide my way. And when I steppd through the side door, I knew Roy was in there. I could smell the Marlboro cigaretes he liked to smoke.

"I'm glad you came," I herd him whisper from out of the shadows. "I didnt want it to end like this. I didnt want you leaving thinking you don't mean nothing to me." Once my eyes adjusted to the dark, I could see his shape in front of me. The horses were rustling about in the stalls and I could feel there nervousness. When Roy came toward me, he moved real slow, like he was approaching a scared colt. I waited until he was reaching out a hand to stroke my shoulder, then I cut him. He didnt expect it, at least not from me. I had the razorblade in my right hand and slashd hard at his palm and fingers and backed away. I'd found it in the shower room of the bunkhouse and had even taped up one side of the blade so it wouldnt cut me. He shouted, cussed at me, then bent over, clutching his fist. I dropped the blade in the straw and ran out the door, my heart pounding like a stampede all the way back to the bunkhouse.

The next day, as we were packing up to leave, I saw him standing in the doorway to the stable. He had a white bandage on his right hand. He didnt wave or try to get my attention. He just vanished into the dim hollow of the barn. But I knew he'd remember me. I knew I'd left my mark. He'd think twice next time he saw a pretty, young girl. He'd look down at his hand and see that scar and think twice about turning something pure and holy into a lie.

After he'd finished reading the story, Kent held the pages in his hands for a moment, sifting through each one and skimming over the paragraphs again. It was raw, uneven writing with innumerable mistakes. But he was stunned by the voice that jumped off the page and the honesty with which she'd told the tale. He read the piece two more times that night and marveled at the skill with which she set up the final confrontation in the stable.

The next day he asked Rachel to stay after class for a moment so they could talk. He waited until all the students were gone, then pulled the envelope from his briefcase and set it on the desk. She remained in her seat and looked shyly down at the carpet.

"I read your story," he began. "Thank you for trusting me with it."

At first she said nothing, her eyes still lowered, almost refusing to look up at him. Then she spoke and her voice was hushed and tentative.

"Am I in trouble?" she asked. "I mean for writing that and giving it to you?"

"No," Kent said. "Not at all. You're not in any trouble."

"My father would think it was the work of the devil," Rachel said. "He'd be ashamed if he knew I wrote it."

"Well, it isn't sinful," Hardin said, "and there's nothing to be ashamed of."

"I know I need to work on my punctuation and spelling. We never did much of that in home school."

"That's easy to fix. Simple editing corrections." Hardin paused for a moment, considering his words carefully. Then he continued. "I think this is a powerful story and that you're a strong writer."

"I am?" she said, finally looking up at him.

"Yes, you are. In fact, I want you to keep writing stories for this class. I'd like to read more of your work."

There was a long silence between them and he let it linger, knowing she was thinking over his words and trying to decide whether to proceed or retreat. She seemed a little stunned by his interest and sat back, her eyes monitoring him, probing the possibility that this was all a trick.

"I like to write stories," she finally said. "All kinds. I never show them to anybody, but I enjoy putting them down on paper."

"And why did you let me read this one?" he asked.

She didn't answer right away, instead let the question hover in the air like a trace of smoke.

"Because of the stories you told about teaching in the Peace Corps," she said. "Some of the kids made fun of you. But I liked hearing them because of what they said about you. You're different from the other teachers. You're not just here for the paycheck. I can tell."

"I appreciate that," he said. "It means a lot."

After that they met at least once a week in his classroom and the stories continued to come across his desk. Every Friday she'd leave one for him and he would read it on Sunday, then arrange a time to talk with her. The stories were always different and he was amazed at their range. The second one she submitted was set during medieval times and was the tale of a young girl named Riva who lived in a castle with her father, the lord of the land, and was susceptible to frightening visions while she slept. In the end she was accused of being a witch by the townspeople and burned at the stake while her own father watched the execution and did nothing to prevent it. Another story was about a young Native American girl living on a reservation who was raped by her alcoholic uncle. A third told of a young black girl in the inner city whose brother, a gang member, had been murdered, and who contemplated revenge until a chance meeting occurred with a mysterious homeless woman on the street.

As a veteran English teacher, Hardin knew how to pay attention to the details when it came to gifted writers, especially one like Rachel. He noticed that her settings were clearly established with well-defined characters. She had an uncanny sense of rhythm and structure within her stories and seemed to intuitively know how to build tension in the narrative. He showed her some of the patterns of mistakes in her spelling and punctuation, and she was a quick study in learning how to correct them. He hoped that she might submit some of her work to a statewide writing contest that happened in late March. During class she remained silent, guarded, reserved. But when they met to discuss her writing, he was always stunned at how animated she became, wide-eyed and observant as he went over the pages and pointed out strengths while also suggesting minor adjustments.

When Kent entered the room, he switched on the classroom lights. He had twenty minutes before sixth hour was scheduled to begin. Rachel went to the front of the room and placed one hand on the dust tray at the bottom of the chalkboard, her backpack slung awkwardly over one shoulder. She looked tired and he said, "Are you okay?"

She shook her head. "I just need to talk."

"I've missed reading your work," he said. "I haven't seen any stories for almost two weeks now."

She frowned. "I've had other things on my mind. There's been a lot going on at home that I've had to deal with." She glanced at the back of the room and the lone window that looked out to the asphalt playground behind the school. Wire mesh covered the exterior to protect the glass.

"I came to say good-bye," she said. She looked directly at him and he could see that her eyes were tired and red. "I'm leaving."

"Where are you going?" Kent asked.

"I can't really say," she said.

"Are you leaving because of what's going on at home?"

Rachel didn't respond and glanced down at her boots. "I just need to get away. I can't stay at home anymore."

"Have you told your parents you're leaving?"

"No."

It is a teacher's legal responsibility to call the Department of Social Services when a student is in danger. The sentence caught him off guard, almost a whisper in Kent's mind. It was a line from the faculty handbook that had stayed with him. He knew that he should handle this professionally and maintain a safe distance from the student involved. It would be what Gillette might want. Something positive to put on his evaluation under professional conduct. Just pick up the phone and contact Social Services. *It was for your own good,* he could tell her later. *Your parents needed to be notified. It was my professional responsibility.*

"How will you get where you're going?" he asked. He was being careful with his questions, afraid to appear like a detective interrogating a suspect on some TV crime series.

"I'm taking a bus," she said. "Don't worry. I'm going someplace safe. People are expecting me. People I trust."

"You're sure about this."

"I'm sure it's what God wants for me."

Kent didn't respond to the last line. He didn't really know how to. It always threw him when she referred to God in that easy, offhand manner, as if she'd just gotten off the direct line to Heaven. He was aware that the students talked about her like she was some circus freak. He'd seen the locker shrine bedecked with pictures of Jesus, crucifixes, and holy items, and heard about the daily sessions in the hall when she'd kneel and pray.

"I'm sorry to put you in this position," she said, "but I had to say good-bye. I know you're supposed to report it when a student admits they're running away."

"To Social Services, then to the police," he added.

"Do what you have to do," she said firmly, "but I'm not going back home."

"Is someone hurting you?" he asked. "Is that why you're leaving?"

She raised her head and looked at the chalkboard. "No," she said. "It's not that. Sometimes I wish it was that easy." She turned away from him and stared out at the desks. "Sometimes I wish he'd just hit me and then everything would be black and white. I'd have a reason to leave. But that's not the way it is."

He waited for her to continue. When she didn't, he said, "How is it then?"

She ran a hand across the worn knee of her jeans. "I don't have a place there. Not a real one. They want me to cook and clean and stand in the background while they make all the decisions. 'Do as you're told,' is what he always says to me. Then he starts quoting the Bible and that's the end of the conversation." She stopped, gave him a sad smile, and shook her head in derision. "Thus sayeth the Lord and the Lord says listen!"

"You're exhausted," Kent said. "You shouldn't be traveling. You should be resting."

She closed her eyes for a few seconds, then said, "I'll sleep on the bus."

He came toward her and took her hand and held it for a few moments.

"Please write," he said. "When you get where you're going, write and tell me you're okay."

"I will," she said, nodding. "I'll send a postcard or something as soon as I arrive."

He squeezed her hand and released it.

"Will you keep writing stories?" he asked. "Will you send me your work?"

"Yes," she said. "I promise."

"I'd like that very much."

Then he reached out and drew her into his arms and embraced her. There was no resistance or awkwardness in the moment. Kent thought of his daughter and how he'd longed to hold her like this. When they parted, he saw that she was smiling.

"Did you know I probably just broke district policy?" he said, laughing. "I'm supposed to refrain from touching students. A no contact clause. Hell, Mr. Gillette would probably tell me I shouldn't be alone with you in this room." Then, in a serious tone, he said, "I know you need to go. I'd suggest slipping out the back. I believe your father and his buddies are still in front and they might feel the need to interfere if they saw you leaving."

"I'll do that," she said, walking to the door.

"Hang on," Kent said as he moved to his desk. "Wait just a second."

He unlocked the middle drawer, then removed a necklace made of white shells. He held it up and said, "This was a gift from my students on the day I left Motu." He took it to her and placed it around her neck. "I want you to have it."

She fingered the shells and looked up at him. "Thank you," she said.

"Safe travels," he said.

After she left the room, Kent went to the doorway and watched her climb the stairs, a bulky pack swaying on her back. *Hai konea ra, Rachel*, he thought, surprised at how easily the words came back to him. *Farewell to you.*

■ ■ ■

FRIDAY, DECEMBER 19, 1997
2:15 P.M.

Eighth Hour

WHEN the bell rang to end seventh period, Kathie left the office and stepped quickly into the hallway. *A confident, low-key visibility is essential to the public school principal's success,* she thought, recalling a line from some administrative textbook she'd once read. The time for which she most desired—3:10—had nearly arrived and the only thing that stood between her and a two-week vacation was a single class period. She stayed in the hall as students streamed by, a few sucking on foot-long candy canes that they'd gradually whittled down to white stilettos of sugar. She smiled, went through the motions of saying hello, and tried to mask the exhaustion that pressed at her temples and chest and shoulders, shadowing her every nuance and gesture with an invisible, unrelenting sense of fatigue.

At one point she felt suddenly dizzy and leaned back, pressing a hand against the cinderblock wall for support. But she quickly recovered and stood up straight, trying to snap out of the daze by visualizing some unbreakable structure under a tremendous strain that refused to buckle or bend. *AP Romero,* she thought to herself. She liked the sound of it, how it reminded her of a tough female detective in one of the crime novels she loved to read in July when she could sit in a lounge chair on her back deck and sip a margarita. It sounded tough and resilient, which was what she needed to be right now. *Bulletproof.*

While Kathie waited in the hall, she kept an eye out for Officer Bradford. She'd called him earlier and asked if he could drop by around 2:15 P.M. She was going to pull Lara Wright from class to question her again. With a police officer hovering in the background, Lara might be more cooperative. And if Leonard Lamb was involved, as Lara had hinted earlier, then Kathie would definitely want Bradford along when she went to haul him out of eighth hour. They could take him into a conference room and do the good cop/bad cop routine until Leonard gave them some information.

As the students continued filing past her, she tried to spot Leonard, but he was nowhere in sight. Perhaps he'd cut out early and headed over to a friend's to party. *Good riddance*, she thought. *I'll deal with him after the holidays.* Suddenly she saw Paul coming her way, his lean frame looming out of the crowd. He seemed in a hurry and was carrying his brown grocery bag that she assumed was filled with hand-carved gifts. He smiled in passing and said, "One more to go and we're home free." She nodded her approval and grinned. *One more—*

—*minute*, S.A.M. Bond thought as he studied the neon dial on his imitation Rolex from the shadowy confines of Paul's closet. His head was pounding again and he braced a hand against the door until the ache subsided. Twice he'd nearly passed out on the cement floor when the pain made him nauseous and dizzy. He probably had a concussion from the fight with Leonard and should be in a hospital. When the watch read exactly 2:18, he slipped casually out the door and blended into the flow of human traffic in the hall, sure to keep his head down as he stayed close to the lockers on the outside perimeter.

Paul had not returned to the closet since their momentary encounter earlier in the day. S.A.M. had appreciated the privacy and reasoned that the janitor was simply allowing him the courtesy of developing a plan of recovery. Even though his masquerade had been partially blown, he trusted Paul to keep their secret until an official debrief could be arranged. Leonard was a different matter altogether, and as S.A.M. moved stealthily down the hall, he wondered if the attaché case's security had been breached. In the wrong hands, the contents could be used with harmful intent, thus resulting in deadly and catastrophic consequences. If the breach had indeed occurred, then S.A.M. would need to take action immediately against Leonard. He glimpsed a yellow sign posted on the wall and paused to read it, then quickly tore it down and stuffed it into his pocket. *When the opponent knows your weakness*, Master Yang once said to him, *then you must find his point of vulnerability and attack. Show no restraint as you overwhelm him. Any hesitation could be your undoing.*

In retro, S.A.M. knew he'd made a mistake during the brawl with Leonard in the bathroom. He'd retreated when his foe was weakened and helpless. He could've easily neutralized Leonard. Another swift kick to the knee. A thrust to the face with his fist. A power punch to the solar plexus. All could have resulted in injuries designed to incapacitate the enemy for an extended period, thus allowing precious time for the agent to complete his mission. If given a second chance, S.A.M. would not make the same mistake. He would finish the job.

He never once glanced at any of the students passing by and kept his eyes riveted on the floor and stairs as he swiftly made his way down to the basement, then into Hardin's classroom, where he quickly took his seat in the back row. He cocked an elbow and rested it on the desktop in order to shield his battered face with his right hand. A few students were beginning to arrive and take their places. Many seemed deliriously happy, their faces illuminated with smiles from a day of class parties, secret gift-giving, the anticipation of the holiday vacation or the surprise flight to Hawaii. They had no idea of the events unfolding below the surface of Ravenhill and the stakes involved, but S.A.M. knew these were matters of life and death and that all of his training, all of his preparation, might not be enough to vanquish a potential wave of destruction.

He studied the classroom and saw a grid with key zones for intervention. The rows of desks could be viewed as obstacles or shields, depending on the circumstances of engagement. Only one entrance and one exit. The window at the rear was secured with an impenetrable steel screen. When fully occupied, the room presented endless possibilities. S.A.M. had formulated a plan while recovering in the closet, one that required patience and cunning. This was no time to allow human emotion or matters of the heart to interfere with his calculations. He would first wait to see if Leonard was bold enough to appear with the briefcase. If so, then a diversion or disturbance could be created in order to secure the stolen property. He had thought through a myriad of alternatives: a fake seizure; a pulled fire alarm; a sudden, verbal attack on Leonard's personal integrity that might trigger hand-to-hand combat, thus allowing him the opportunity to grab the case and possibly escape in the ensuing melee. *Whatever the situation requires—*

—whatever, Lara thought as she came down the steps and immediately saw Kelly waiting for her at the bottom outside Hardin's room.

"Check this out," Kelly said, pointing at the row of gray lockers across from the classroom. "Someone's been busy *again.* Only this time, you're not the target."

Sprayed over the metal exterior in the same vibrant red were the words **HARD ON MUST DIE!** The huge letters seemed to pulse against the gray backdrop and Lara could feel the heat rising in her face. She imagined Leonard sneaking down into the basement during passing period, telling his friends to keep watch on the steps, all the while grinning as he went to work with the can of paint.

"Psychotic," Lara said. "Gillette's gonna go ballistic."

"Definitely certifiable," Kelly added. "I wonder if Hardin has seen it yet."

"I know one thing. When he does, he's gonna call the police."

The girls entered the room and saw Hardin at his desk, intently sifting through a stack of papers.

"Hey Mr. Hardin," Kelly called out. "Have you seen the message someone left outside in the hall?"

Hardin looked up, his face pale and tired as he stared at them. Lara remembered this morning when she and Kelly had spooked him on the stairs and he'd retreated against the wall as if they were evil specters. It had been a rush to scare him like that and witness his fear.

"What message?" he asked, his eyes agitated, darting about. He went into the hallway for a moment, then returned seconds later, his pace slow and mechanized. He stopped a few feet in front of them but didn't speak.

"I saw your signs upstairs," Kelly continued. "Any leads?"

"Not much," Hardin said, without looking at her. He seemed lost as he stared down at the ragged weave of the carpet. "Only a few less than credible sources."

"I might have something for you," Kelly said. "I was around school this morning. I saw something that seemed odd."

Hardin looked over at her, then took a few steps closer. "Such as?"

Kelly moved toward him, then lowered her voice and said, "Such as Leonard Lamb coming out of The Pit."

"At what time?" he asked.

"Before seven. My mom had an early shift so she dropped me on her way to work."

Hardin looked eager, his eyes wired. "Would you be willing to tell that to Mrs. Romero after class?"

Kelly smiled. "Did that sign say a hundred dollar reward?"

"Yes," he answered.

"In that case, it would be my pleasure to speak with Mrs. Romero."

Lara took it all in, admiring the cool, professional way Kelly handled herself as she talked with Hardin. Kelly wasn't afraid of Leonard or his friends or even the repercussions of ratting on him. If anyone could shut him down, it was her.

As they went to take their seats, Lara glanced to her left and suddenly paused. S.A.M. Bond was in his regular desk in the back corner. Only it wasn't the same S.A.M. Bond who had stood in front of her locker this morning. The dark clothes and sunglasses were gone, replaced by a white T-shirt, denim jacket, and jeans. All that remained of the mysterious stranger was the shock of jet black hair. But even that was different now. Unmoussed, his hair was spiky, jutting up in a punkish mop. He looked strangely ordinary. She could tell he was watching her, perhaps even studying her reaction to this new look, his hand partially covering his face in a shy pose. She smiled at him, but his eyes glanced away, so she quickly took her seat behind Kelly. *Strange days—*

—and strange are the ways of the world, Hardin thought as he perused his lesson plan. He only had a minute before class was to begin, but his pulse was racing and he felt an odd, exhilarating high, as if he'd been trapped within the confines of some invisible force field and suddenly it had evaporated, allowing him to roam freely. All afternoon he'd been frustrated, anxious, badly in need of a drink. It hadn't just been Rachel Riley's sudden good-bye and his complicity in keeping her running away a secret. Yes, he was worried about her getting on a bus and taking off for parts unknown, and he trusted that she'd made contact with a relative or a distant friend of the family. But it was more than that. The students who came forward in response to the reward posters had been ridiculous and pathetic, telling him

wild tales that could not possibly merit any truth. And not one of them had mentioned Leonard Lamb as the culprit.

The 3:30 meeting with Gus and the administrators from Central Office weighed heavily on him as images of job application forms for Wal-Mart, Kmart, Sofa Mart, Food Mart, even the dreaded PetSmart filled his brain. The last straw had been the new message spray painted on the lockers outside his room. In a moment of pure hatred, as he stared unbelieving at the writing and its hideous message, as he listened to the muffled laughter and jeering chuckles from the students as they walked by, he wanted to kill Leonard Lamb.

But who would have thought that Kelly Mason, Miss C average, would be his salvation? Yet here she was, an eyewitness with the necessary information to implicate Leonard and get him expelled. Perhaps this was the break he needed after such a bad day. A fresh start. A new beginning. Maybe he'd even follow through and take Kathie Romero to The Lighthouse over the holidays. Nothing pushy. Stay cool. *I was surprised*, she might say, *when I found out you were my Secret Santa.*

I'm full of surprises, he'd say. *More than you know.*

Kent was sweating and his right hand trembled as he touched the desk. Fifty minutes left. The opening of class was the key. Don't even give them time to breathe. Take attendance, then explain what had happened to the papers. He'd be straight with them up to a point. *Sometimes honesty is the best policy.* There'd been an accident and something had spilled on the essays and they were ruined. He was going to give them a chance to rewrite today. Open notes. Open book. Use whatever resources available, as long as you do your own work. Don't even bother taking questions from them. If Leonard, or anyone else for that matter, starts to whine or tries to take him on, don't hesitate. Pull the trigger. Make it snappy and boot them into the hall or send them upstairs to Gillette.

Then he'd rip through the directions for the essay. *Take out some lined paper and a pen or pencil. The topic: which of the spirits that haunted Ebenezer Scrooge had the most impact on him and therefore caused him to change? Support your answers with specific examples from the text. Write on every other line, one side of the paper, in cursive, with a full heading in the upper right hand corner. When finished, place your paper face down on the desk. No talking. The clock is ticking. You have thirty minutes. Begin.* As the bell rang for class to start, Hardin looked down at his attendance chart, then out at the students in their desks and, for the first time all year, he hoped to see Leonard Lamb present and accounted for. *How—*

—sweet, Leonard thought when he heard the bell announcing the beginning of eighth hour. He was cruising down the hallway, holding the recently unlocked Executive Attaché in his hand and taking his own sweet time getting to class. *Executive my ass,* he thought. It had been much too easy. During sixth hour Industrial Technology he'd been down in the shop with Mr. Bosch when the old fart went to help some special ed kid finish his knick-knack box. So Leonard had simply heisted a drill, a hammer, and a chisel, then went off to a corner where he proceeded to crack open the sucker.

He made sure to swagger into Hardin's room with the briefcase swinging from his arm like a professional, his strut methodical and slow as he made his way to the desk directly in front of Kelly Mason. Leonard knew Hard On was watching, but he checked to see if S.A.M. Bond, the creep in the back row, was paying attention as well.

"How nice of you to join us, Leonard," Hardin said. "You're late."

"Yes I am," Leonard responded, placing the case on his desktop with a smack that startled those around him. He then made a production out of removing his leather jacket and draping it on the chair. He enjoyed having all eyes focused on him, the main event, as the class held its breath and waited for the inevitable explosion of shouts and accusations that had become the norm.

Only Hardin didn't bite this time. He remained at the front of the room leaning against the desk, arms folded across his chest, looking almost relaxed. He stared quietly at Leonard through wire-rimmed glasses, a calm look on his face. When Leonard finally lowered his massive frame into the seat directly in front of Kelly, Hardin said, "I was in the middle of talking about the *Christmas Carol* essays that you wrote last week."

Suddenly Leonard's hand shot into the air and a few students giggled at his mock enthusiasm. Even though they'd all seen his act before, Leonard also knew they still found it amusing when he played the hell-raiser. Only this time Hardin didn't look perplexed or annoyed and it made Leonard uneasy. Instead, the teacher smiled in a laid-back way.

"Do you have a question, Leonard?" he asked.

"Yeah," Leonard answered in a serious tone. "It's about those reward signs you hung in the halls. I was wondering if you'd found out anything."

"Why do you want to know?"

"Because I think I know who did it."

"And what exactly was done?"

Leonard knew Hardin was baiting him, trying to force a mistake. But he was ready.

"Miz Romeo said that your room was vandalized this morning. Then at lunch, I heard Rory Knowles bragging about ripping somebody off. You should check his locker."

Hardin paused and took a step back toward his desk. "Thank you, Leonard. Why don't you see me after class."

"And if I'm right, do I get the reward?"

"We'll see," he said.

As Hardin went to write on the board, Leonard thrust his hand into the air once again. When the teacher turned and saw him, he said, "Last question, Leonard. Then we need to move on."

He rested his arm on the briefcase. "Since it's Friday, I was wondering if we were having Author's Share." Leonard knew it was a tradition in Hardin's classroom to give the students an opportunity each Friday to share aloud something they'd either written or read that week. He also knew that Hardin gave extra credit points to those who participated. Rachel Riley was the queen of Author's Share and Hardin was always begging her to get up and read one of her stories.

For a moment Hardin seemed frozen by the question, especially considering the source.

"So are we?" Leonard asked.

"And why are you so interested?"

"Because I got something to *share*," Leonard said, patting the briefcase with his hand. He turned and glanced quickly at S.A.M., then gave his full attention to the teacher.

"I hadn't planned on it," Hardin said. "We have a lot . . . "

"C'mon, man!" Leonard retorted, cutting the teacher off in mid-sentence. "It's the last day before break and all the other classes are partying. All but *yours*. And how often do you get me to volunteer for anything?" A few of the students were laughing now, and a couple in the back row even shouted, "Let's hear Leonard!" and "Give 'em a chance!"

For the first time since he'd set foot in the room, Leonard saw that Hard On was off balance, unsure about what to do next.

"I suppose we could take a few minutes," Hardin finally said, relenting. Cheers broke out in the back and Leonard pumped his fist in victory. "But what are you going to share?"

"It's a surprise," Leonard said.

"Is it appropriate?"

Leonard feigned a hurt look. "'Course it is. But it's private stuff." He swept the class with a menacing glare. "I don't want anyone laughing. This is personal."

Leonard rose from his seat with the briefcase in hand and moved to the front of the room. He set the case on Hardin's desk and turned to face the class. Then, with a dramatic flourish, he slyly snapped open the lid like some magician about to reveal his favorite trick. He glanced inside at the contents, then over at Lara Wright for a moment. *This is killer*, he thought. *Wait till she sees this—*

—wait, S.A.M. thought. *Patience is a weapon of the soul. Let the moment of weakness present itself.* And when Leonard lifted the black book out of the briefcase, its cover gleaming like polished ebony, S.A.M. gripped the desk with a steely resolve. Leonard glanced at Mr. Hardin and said, "Probably didn't know I'm a writer, but I been working on this in secret. That's why I carry it in this fancy case." He held the book out in front of him so everyone could see the detailed cover illustration of a young woman, dressed all in black, rising from a dark pool that glistened with moonlight. "I can draw too," he said.

S.A.M. could tell that Hardin was stunned, his face suddenly flushed as he stared at Leonard with a look of disbelief. Once he regained his composure, he finally spoke. "This is impressive. When did you work on it?"

"At home," Leonard said. "I put in hours and hours of time. The pictures were the hardest. Just look." He held the book up and flipped through the illustrations for the class to see. "This should be worth a lot of extra credit. A ton," he said.

S.A.M. recognized the illustrations, each one drawn on ivory parchment specially ordered from Denmark. He recognized the classic binding, hand-stitched with gold thread that was guaranteed to last a hundred years. He recognized the calligraphy, each letter created with special calligraphic brushes from China that he'd practiced with for hours before ever touching the page. It was his masterpiece, a tribute for his beloved that would reveal his true intentions. A gift to Lara.

"Perhaps we can talk about extra credit later," Mr. Hardin said. "Is it a story?"

"No," Leonard stammered. "Poems."

"And where did you get the ideas for these poems?"

Leonard hesitated. Then, with a wicked grin, he looked at Lara Wright and winked. "I was inspired," he said.

"Does the book have a title?" Mr. Hardin asked.

Leonard stared directly at S.A.M. "It's called *Goddess of the Night* because it's about this weird girl who lives in the dark."

"Go ahead," said Hardin. "And please remember we only have a few minutes."

"Right," Leonard said. He flipped carefully through the pages, his face a study of mock concentration. "I'll read this one poem. I worked hard on it."

S.A.M. bit his lip and fought the urge to rush Leonard, to rip the book from his hands and claim it as his own. He wanted everyone to see what he'd created for Lara. But he waited. S.A.M. was sure that Leonard had already torn out any pages that contained the author's true name. *When the opponent knows your secret fear,* Master Yang would say, *look for him to reveal his own.*

"In the nightshade of forest,"—Leonard began, his voice too loud—

"in the blessed dark of midnight's hour,
her slumber is broken
by that she ... "—
he stumbled, then tried to correct—
"that which she longs for,
the lux-lux-*lux*-... "

He stammered, struggling with the syllables, his mouth contorted in a grimace as he tried to pronounce the word.

" ...*the luxury* of dusk,
the courage to remove the mask of evening
and be trans-, transphoned-... "

He stuttered again, caught himself, then finally blurted it out—

" ...*transformed,*
to awaken in a world

where there's no need to hide,
to slick, *slink* from shadow to shadow
under the curtain of night."

Leonard paused and S.A.M. saw he was struggling to maintain control, his scowling face showing all the classic signs of panic. He looked up at the class and flashed an uneasy grin as if to say, *Cut me some slack, this is hard stuff,* then began again, only not as loud as before. When he spoke, S.A.M. felt a sudden stab of pain in his skull, a throbbing that made his head spin. For a moment he thought he might black out, but he held on, stayed focused until the discomfort began to ebb. Leonard continued:

"Sunlight, moonglow,
all stages to pass through
in the trans-, transfig-, *transfigur-...*"

S.A.M. could stand it no longer, this butchery of the text he'd spent hours crafting, honing, perfecting, only to have it massacred by Leonard.

"*Transfiguration!*" S.A.M. shouted, enunciating the word with vigor as he silenced Leonard, then stood and looked directly at Lara. He continued, his voice strong and resonant as he recited the words from memory:

"The goddess waits
for the awakening to true morning,
when night is no longer night,
day no longer day,
and she emerges whole, chaste, unadorned
into the light of moon and sun,
the mask torn away from her brow."

He hesitated, aware of the silence in the room, then closed his eyes, praying that the pain in his head would stay away, and spoke the final stanza the way he'd imagined it so many times in his mind while watching Lara from afar, always separated by an expanse of classroom or hallway or cafeteria or parking lot.

"She is unafraid to face the dawn, the dusk,

to touch the hand reaching across the void
that brings her *willingly—*
unashamed—
into the arms of daybreak,
into the light of acceptance,
into the shelter of truth."

When S.A.M. stopped and opened his eyes, he realized that the other students were staring as if he were some strange, exotic creature. Leonard was still in front, clutching the book in his hands, and the room was dead quiet. Lara was gazing directly at him, unblinking.

Truth—

—The word resonated in Lara's head like a tremor just below the surface of the skin, a pulse that grew stronger and more vibrant with each second. She turned for a moment and saw the book in Leonard's hand and knew the words were intended for her. She'd seen the briefcase this morning attached to S.A.M.'s wrist and knew Leonard must have stolen it, then tried to pass the work off as his own. Perhaps she should be afraid that some strange guy had written a poem for her. But the truth was that no one—not her parents or relatives or even the boys with their silly crushes and ID bracelets and love notes—had ever done anything remotely like this for her. Not this bold. Not this honest. And ever since the encounter with S.A.M. at her locker, she'd felt there was a possibility that he knew her better than anyone. She'd even thought about calling him over the holidays when Shannon and Kelly weren't around, so they could talk on the phone, maybe even take a walk or go to a movie. And now this. All this. For her.

She saw S.A.M. glaring at Leonard from the back of the room. "I'd like returned what was stolen from me," S.A.M. said sharply. "And I'd like it *now.*"

Leonard lifted the book in his meaty hand and pointed it at S.A.M. like a preacher waving a Bible in order to get his point across. "Siddown," Leonard said. "You tried once to take away what's mine. Don't try again."

Mr. Hardin suddenly moved between them. "I need you both to settle down," he ordered. Then he turned to Leonard. "Please return to your seat," he said. "And leave the book with me so we can resolve this after class." He reached for it, but Leonard would have nothing to do with him. He jerked it away with a sneer.

"Stay out of this," he said to Mr. Hardin. Then Leonard gestured at S.A.M. with the book and took a step down the aisle toward him. "If you want it, come and get it. No ambush this time. Or are you afraid of what else I know?"

Lara looked at S.A.M. He was rooted to the spot, unmoving. Suddenly he winced and put a hand on a desk to steady himself. She heard Mr. Hardin again as he said firmly, "Leonard, I need the book."

But Leonard ignored him again and moved down the row until he was standing only a few feet from Lara. His voice was menacing as he spoke to S.A.M. "Do you want me to tell them, faggot? You want me to tell them you're a freak? A real she-man?" Leonard reached into his jeans pocket and pulled out some small cards, then thrust them into the air. "I got these from the briefcase," he said. "Show 'em your ID, *Samantha*. Show 'em who you really are."

"That's enough!" Mr. Hardin shouted.

"I only want what's mine," S.A.M. said, fists clenched at his sides.

"I said that's enough!" Hardin yelled again as he rushed down the aisle and tried to position himself between Leonard and S.A.M. "This needs to stop!"

Suddenly there was movement in the doorway and Lara turned to see Rachel Riley standing just inside the room. She seemed out of breath and was panting, her cheeks red from exhaustion. She had a lost look on her face, the kind reserved for new students who accidentally stumble into a class, uncertain as to whether it's the correct one on their schedule.

Mr. Hardin took a few steps toward her, a puzzled expression on his face, then said, "Rachel?"

"I had to come back," she said, still trying to catch her breath. "There's something you need to know."

"It'll have to wait," Hardin said, waving a hand at Leonard. "We have a situation here that must be addressed."

"I had to warn you," she said, her voice desperate with panic.

"Warn us about what?" Mr. Hardin asked.

Then Rachel saw Lara in the middle of the classroom and her face softened and she smiled at her. It was a knowing smile, as if she and Lara shared some secret that only they could possibly understand. Then she made a slow, deliberate movement with her right hand as if tracing a pattern in the air in front of her body. It took Lara a moment to figure out exactly what she was doing, but then it came to her and it made perfect sense. *The sign of the cross. A blessing.*

Out of the corner of her eye, Lara saw a sudden flash of red. She turned long enough to see Kelly's hand sliding forward into Leonard's jacket pocket. She was quick, hardly a blip on the radar screen since all the attention was focused elsewhere. "Someday I'd like to be a pickpocket," Kelly told her once. "The old five-finger discount. The hand is quicker than the eye." Within seconds, Kelly was leaning back in her chair and waving a hand in the air. "Mr. Hardin," she called out, "I think you need to see this."

Hardin didn't respond immediately. He shook his head, looking perplexed, and turned away from Rachel.

"See what?" he asked.

Kelly paused, glanced at Lara for a moment, then back at Hardin. "I think you need to check Leonard's coat pocket. I saw something."

Without hesitation, Hardin quickly moved over to Leonard's desk, then reached down into the pocket of the jacket and pulled out a can of spray paint with a top as bright as flame. He studied the can for a moment, then turned and faced Leonard with the evidence thrust before him like a weapon.

"This can't wait any longer," he said. "Come with me to the office."

Lara could see that Leonard wasn't budging. Not an inch. He stood there, his massive frame towering over the row of students and fixed Kelly with a murderous glare. "You bitch!" he screamed at her. "Lying bitch! You set me up!"

Then he charged down the aisle to get at her and Lara was surprised by his quickness. Hardin blocked his path for a moment, but Leonard rammed into him and the teacher tumbled over Sara Gleason at her desk, sending them both sprawling onto the floor. Then Leonard was upon Kelly, yanking her from the desk and throwing her onto the carpet as his hands throttled her neck, his strong fingers digging into the skin at her throat. Kelly fought him, scratched at his face and eyes, her legs kicking at his torso, but to no avail. Lara rushed him from the back to pound on his shoulders and head with her fists and yell for him to stop, but he was oblivious, so intent was he on the task at hand. Leonard hunched over Kelly as if wanting a kiss, wanting to see the light fade from her eyes, his mouth close to hers as he squeezed out every last breath.

Pure nightmare. A rush of panic flooded Lara's mind. She could hear the gargled sounds of Kelly as she was being strangled and the grunting of Leonard as he bore down on her. Students were screaming and a few shouted, "Get a teacher!" or "Get Gillette!" Lara searched for Hardin, but he was collapsed on the floor, clutching his knee in obvious pain. She glanced up and saw S.A.M. slumped over a desk, a dazed look of anguish on his face.

In a moment of sudden, almost hypnotic clarity, she knew exactly what needed to be done. *Desperate measures*, she thought, *require desperate acts.* She grabbed her backpack, then quickly reached inside and slid her hand to the bottom, digging around until she felt the shape, wrapped carefully in a piece of downy flannel. When Lara yanked it from the pack, the gun felt powerfully redemptive as she leveled it on Leonard, her arms locked and extended, just the way Gary had taught her. Two days ago she'd gone into her brother's room when he was out and slipped the little 9 mm out of his duffle bag. *Just to scare Leonard*, she told herself. *If he follows me again, I'll pull this out. He won't mess with me after that.*

"Let her go!" Lara screamed. "Get off or I'll shoot!" The last line got Leonard's attention and he jerked his head up, saw the pistol aimed at his face, then released Kelly and backed away from her. Lara could see her friend on the floor, her terrified, wild eyes as she held her bruised throat and gasped for air, still choking. "Move away," Lara said, trying to sound firm even as her voice broke on the last word. Leonard took a step back, but an eerie smile flashed across his face. She felt the adrenaline like a wicked rush and noticed that her arms were shaking. A part of her wanted to fire point blank and put him down with a bullet. *Try not to think.* The fear left a bitter metallic taste in her mouth, and she thought about the consequences of shooting someone, the inevitable blood that would surely flow. And that's when she knew Leonard saw her doubt, saw the panic setting in like a veil over her eyes, and she realized he was coming for her and there was nothing she could do to stop him. He rushed her like a wild animal bursting from cover to assault its prey, his hand twisting her wrist and wrenching the gun away as he slammed into her chest and shoved her backward.

For a moment Lara couldn't breathe, the impact knocking the air out of her as she hit the floor. But she grabbed a chair and pulled herself upright, then saw Leonard aim the pistol at her. Only he didn't shoot. He held the gun on her, the veins in his neck straining as he bared his teeth. Lara saw a change in his face, his eyes, if only for a moment, and there was a sudden innocence in the way he looked at her. It was as if he'd lost his grip on something fragile and was watching it plummet to the floor where it might shatter. But Lara knew it was fleeting, knew she was going to die, and she opened her mouth to cry out when a dark figure dashed in front of her. *No—*

—stop, S.A.M. thought as he rushed Leonard. Until that moment he had witnessed it all through a filter of pain he could not understand. The poem had come to him quickly, nearly exploding from his mouth as he'd recited it. But this was different. He wanted to go on the offensive and attack Leonard as he taunted him with the book, but his body seemed crippled, shut down, unable to respond to the simplest motor commands. *Concussion—an impaired functioning of the brain caused by a violent blow*, he thought with a certain medical cool. Then he saw Lara Wright with the gun pointed ahead, her arm as straight as a compass needle, and he was sure he had never seen anything so beautiful. *My avenging angel.* But when Leonard attacked her and took the pistol, S.A.M. knew instinctively that the enemy would attempt to remove the initial threat. He understood the ways of vengeance and knew he only had seconds to force the pain in his head aside and place himself as a shield between Lara and the path of the bullet, his own destiny controlled by a force that exceeded all limits of time, space, distance, speed. *God—*

—help me, Hardin thought as he tried to rise from the carpet. *God help us all.* His right knee was on fire from where it had struck the floor. He hoisted himself up by using a desk for support, and when he finally stood, he saw Leonard Lamb shoot S.A.M. Bond point-blank with a gun as blood spurted from Bond's white T-shirt.

Hardin was only twenty feet from Leonard and he made a fierce, staggered run at the shooter, blindsiding him from the rear with a savage tackle, his right hand going for the pistol as he seized Leonard's wrist. "I'll kill you!" Leonard shouted at Hardin as the teacher clung to him, gripping the gun arm with both hands as they did a crazy dance, the weapon now thrust above them and pointed straight into the air. A shot was fired into the ceiling, and plaster rained down on them like snow. Then the pistol swung violently around in a pendulum motion and more shots erupted as the two struggled for possession of the weapon.

Within seconds Hardin realized that Leonard still had his finger on the trigger and was shooting wildly, randomly, spraying the room with a mad carousel of gunfire—three, four, five shots—as the pair spun around. He heard Leonard gasping for breath as they wrestled for the gun and Hardin smelled the odor of his skin, the sweat of his scalp. His good leg was taking the brunt of the weight, while the bum knee was locked straight, no flex, and Hardin knew he only had a moment before he went down for the pain was excruciating and too much to bear. So he lunged for the pistol and gripped the hot barrel, then smashed an elbow into Leonard's face and tore it from his grasp. Leonard fell hard to the floor, clutching his nose.

Panting for air, Hardin held the gun on Leonard and surveyed his classroom while a number of hysterical students ran screaming out the door. Kelly Mason lay motionless, a few girls crouching at her side, as a small pool of blood formed on the carpet. Amanda Rice crouched near a desk, sobbing uncontrollably and holding a bloody arm from where a bullet had struck her. Lara Wright knelt on the floor and cradled S.A.M. Bond's head in her lap, her hands coated with red. A small body lay face down in the corner, and Hardin could see the wine-colored stain on Blair Hull's shirt growing larger from where the shot had hit him square in the back. And by the door, her body in a crumpled heap, lay Rachel Riley. She was only fifteen feet away and a dark, syrupy liquid oozed from under her still form.

"Run upstairs!" Hardin shouted to a student. "Now!" He kept the gun pointed at Leonard who had risen from the floor, blood seeping from his nostrils.

"I don't need this shit," Leonard hissed at him. "I'm outta here."

He began walking for the door, but Hardin shouted, "No!" and thrust the pistol at him. "You look at this!"

Leonard froze in place and glared at Hardin. He gestured at the gun. "Do it," he said, grimacing. "Go ahead. Shoot to kill."

Hardin limped forward, one hand on his bad knee, and pressed the barrel of the pistol against Leonard's forehead, pushing him until his back was against the wall. He could visualize the brains and blood on the white plaster if he fired at such close range and imagined the bullet as it passed through the skull and lodged deep in the cinderblock. *The End.*

Hardin leaned closer until his face was only inches away from Leonard's. "Remember this," he said, gesturing with his free hand at the room. "Remember it all." Unblinking, he stared at Leonard as the gun began to tremble in his hand. Then he clicked on the safety and began to lower the weapon.

The shot struck Hardin in the abdomen, slamming him backward a few steps. It was a blow unlike anything he had ever felt before, a pain in his stomach that left him stunned at the power of steel piercing skin and muscle. Somehow he remained standing for a moment, but then collapsed onto the floor, striking his head against the wall as he went down. At first he couldn't feel his legs or arms, only the stinging in his head. When he finally looked up, he saw the officer standing by the door. It was a crooked view and the man looked enormously tall because Kent was on the floor now and the overhead lights had never looked so blinding and harsh. *Officer Bradford,* he thought. *To protect—*

—and serve. Bradford crouched in a shooter's stance, his 9 mm poised out in front. There had been so much to take in when he first stepped over the threshold of the doorway. The fallen students. The blood on the carpet. The cries for help and screams of the wounded. So much. He felt adrenaline surging through him like a train. Then he saw Hardin with the gun, how he'd pinned Leonard to the wall as if ready to execute him. Bradford knew there wasn't time to call out a warning, only

time to shoot, and he had a clear line. *Terminate the threat.* So he fired.

The moment would stay with him in the days and nights to come, haunting him so he could not sleep and rest would become an impossibility. Hours later, long after he helped to sta-bilize the wounded, long after the EMTs had arrived, he would remember it all so clearly when he reported the incident to the Shoot Team at the police station. In the weeks to come he would remember the details as he talked with Leary, a trusted veteran, over stale cinnamon rolls and weak coffee, trying to justify why he didn't call out a warning, why he didn't hesitate before firing, why his instincts were so automatic. Finally, he would remem-ber it all on a cool night in early March when he was huddled alone in his squad car out by the landfill and suddenly recalled a line from a poem that a grade-school teacher had forced him to memorize as punishment for yanking down a girl's skirt on the playground. *Miles to go before I sleep,* he thought while gripping the 9 mm pistol in his hand.

Bradford suddenly thought of Leonard Lamb in his cell at the detention center and wondered if the young man had considered suicide in the days after the shooting. He could've hung himself with a braided bedsheet or slit his wrists with a sharpened piece of plastic. Bradford carefully slid the gun back into its leather holster. He was sweating and took a deep breath, then exhaled slowly. He had a plan. In the morning he'd rise early and drive to the detention center where Leonard was being confined. *It's a beginning,* he thought. *Try to reach out to him. Let him know he's not alone. At least it's a start.* Then Bradford turned the ignition on and drove the police car back to the station. Along the way it started to rain and he kept his window down so he could smell the fresh scent of the March storm as it moved through Old Town.

■ ■ ■

SUNDAY, DECEMBER 21, 1997
7:00 P.M.

Kathie

S HE was resting when Josh, her oldest, came into the bedroom to wake her.

"It's time, Mom," was all he said, yet Kathie understood
immediately. She eased out from under the comforter, then
slipped on a wool sweater. She went into the kitchen where the
boys were waiting for her. Josh and Ben had already bundled up
in their warmest down coats and snow boots. A few candles
were on the wooden table's surface and Ben handed her one.

"Thanks sweetie," she said and he smiled back at her.

Since Friday the boys had been amazing, never once complaining about having to cancel the trip to Chicago to see her
parents. In their own quiet way, she knew they understood.
Even Ben, her angry little man, would crawl into bed with her at
night so she wouldn't have to sleep alone. When she came home
after being at the Shoot Team headquarters or the police station,
she would go into her room and cry for what seemed like hours.
Inevitably, she'd hear a light tapping at the door. After wiping
her eyes with a tissue and opening the doorway a crack, she
found a gift placed on the carpet near the threshold. A candy

nugget wrapped in foil. A picture that Josh had drawn at school. A favorite toy from one of Ben's Galactic Guardians collection. Their offerings to her.

After turning out the lights in the house, they got into the Subaru and drove quietly across town. There wasn't much traffic on a Sunday night and Kathie drove slowly, deliberately, occasionally glancing at the passersby on the sidewalks. For two days she'd hoped to spot Lara Wright somewhere on the street or possibly emerging from an alley. Lara had vanished after the shooting on Friday afternoon and the police were conducting a massive search for her throughout the town. Kathie knew they had questions to ask Lara about the gun and why she'd smuggled it into the school, but she was more concerned about her student's well being and less about the case itself. Had she run away? Was she hiding out in some desolate, cold place? On both Saturday and Sunday afternoon, before Kathie went home to relieve the babysitter with the boys, she drove around town, hoping to catch a glimpse of Lara walking aimlessly across an abandoned lot or field. But there was no sign of her anywhere.

As they traveled over the dark, wet pavement, ice formed inside the car windows and Ben made drawings on the frosted glass. Cars passed by and their headlights illuminated the pictures so that they glowed with silver tracings as if drawn by a magic brush. When Kathie turned right onto Main Street, Josh said, "There they are," and pointed at the crowd that had gathered in front of the school. "Is it bigger tonight?"

"It seems bigger every night," Kathie answered.

She parked a block away because the main lot was already full. As they crossed the street and approached the gathering, Kathie saw that someone had lit the candles on the makeshift memorial in front of the school and the entrance glowed with a warm light. *Something for the dead*, Kathie thought. *Something holy.*

When the boys reached the sidewalk, she paused for a moment to take it all in. They looked up at her and waited.

"Go on," she said with a wave of her hand. "Go ahead. I'm sure Gus and Marilyn are up front. I'll be there in just a moment." The boys looked at her with puzzled expressions, then shrugged and moved on. Soon they were enveloped by the crowd. "Stay together," she called after them, almost an afterthought. But they didn't look back.

The sight of Ravenhill made her freeze up. She hadn't actually stepped foot inside the building since last Friday. There were moments when she wasn't sure she ever could. Even now she had to calm herself to move toward the school, as if the physical proximity to the site unleashed a flood of images in her head that she couldn't control.

She remembered being in the hallway with Officer Bradford when they heard the shots. He immediately bolted ahead, his pistol drawn, and she tried to follow but couldn't keep up. Kathie had waited at the top of the steps, feeling for a moment as if she stood at the edge of a vast pit. Then she heard the crack of gunfire and proceeded down, all the while being met by panic-stricken students who raced past her. A ninth grader, Anna Foster, was screaming hysterically and Kathie embraced her, then led the girl outside to safety. She tried to do her job and direct the fleeing students away from the building to the south field. Eventually she made her way back into the school and down the stairs to Hardin's room where she saw the dying and wounded. The blood seemed to be everywhere, splattered across faces and shirts and carpet.

Soon Kathie followed Josh and Ben and made her way through the somber crowd. As she proceeded, people acknowledged her presence with small gestures. A simple nod of the head. A hand placed momentarily on her shoulder. Few smiled, but many said reassuringly, "Glad you're here, Kathie," or "Good to see you again." Some waved to her from a distance. When she saw Gus and Marilyn near the front with the boys, she walked over and they embraced. Gus looked terrible. She could see that he was exhausted from the grueling sessions with the Shoot Team as well as the long meetings with school district officials in the aftermath of the tragedy.

"You should go home and get some rest," she said to him.

"I'll sleep later. This is where I need to be tonight." He looked around at the crowd, then nodded at Josh and Ben. "And I'm glad you brought the boys. It's good they're here."

Every night since the shootings, a crowd had gathered in front of the school. Some brought gifts for the memorial. Some left candles and flowers on the steps and pavement. Eventually banners and posters were taped to the walls and fence near the entrance, along with photographs of the victims. There were handwritten poems and drawings, as well as an assortment of stuffed animals, a baseball cap, and a pair of white ballet slippers. As the shrine grew larger, so did the gathering, expanding to a few hundred people by Sunday night.

Kathie glanced behind her at the street. "Not as many TV cameras as before," she said. "The network vans aren't around."

"I guess they've decided to let us mourn in peace," said Gus.

Soon more people streamed out of the school auditorium at the south end of the building. The mayor's office, the school board, and the police department had brought in a national expert on youth violence to lead a public forum on the Ravenhill shootings. Kathie and Gus had deliberately chosen not to attend so that parents and students could speak their mind without worrying about offending any of the school administrators. In the end, it had been a wise decision for Kathie to return home and get some sleep.

She felt a tug at her sleeve and looked down at Ben. "They're lighting candles now, Mom," he said, holding his out. "Did you bring yours?"

"Yes," she said, slipping it from her pocket. She glanced over and saw a wave of light spreading from one end of the crowd as candles were lit and flames exchanged. The world became abruptly still as Kathie held Ben's hand and gazed at the scene around her. Many people bowed their heads and closed their eyes as if in prayer. Kathie needed to take it all in, soak it up like rain so the moment could sustain her. Each time she came to the evening gathering and looked into the faces of those who welcomed her and stood next to her in the frigid night air, she felt accepted once again. She knew deep inside who was directly responsible for the deaths last Friday, but she was somehow forgiven each time she stared into the face of a parent or student or one of the townspeople and they looked back at her without asking the questions that haunted her at night. *Where were you when my child was killed? How could you allow a gun in your school? Why wasn't Leonard expelled weeks ago?*

Kathie looked up suddenly and saw something that caught her eye. At the farthest edge of the gathering, a hooded figure was standing near the front. There was a certain familiarity about the way he stood, hands stuffed deep into his pockets with shoulders hunched to the cold. A loner's pose, more protective than defiant. A wounded soul. When the flicker of candle glow reached the stranger's face, Kathie saw the profile, visible only for an instant, then quickly turning away. In that brief second of recognition, Kathie's pulse quickened for she knew immediately that the cowled figure was Lara Wright and that she had returned to mourn the dead.

■ ■ ■

SUNDAY, DECEMBER 21, 1997
7:30 P.M.

Lara

SHE held the candle close and cupped her hand around the flame to protect it from the frigid wind. Even the slightest warmth felt good on her icy fingers, and she moved them as near to the tiny fire as she dared without burning her skin. Lara lifted her head for an instant and tried to spot Mr. Munn, the tall custodian, but she couldn't see him and pulled the hood around her face. He'd persuaded her to come tonight, even though she hadn't wanted to. More than anyone right now, she trusted him to help her do what was best.

Last Friday seemed months, even years ago. A piece of nightmare, a sliver of dream that would not let her escape the fact that it had indeed happened. The gunshots. The screams. Kelly's silent, unmoving body. The blood of S.A.M. Bond on her hands and dress as she held him. She wasn't sure how long she knelt on the carpet next to his body, but when the policeman came in with his gun drawn and shot Mr. Hardin, she felt a shattering within her and fled the room, pausing long enough to see Rachel Riley's still form on the carpet. Somehow Lara knew that Kelly and Blair and Rachel and S.A.M. were all dead, shot with the gun she'd brought into the school. *Your gun, your murders.* Before she bolted past the door, she glanced down and saw the black book on the floor and stooped to pick it up. Then Lara ran, clutching it tightly to her chest.

She could hardly breathe as she rushed to get outside where there was air and no screaming and no blood. Somehow she must have veered right instead of following the other students up the stairs, then exited out the rear door next to the old furnace. Dazed, it took her a moment before realizing she was at the back of the school, not the front, and the wailing sirens of police cars and fire trucks swirled around her in a relentless, dizzying blur of noise as if a swarm of electrified hornets encircled her head. She ran from the hideous sounds in a frantic sprint across the snow-laden football field, her breath exploding in cold bursts. At one point she stopped and realized she'd lost her shoes and was barefoot, yet she didn't feel the cold or even notice the hard crust of ice on the ground that dug into her toes.

She hit the street and kept going, not clear about where she was headed, only sure that it was away from the school. She ducked into a long alley that was narrow and empty and seemed to stretch in front of her forever like some secret passage to safety. She kept looking behind her, expecting to see Leonard with his wicked grin emerging from behind a dumpster or a policeman with his gun drawn taking aim at her back. She kept running.

Time must have passed, but Lara didn't notice. When her legs burned from the grueling pace and started to buckle, she slipped into an open garage facing the alley and slumped onto the cold cement. She began to cry, but couldn't catch her breath and thought she was choking, maybe even dying. Her feet were bleeding, but she felt no pain. Questions whirled through her mind like a tempest. How did she escape unharmed? Why did S.A.M. Bond step forward to take the bullet that was intended for her? And why did the policeman shoot Mr. Hardin?

Eventually Lara got up and started running in the alley again, uncertain as to how far she'd come or which direction she was going. Then she saw the steep tower looming out of the houses and ran for it, the cross affixed to its pinnacle her only sign of recognition. When Lara reached the church, she ran straight for the front doors and slipped inside. It was dark and empty, but she glimpsed a side stair and took it up to the balcony where she collapsed in a corner in the back, her chest pounding.

Eventually her breathing grew easier, more under control, and she saw the streaks on her bloodstained hands. There was a door to her right and she crept through it, then turned on the light. Lara saw that it was a small restroom with a sink and toilet. She set the black book down, ran cold water on her face and hands, and watched as the white basin turned pink from the blood. Afterward, she closed the door and turned off the light so she could curl up on the floor. All she wanted was rest, a deep, muted sleep that was void of dreams and sound and image. She pressed the book close to her body and drifted off. *Comatose*, she thought. *Zombieland.*

She did not awaken until the afternoon of the next day, when Paul Munn, who was cleaning the church to prepare for Sunday services, found her huddled in the second floor restroom. At first Lara didn't recognize him and she screamed when he entered, holding the black book like a shield over her chest. He jumped back, startled from her presence, then slowly, gradually, sat down in one of the wooden benches just outside the door.

"I'm not going to hurt you," he said calmly. "I'm just cleaning up for church tomorrow morning."

She still did not speak, her eyes wide with panic. He looked familiar but her mind still raced with the ghastly images from yesterday. Suddenly she saw his face soften with recognition as he stared at her.

"Lara," he said. "You're Lara Wright. I know you from Ravenhill." She slowly nodded, brushing a strand of hair from her eyes. "I'm Mr. Munn, the custodian at the school. I live next door to the church." He paused, letting the information sink in. She recognized his tall, lean figure from the hallways, where he was usually pushing a trash cart or wielding a dust mop. "Have you been here all night?" he finally asked.

Lara nodded again, lowering the book so that it rested in her lap.

"And were you in Mr. Hardin's class when the shooting happened?"

"Yes." Her voice sounded foreign, as if the words came from a stranger. "I was there," she said.

"Are you okay?" he asked. "Were you hurt?"

She shook her head no, then stared past him at the stained glass panels above his head to the rear of the church. It was overcast outside and the image on the window was hard to decipher. An angel? A saint? She could not tell.

"Do your parents know you're here?" he said.

Lara hesitated, unsure of what to say next. She felt cornered by him and wanted to make a break for the lone door on the far side. But she was too tired to run and stayed put without answering his question.

"They need to know you're okay," Mr. Munn said. "They're probably worried sick about you."

"They'll want to know I'm all right," she finally said.

"We can use the church phone," he said. "It's downstairs."

She pulled back from him, shaking her head vigorously. "I can't call them because of the police. They'll be waiting for me."

"Why?" he asked.

Lara hesitated, uncertain of what to say next and whether he could be trusted. Finally, she spoke. "It was my gun. I took it from home and brought it to school in a backpack. I just wanted to scare someone so he'd leave me alone."

Then Lara told him everything because she didn't know what else to do. She told him about Kelly's plan for revenge and

S.A.M. Bond's protecting her and the black book in the briefcase
and how Mr. Hardin had saved them from Leonard. It came out
in a crazy, cracked-up blur of a story, and she was crying when
she finished telling him all she knew.

"I'm responsible," Lara said. "None of this would have happened if I hadn't brought the gun."

Mr. Munn listened quietly to her. When he finally spoke, his
voice was even and calm. "You're going to be okay. You made a
mistake in bringing the gun to school, but never intended to
hurt anyone, right?" She nodded in agreement. "I'm not going to
turn you in. You'll do that when you're ready. In the meantime,
you need to call your parents and let them know you weren't
harmed and that you're safe. It's up to you if you want to tell
them where you are."

"I can't," Lara said. "I'm not ready to see them yet."

"It's your decision."

Then he took her downstairs to the church basement where
there was a phone. He left her alone to make the call to her parents and when she was done he took her across the street to his
apartment below the rectory. He gave her a clean towel so she
could shower later, then fixed some hot soup. While she ate, he
said, "You're welcome to stay here for now. In the meantime, I
can sleep over at the church on a cot in the basement. When
you're ready to go to the police station, I'll come with you."

Between sips of the hot broth, she studied him, weighing
each of his sentences carefully. Finally, she asked, "Why are you
helping me? You don't even know me."

Mr. Munn stood up, his head nearly touching the low basement ceiling. "I used to be a priest and I liked helping people. I
still do. I guess it's a habit that's hard to break."

Lara stopped eating the soup and rested her spoon on a nap-
kin. She glanced up at him and held his gaze for a moment, then
looked back at her food.

"Thank you," she said.

"You're welcome." He smiled at her, and walked over to the basement door. "I'll be at the church if you need me." Then he was gone and she was left alone to finish her meal.

Lara stayed at the apartment that night, her sleep disturbed by recurring images that would jolt her awake in the dimly lit room. Kelly's blood-soaked dress. The piercing echo of the gunshots. The weapon in her hand as she aimed it at Leonard, wanting to pull the trigger. The way Mr. Hardin's body jerked back when the bullet struck him. Once she awoke and went to the door and saw Mr. Munn outside with a blanket wrapped around his shoulders. He was sitting on a folding chair in the entryway to the basement, his head tilted back against the frame as he dozed. It felt good to know he was close by, just in case. Then she returned to bed and slept.

In the morning, Mr. Munn came by with some clothes for Lara: a wool parka, a hooded sweatshirt, jeans, and a long-sleeved T-shirt. They smelled of laundry detergent and were neatly folded as he handed them to her.

"Straight from the church's relief box," he said with a grin. "Nothing fancy, but it'll keep you warm." While she changed in the bathroom, he fixed her scrambled eggs and toast, then sat across the table drinking coffee as she ate.

"There was a gathering in front of the school last night," he said. "Some kind of memorial service. Almost a hundred people showed up. I heard they'll be meeting again this evening."

Lara nibbled at the eggs and drank deeply from a mug of hot tea. The donated clothes hung loosely from her thin body.

"Perhaps we should go," he said. "If we wait until after dark and you put up that hood, no one will even recognize you."

"I don't think so," she said without looking at him, instead keeping her eyes fixed on the plate of food in front of her.

"I'm not talking about going to the police," he added. "You do that on your own terms. But it's a way to start healing. That's why they're all coming to the school. They've all been wounded in their own way."

"And what if I'm not ready for that?" she said sharply, her voice rising. "What if someone recognizes me and turns me in. What do I say to the police?"

He leaned forward, his elbows resting on the table, and looked straight at her, his gaze unwavering. "You tell them what you told me. You tell them the truth."

Lara pushed the plate away and got up from the table. She walked across the room and sat on the edge of the bed, glaring at the flimsy wood paneling. Mr. Munn stood and cleared the dishes from the table, then set them in the sink. He went to the doorway and said, "If you decide to come to Ravenhill tonight, I'll be there." She turned toward him, wanting to respond in some way to his invitation. But before she could speak, he was already gone, the door closing tightly behind him.

In the end Lara chose to go. At dusk she pulled on the sweatshirt and wool parka, then drew the hood tight over her head. She walked quickly down the sidewalk, wanting to be seen as little as possible on the street. As she made her way to the school, Lara thought of S.A.M. Bond and wondered if this was how he felt each day when he wore his disguise and concealed his true identity from the world around him. She was in hiding now, just as S.A.M. had been for so many months at the school.

Lara stayed on the outer fringe of the crowd, afraid to be drawn into the heart of the gathering where a parent or student might recognize her. She looked for Mr. Munn, hoping to glimpse his sturdy figure rising out of the throng, but never saw him. Soon the candles were lit and the crowd pressed toward the makeshift memorial as the low hum of conversation filled the air. They grew quiet when a figure mounted the steps and turned to face them. It was the principal of Ravenhill, Mr. Gillette, and he waited until all were silent and the only sound was the occasional hiss of tires as a car passed by on the wet street behind them.

"Thank you for being here," he began. "We met last night in order to provide some comfort for our community after the tragedy on Friday. We're here again this evening for the same reason. All are welcome, no matter what your faith or beliefs might be. This is simply a time to mourn together." He grew quiet and looked out over the people and the multitude of luminous candles flickering in the darkness. "Let's have a moment of silence for the victims and their families. Let's hold them in our minds and in our hearts."

The world became abruptly still and Lara was aware of hundreds of people bowing their heads. She stared down at the wavering candle flame and thought of Kelly, S.A.M., Blair, and Rachel. She remembered Mr. Hardin and how he'd charged Leonard and eventually wrestled the gun away from him. Suddenly there was a hand at her elbow, gently squeezing her arm and she looked up to see Mrs. Romero standing there. Lara started to pull away, but she held on.

"I'm not here as the assistant principal," Mrs. Romero whispered. "I'm here as your friend."

Lara stood frozen in place, waiting. She expected the police to close in and hustle her off to a squad car. But there was only Mrs. Romero, still touching her arm.

"Do you know about the gun?" Lara asked. "Do you know it was mine?"

The assistant principal nodded, then moved a step closer. "I can help you," she said. "You don't have to go through this alone."

Lara felt tears welling up in her eyes. "I didn't mean for it to happen the way it did. I didn't know what Leonard would do."

"Of course you didn't," she said. "But you have to talk to the police. They need to hear your story."

Lara looked up and saw Mr. Munn standing beside them. "Mrs. Romero knows the police," he said. "She can help if you let her."

Lara was still holding the candle and she saw that her hands were shaking as hot wax dripped onto the ground. She leaned down and blew out the flame, then looked at the two of them. "Okay," she said. "Will you come with me?"

"Yes," Mrs. Romero said, "but give me a few minutes so I can make arrangements for my boys." She slipped away through the crowd, leaving Lara with Mr. Munn. There was a woman on the steps of the school who was speaking to the crowd now. Lara recognized her as a cashier over at the Safeway store. She was a heavyset woman, maybe in her fifties, with silver hair and wearing a long black coat.

"I sold candy and pop to Kelly Mason at least once a week after school," she told the gathering. "Dr. Pepper and Paydays were her favorites. When she came up to my register, I'd always say, 'What's your pleasure?' and she'd say, 'The usual; just put it on my tab,' and we'd both laugh. I'm going to miss that girl's smile."

The next speaker was a bus driver with a dark beard who had known Blair Hull since third grade when he started riding on his route. "Blair was always a little guy and sometimes the other kids tried to take advantage of him. But he was smart as a whip. He knew the safest seat on the bus was right behind the driver. And I always did my best to save it for him."

When the driver was finished, Miss Healy, the art teacher, stepped up to speak. She'd brought a portrait of S.A.M. Bond to display at the memorial and she leaned the framed picture against the brick wall among the scattered flowers. "I drew this caricature of S.A.M. last week," she said. "I guess it's my way of remembering him for who he was: a gifted artist and a talented poet." Miss Healy lowered her head for a moment and stared down at the picture, then brushed back her wavy hair with a hand. "As a teacher, whether we want to admit it or not, we all have our favorites. S.A.M. was one of mine. He saw things in the day to day that the rest of us don't pay much attention to. Invisible things. Hidden passions. Sometimes I think S.A.M. looked at the world as if it was this crazy maze of a museum that we have to find our way out of. If so, then I'd want S.A.M. Bond as my guide. I'm going to miss him terribly."

241

As Miss Healy walked down the steps, Lara felt the weight of the black book under her parka. She'd brought it with her out of fear. If she left the book behind, it might somehow be found and given to the authorities. After all, S.A.M. was a young woman. *Samantha* was what Leonard had called her in Hardin's classroom. So when S.A.M. Bond had stood next to her locker and Lara had wanted to kiss him, it was all a mistake because Lara thought he was a young man, not a young woman. She'd been tricked, pure and simple. After all, some of the jocks already called her *Lara Lezbo*. What would they say if they found out she was in love with another girl?

At one point that morning, Lara thought about using the gas stove to burn the pages of the book. *Destroy the evidence*, she thought. *No one will ever know*. But she couldn't bring herself to do it. She kept reading the poems and studying the detailed drawings, each one containing her image and likeness. It was hard for her to imagine the amount of work that had gone into it. And for what? A high school romance? Lara kept seeing S.A.M.'s face resting in her lap after the shooting, his nostrils flaring as he struggled for air. The eyes were wide open and Lara saw the fear in them, how S.A.M. didn't want to die. "Hang on," she'd said to him, "you'll be okay." Then a tendril of blood trickled from the corner of his mouth and Lara wiped it away with her own hand. Only S.A.M. clutched at her arm and Lara was surprised at the strength that remained, the urgency in his grasp. He brought Lara's fingers to his lips and kissed them. All this before S.A.M. closed his eyes and died.

When Lara read the final poem in the book at Mr. Munn's apartment, she felt dizzy and confused by the words. It was called, "The Goddess Rests," and when she came to the last stanza, her hands trembled.

The Goddess knows
that somewhere a lover rests,

> her face masked in twilight,
> her lips like two blossoms
> waiting to open,
> yet untouched.

Am I this lover? she asked herself. *If S.A.M. had lived, could I have returned that love? Does it really matter that S.A.M. was a young woman?* Then she'd closed the book and wept.

After Mrs. Romero returned, the three of them walked around the outer edge of the crowd and crossed the street.

"When we get to the station, you'll need to call your parents," said the assistant principal. "They'll want to know where you are."

She nodded her head in agreement as they walked together. When they reached Mrs. Romero's Subaru wagon, Lara suddenly paused on the sidewalk and turned to them.

"I have a favor to ask," she said. "There's something I'd like you to keep for me." She withdrew the black book from under her parka and held it out to Paul Munn. He took it in his large hands and studied the cover for a moment. "It was a Christmas gift from S.A.M. Bond," Lara said, "and I don't want to lose it."

"Of course we'll take care of it," Mrs. Romero answered.

"That's a promise," Mr. Munn said, looking directly at the assistant principal. "I don't think the authorities need to see this, do you?"

"No," she said. "It's our secret."

Then he stepped toward Lara and took something from beneath his coat. "I'd like you to have this." He held it out to her and she saw that it was a folded quilt. The colors had faded, but she could see tiny names sewn into the fabric of each square.

"It's Mr. Hardin's," she said, suddenly recognizing it. "He hung it on the wall behind his desk."

"Yes," Mr. Munn said. "I cleaned it in the big washing machine at the church and was planning to leave it on the steps of the school tonight." He paused and stroked the fabric with his fingers. "But I think you should have it. It was a gift from his students a long time ago."

Lara held the quilt close for a moment, studying the pattern on the cloth. Then, without glancing up at Mr. Munn or Mrs. Romero, she said, "Thank you," and tucked it under her arm.

When she got into the backseat of the car, Lara turned and looked out the rear window before they drove away. She could see the school and the radiant glow of hundreds of candles illuminating the front of the building. She closed her eyes for a moment and imagined Rachel Riley standing in the crowd as part of the gathering. *Rachel would've loved this*, Lara thought. *A holy shrine for Our Lady of Lost Souls.* Then they pulled out of the parking lot and drove down Main Street toward the police station.

■ ■ ■